I0778876

STARHEART

STORIES OF OSSYNTHORE

BOOK ONE

DEVON REDMOND

Table of Contents

CHAPTER 1

LONG WAY HOME

L et's say you'd been granted three wishes the moment you encountered a genie. "What would you wish for?' I asked myself in the rush of kids pushing through the door to reach the cool autumn air of a day not yet dark. I hold the door for someone behind me, then continue through the crowd. As I walked, my thoughts return to the genie; I figured I'd first ask for a large house, with a hundred rooms and a bedroom balcony. Then, I'd want a nice flashy car, a polished red two-seater convertible. Finally, not being too sure, I would wish for a ton of money, which was a bit lame, I thought, because if I just wished for a fortune in the first place, I could have bought any house or car and still have two wishes remaining. I looked up just as the surrounding herd of students began to scatter. I turned right and began to walk down the sidewalk. I had nothing to do and nowhere to go. I'm taking the long way home.

The wind hit my shoulders gently as I walked with the autumn leaves rolling along at my pace. I looked down at the holes in my all-star sneakers and slowly began to zone out. It's easy for me to disassociate and fall into an old trap. It's been a long week, but it's finally Friday. The Bio-lab I had at noon went on seemingly forever, which was weird because I typically find botany intriguing. The study of plants is very fascinating, though it can be a bit complex, especially when delving deep into their evolution and development. Plants aspire. Their abilities come naturally. They're self-sufficient and provide for themselves using photosynthesis. Of course we've been studying plant life since prehistoric times, over 10,000 years ago, and the topic covers literal billions of years.

My professor explains plants in ways that make you think and question them. You think about function, productivities, and the new uses discovered every day. Lately, I've struggled to keep up with the other guys at my lab table. I still try to participate. I try to understand what I can, but today, I was just too out of it and ended up daydreaming until it was time to wrap it up.

After that, I had a History test. Not only is this professor interesting, but he's also very fair and lenient. I could listen to his lessons all day. He doesn't give out homework, making his exams critical to our grade. The exams can be lengthy, wordy, often covering multiple topics. I've spent the last few nights studying and reviewing everything from class. His essays are a critical part of the exam and he's demanding on specifics like places, names, and dates. He prefers precision, so I do what I can. I read the assigned articles, filled out the review sheet, and looked over my notes until the moment the exam began. You know that nervous feeling you get when you're sitting at your desk with nothing but a pen right before a test? Yeah, I get that. I was a little iffy on a few answers but still, I studied.

Being enrolled in five classes can be tricky. Two exams, two papers, and a presentation. Don't you just miss that? Then there's Journalism class, and I won't lie, I imagined it very different from what it turned out to be. For some reason, when the class was offered last semester, I pictured this whole syllabus focusing on personal and creative writing. I didn't care at all when I realized on the first day that Journalism was much different from what I expected it to be. You already know how news coverage goes. Gathering specific information and details about a particular subject or event to analyze and arrange that information for a news story. My professor is kind and outgoing. She has blonde hair and wears glasses. She lets us pick our assignments and tells us about campus events for story ideas. One came to mind the other night when I passed a flier for a video game tournament on campus next week. The best nights are when we show up, sit down, and the professor tells the whole class to grab everything after taking attendance because of something exciting on campus. Just the other night, she brought the whole class over to an art gallery. There, we gazed at sculptures, paintings, and illustrations. I focused on historic photography. I closely studied a few political cartoons. The professor works for an exciting experience and that's what makes the class one of my favorites. I still feel like the semester just started and we've already learned so much about journalism. I like when we go into depth about its history and originality and compare it to how news reporting works modernly. We've established relationships with one another after we interviewed each other, one on one, and listened to ourselves. We discussed simple things, like who we are. You never know who you're sitting next to.

I've come to really enjoy the class and found it a fascinating subject taught by a professor who told me I was a good writer. While walking, I checked online to see if my draft paper had been viewed by my professor. 'Unopened' was its status. Submitted 7:42am 10/02/2018.

It's October second. I'm turning twenty in a few days, I thought to myself, *October second. The beginning of a new month.*

Suddenly, I saw a five dollar bill fall from a girl's pocketbook up ahead. It landed on the pavement as she was pulling some transit-card out of her bag.

I yelled for her and chased the bill as it slowly blew with the breeze, but I was too late. I didn't catch her, and she clearly didn't hear me. Her back didn't even turn before she stepped on the bus. She rode away. I finally got to the $5 and stepped on it. It unrolled softly with fades and wrinkles when I picked it up. I was about to put it in my pocket, until I turned the corner and saw a homeless man sitting, his back resting against a brick wall. I didn't think before dropping the money in his styrofoam cup.

He pressed his hands together and gave me a look of gratitude before he lowered his eyes and leaned back again. I knew he needed the money more than I, and I guess in a way, the money was never really mine to begin with.

I was about to keep walking until I heard a rowdy commotion of yells, howls, and chants coming from the grassy field across the corner. I turned around and took a few steps towards the curb. From across the street, I could see school boys hyping up in their football jerseys outside the high school. Over the crowds, I heard the announcer doing audio checks as the scoreboard lights flickered to life. Nothing gets you more hyped than a football team finally getting to pregame in some nice autumn air. I'm sure hell week conditioning seemed like yesterday for them. I played football for six years. It's not something I allow to shape my personality. Now, *those days* feel long ago. I was never too good and my coaches never thought much of me, but I still showed up every year because I loved the sport. That, and because my brother played on the team with me. That sport saved my life. Football was discipline. And still, no matter how long it's been, there isn't a moment I don't feel a heavy bump in my heart at the thought of all my boys and I playing together in the same color. 2014 was the year. I was only a junior, but there was something special about that year. That was my first year playing on varsity. I was so young when I was finally handed a jersey with black threads.

Then, in some kind of cosmic coincidence, a glint on the ground caught my eye. I kicked away the orange leaves and saw a shiny new penny facing heads up. It's a wonder I caught its glare. I'm usually always stopping to flip these things over when I pass them on tails, even if it's raining, so yes, I was happy to find this one looking right at me, Lincoln as serious as ever, after I moved the leaves.

I waved the penny in the light and a sharp glare shone over its face. The penny looked like it was washed in a pool of light. *Where's a fountain?* I wondered. I admired the coin's fine condition as I flipped and rolled it around. I brought the penny close and read its date. It was minted years ago. It wasn't anywhere near as young as it looked. I wondered how it could still be so fine and brilliant without a scratch.

In my steps I began to reminisce further. Your coach tells you to run. They tell you to be strong. They break you down, and then they do it again, and again. After the thousandth time, you look down at yourself, see the progress you've made, and realize they weren't being cruel. Not too far up ahead still stands what's left of my old gym. The place closed for good a while back. I was far from being the biggest guy there, but I remember feeling unstoppable in that place.

I passed my favorite book store. Actual guitars hang in the front window. Inside is a paradise with books stacked from carpet to ceiling. So many books, one could trip inside if they weren't careful. I remember how excited I was the first time I walked in. I told the owner all the titles and authors I was looking for. Mostly classics. I refer to them as "Initial pens." Anything more original than that simply doesn't exist yet. That's why I like them. The bookseller brought me to a crammed bookshelf for what I was after. Then, he headed off to search another section of the store. I climbed a step stool, reached up and pulled a title out of a stack, sending all the rest of the hardcovers toppling down. I immediately stumbled back and kicked over another stack of books, all while he searched in another row very close by. I've only been there twice and I walked out the first time with a box full of books, lying to my mom about how much I spent.

My thoughts flowed as I walked over the cracks in the concrete, making sure not to step on one. I looked to my side and stopped as my eyes locked on my own reflection. I was standing in front of the window of my old gym. I glanced up at the old sign that still hung above. "Crown Fitness." Instead of continuing to walk, I took a moment to look back at myself. The glare against the glass reflectively burnishes the outside streets of the town, so alive and active as I stand alone in the storm's eye. Most of the stores and firms have yet to be locked and the lamps on the pavement have yet to be lit. The trees above town appeared in massive beautiful splats of yellow and orange, like a mountain range of fireworks set to be painted. Just your average autumn evening. I was wearing my black thermal. My dark blue jeans were somewhat contrasting my shirt, but any darker, they'd probably be black too. I think of black as a sharp color. One that's clean and makes you hard to define. That's why I rock it.

I dug between my books and tablet to reach for a red and black flannel I didn't think I was gonna need. I threw it over and loosened its collar. I was about to zip my bag back up when I noticed a black beanie all ruffled up in its bottom corner. I tried to fix my hair up as best I could earlier, but the wind clearly didn't have a problem messing it up again. I had the top pushed up and the sides pushed back earlier. Now it's all over the place in curly blonde twists and waves. I swung my bag back over my shoulder and from there, sank into my own eyes. I've been told before that my eyes resemble the color of the water in Saint Martin, a bright aqua. I looked beyond the windowpane and a part of me felt as empty as the inside of the place. I saw nothing but only the bits and scraps of what remained from the gym that it once was. Inside, it was dark. Loose wiring hung from the ceiling and most of the floor was ripped up. The walls were a pale faded gray with rectangular marks left from the mirrors and posters that used to hang.

If it weren't for the giant sign high above the doors, one wouldn't even be able to guess what this place once was. I'm a bit thinner now, and probably nowhere near as conditioned as I used to be. My boy and I would go here every day after we got out of school. He was the strong one. Still though, he and my coach helped me get stronger and showed me everything I needed to know to do it on my own. I remember holding a wider build.

The front of my hair stuck out from under my hat. It's a dirty blonde. It only comes out bright when the sun illuminates it. My hair still carries a few drops of highlights from the last few days of the August sun; but again, the swirling leaves at my shoes tell me the days are getting colder and the nights are growing longer. The months change and the seasons follow. Soon my blonde will dim. Sometimes your reflection will be the only one in the room that knows what's exactly going on inside your head. It's who you are. Stay as true as you can to it. I stood and stared with my pinky ring in hand. I rolled its spinner around its cloud silver band. My eyes broke away the moment I felt a sudden vibration in my pocket.

A text message from a boy J: "We out to the shore point tonight, you comin' through?"

I'll get back to him later. Right now I just need to get home. I walked away from the gym doors just as the street lamps lit up. There was a charm in the air. I could sense it. I continued ahead.

The hot pink sky was clear as the day approached twilight. I watched the sun set another day over a town that shaped my life. Cars swung around the center ring where an orange oak tree stands. Shoppers flooded the streets as they walked up and down the sidewalks and passed in and out of shop doors. At the end of the road stood a massive red tree. I began heading in its direction. I suddenly stopped short for a lady rushing out of a craft store. Her hands were filled with bags holding long rolls of fabric. Shortly ahead, I passed some kids gathered on their bikes. I walked through the fruit markets and passed men wearing flannels hauling loads of fresh fruit. They placed each bag on the sidewalk. I passed the apples and I noticed a young couple about to pass me. They walked hand in hand down the sidewalk as the girl gracefully ran her fingers through the small light yellow trees planted in the dirt beds along the pavement. I courteously moved aside for them and continued to walk under the overhangs of the shops. I began to gaze at all the window displays. I peeked in a videogame store and saw that the open sign behind the glass was still lit. I then figured that I already had enough video games and pulled my hand away from the door handle. I passed a costume store, a magic shop and further down I pass the window of a clothing store. I'd like to check out what they got and maybe get a new pair of sneakers. I have no guess where the ones I have now are taking me. Suddenly, I almost tripped over a sign that said, *School sale - Discount on All supplies.* I got down and read, 'Forty percent off,' as I straightened it and backed away. *That's, how many cents a notebook?* I briefly wondered to myself. I walked away like nothing happened. I could go there in my free time and pick up some notebooks. My favorite book is a blank one. As I was looking down, my head waltzed straight into the pipes of a wind-chime. It was dangling above on one of the hooks on a vine-strung trellis, outside of a coffee shop. The silver pipes danced, rang, and shimmered. It was a bit awkward to look beside them and see a whole row of chimes hanging along the hooks. I didn't notice a single one of them at first. A chrome dragonfly sat on the cap of the chime I bumped into. I moved over and kept walking.

I'm still not sure what I should do tonight. I'm not scheduled to work so I always have the option to just break my cage, go out, and chill with some good people. You'd think of a cage as something to fear, but for a while, it's been a haven for me. A barrier. A place of security. I don't wanna call it a bubble.

I'm never against just layin' low. After I dropped my bookbag, I could just chill on my bed, find a movie, or maybe even open a book. I'll just unwind until I fall asleep. I'll stare at my ceiling for hours, even if it doesn't change. I met my reflection passing the window of an art gallery filled with some of the most brilliant, spontaneous art. Imagine a world made of that stuff. Imagine its whole surface permeated. It's as though these guys paint with the stars. Anything can be brought to life with the tip of a brush. Inside, there's paintings of vast cosmic universes consisting of exotic planets and galactic phenomena which I particularly find the most extraordinary. There was a portrait of a trail that led through a blossoming forest. Then another of a waterfall deep within a rainforest. Above that, a painting of a leafless curvy tree with a wide eyed pink and white owl perched on a branch before a blaring moon.

"Hey," I hear someone say to me.

I turned from the glass and I caught an apple tossed by a girl at a flower stand beside the art gallery. She looks my age and she was standing alone. She was selling mums. A crate of apples was on the sidewalk next to her stand. She looked at me and smiled. She had curly short blonde hair that twirled and bounced over her blue denim coat. We shared a look while I passed. She was wearing a wavy yellowish-orange shirt, the same color as the flowers, underneath an open red flannel. Her flannel collar peaked over her denim jacket.

"Huh," I muttered, eventually forming a simple "Thanks" while smiling at her bright blue eyes. She smiled back. With gratitude, I walked ahead wondering why she even threw it to me. The apple was round and ripe. I wiped it on my shirt before crossing the road. I continued along the painted lines of the crosswalk and hopped back to the sidewalk. I pass under the giant red tree I saw from down the street. I took my first bite into the apple's ruby red outer layer. Its juice was phenomenal. I looked back.

"What a lovely girl," I thought.

There should be dozens of people lined up at her stand but I was the only one that passed it. She threw the apple to me for free. I would have said more to her if the moment wasn't so sudden. I could have walked away with her name. It was not only upsetting, but bewildering, to look back and see the girl was gone. Not only her, but her entire flower stand as well. The flower displays that were arranged out front had mysteriously vanished. I looked to the sky. The leaves above flew in a spiral. They fluttered past the massive red tree. The leaves withered and fell beside me. An empty tire swing spins in the breeze. Under the tree is a short white picket fence that lines the whole corner yard. The white tips of my shoes kicked and crunched in the leaves on the sidewalk as I tried to decide whether tonight was a good night to go out. I still couldn't make up my mind over the next few blocks. I stepped onto the long street where my job is located, the local public library. The lights inside were shut off. I hear of ghost sightings all the time. This town is old.

It may be a secret that I work here. When I started out as a cleaner, it was only on the weekends. I thought it was a good gig. I would begin by dusting and after I would sweep the floors. I'd dust books, wipe away cobwebs, wash the windows. It was usually pretty empty and very quiet, even for a library. Usually after I finished, I would return to all the titles and covers I pulled from the shelf and found interesting.

What I personally like is the classic section that's deep toward the back. There's this one lady who tends to accuse me of using it as a place to hide. Well, she's not wrong. Most books are written expressively. Some use past experiences to create stories. Some use their imagination. It's how we communicate with our past, present, and future. Words come from deep within. They're free and infinite. They're there for us to use as we wish. To compose in our own way, like notes in a melody. Regardless of who you are, out of all the writers that once were, are now, and ever will be, you'll find something that speaks to you. They could have been just like you. Once everyone's gone and I'm certain the inside doors are locked, I got the whole place to myself. You can say working there has its benefits, so I don't complain. It's usually peaceful and often therapeutic.

I keep walking past the library until I came to a street shaded by trees and greenery. A scarecrow sat below the street sign. He had a mischievous, wild-eyed leer. The pupils were looking towards the street from under a droopy felt hat. The brim of his hat was curved like his stitched grin. The holes in his hat were dark and web filled. When a spider dropped out of his hat, I backed away. The spider crawled away and I did the same. Its face was unusual. The wind blew and his head turned towards me. His head bowed and now his eyes seemed to be a bit more menacing. He was looking at me as if there was something ahead I shouldn't trust.

The street led through a small forest. I was surrounded by green trees draped with long vines. Only half the sun's light shone through. I can remember kids always gathering here. This place was the go-to spot every Halloween when I was younger. Up ahead lives a guy that used to decorate his house for the holiday. He'd do it up big for the town when the autumn season came around. Sort of like a witch's house. There were plenty of haunted houses in town but the one up ahead was quite the attraction. That was back when I'd just grab a mask and a pillow case and follow my brother until we eventually met up with everyone we knew. They would already be covered in shaving cream by the time we met up and my brother and I would be there just in time to raise hell.

A lot has changed since those past days, I thought. Suddenly, a rustling in the bushes behind me stopped my stride. *It's the scarecrow*, I thought. I turned around and noticed a commotion up in the trees. I didn't move. I tried to make out what was causing it but I couldn't.

A squirrel? A racoon? No, it had to have been a cat. Something aggressive. Whatever it was, it was angry. That's sure what it sounded like. All went quiet once the ruckus stopped. The branches continued to shake for only a moment; afterwards, I was just standing on the sidewalk, staring at a bunch of still greenery.

All I'm really tryna do is hit my pillow now. I continued up the street until I eventually passed the lawn of the house which marks the center of the road. The bushes were speckled with orange lights underneath a layer of stretchy spider webs. The webs were purple, green, and white, and pulled from the bush tops to the grass blades. A jack-o-lantern candy bucket crowned each fence column. I'm always impressed by his functional guillotine. I saw a werewolf made from a mask, a torn flannel, and a faded pair of jeans.

I gave a view up to the house and in the window, I saw a man watching me from behind the curtain. He turned away and the curtain fell.

I should probably get out of here, I thought.

The memories of all the nights I came here slowly returned with every step. I remembered being here with my dad and dog. Even back then, the whole lawn was spread with gruesome Halloween decorations. Animatronics would come alive and the mechanisms would run. Lights would glow pale and ominous all around the graveyard. The whole town would be gathered in the street outside. Everyone you knew would pull up wearing some funky thing, with some crazy story to tell. Good times.

From out of nowhere, I heard a caw. Something about it was strange. I wasn't sure what type of bird it came from. As I started walking again, I heard it once more, except this time it was overhead and louder. I threw a glance up. I didn't see anything nor did I notice any movement. Then, *KAWWWW* again. I cringed. The sound irritated my ear. I didn't know where it was coming from. It was the caw of some type of crow. I wouldn't be surprised if it was hurt. I could hear its caw coming from all around now. I thought the mysterious bird may be circling above, yet there wasn't a thing in sight.

Then suddenly, as if it were right over my shoulder, I heard one last clear *Gawhh*. I whipped around to see something vanish within a poof of black feathers. I stood still, questioning what I just saw. It was the most bizarre thing. I backed away from the trees and moved along. I held my eyes on the branches above me and hurried until I was beyond the horizon. I turned onto another street and headed for the sidewalk. I felt in touch with the pink and yellow sky.

CHAPTER 2

ALL THE LIGHTS

I wasn't too far from my street. I just considered the events as I walked my way. I've also yet to decide what I want to do tonight. If the house is quiet, I can go straight to my room and just stretch out. I'll probably just watch TV until I fall asleep. I do have an eBook I've been working on. I haven't really gotten around to it lately and it's about to expire again. I pass each house and considered how I could spend the rest of the evening. I was about to reach the end of my street when a thought came to mind. What I'd really love to do is get working on this new story I have. There's an unfinished monologue just sitting in my room. It's a little side project I started. I kept it to myself.

I walked up my pathway, passed my kitchen's bay window and noticed the lights were off inside. I opened the front door and entered my den. The sectional was exactly the way it was left last. An orange patch quilt was folded over its backrest. Its pillows were jumbled. The remote was lodged between the cushions. Books and magazines were left in a messy stack on the ottoman. I stepped in and closed the door behind me. A hard push always rattles the walls and makes the plates on the shelf wobble and clink. The herb dryer dangled from side to side above the window curtain. On one shelf, a display of old novelties and candle holders, while the other shelf holds knick knacks from years of growing up.

I pulled the beanie from my head and hung it on the wobbly coat rack. From my dining room, I could see heavy clouds roll past the windows of my living room. Good thing I got home in time. I never have any insight on when it's about to rain. I quickly turned at the bottom of the stairs and continued to my bedroom.

I didn't turn on my bedroom light so my room was dark. I was wearing the green and teal shine casted from my lava lamps. I shifted the mouse on my desk to awaken my monitor. When the screen lit up, I saw my story where I left off. I was only on the first chapter. I dropped my bag and read the last few lines. I pulled off my flannel and tossed the rag on my bed which was made but only in a lousy, thrown together type of way. A dark blue hoodie laid at the end of my bed. If I decide to go out tonight, I'll wear it. I opened a small drawer in my desk and pulled out a lighter to light my candle. The flame had a bright yellow blare. The candle burned with a warm glow, its yellow light shining on the ceiling as the flame danced. Across my room stood a dusty turquoise motion lamp that I haven't used in a while. Lighting flows through its glass when you switch it on. I walked over and reached my hand around its back. I flipped on the switch and stood back in its blue glow. Afterwards, I looked over at a small red glass lantern I keep on the corner of my dresser. I grabbed a smaller candle from a miniature black drawer then propped open the glass lantern's black iron door. I lit the candle's wick, placed it within the lantern's candle holder, then shut the small door. I watched the flame flicker through the red glass panes. A bright red glow shone throughout my room. From there, I walked over to the nightstand on the right of my bed, and rolled the switch to my salt lamp. I rolled onto my bed and looked up at my ceiling with my hand placed under my head. Soon, my mind began to slowly drift off.

My room was filled with yellow, green, blue, turquoise, red, and orange. I found serenity in every light. In every color, I saw a charm. For a moment, I felt away from this world. Out of touch. I love that feeling. Out of boredom, I turned over to my nightstand and lifted a heavy silver magnifier. The magnifier was sitting on its flat blue holder. Its holder can be used as a paperweight. I grabbed both, rolled back over, crossed my feet, and held up the magnifying glass. Through it, I looked at all the lights on my ceiling. I was thoughtless while looking at the warmth of each color blending into the other. I flipped over the magnifier and looked through its other end. The magnifier possessed no handle. Its glass was contained within a circular silver hoop meant to be held at the edge with just your thumb and pointer finger. It belonged to my mother's parents. It's been around a lot longer than I have. Its minor rust and slight scratching couldn't cloud its bright shine. It always brought me to wonder where it came from and what it was even used for. I wasn't sure what it was the first time I saw it until I looked through it. I asked my mom about it, but all she could say was that it belonged to her parents and that it had been around forever. I don't know why, but I liked gazing through its window.

Slowly, my head started to sink heavier and heavier into my pillow, while at the same time, I began to feel weightless. I shut my eyes and rested calmly in a meditative state. I felt completely spaced out. Right when I felt like I was about to fall fast asleep, I jolted forward and opened my eyes. I was surrounded by nothing but darkness.

"I've gone blind!" I yelled. My hands were still visible. They could be seen clearly as I waved them in front of my face. It appeared as if I was slightly glowing, yet the world around me consisted of only boundless blackness. I was no longer laying down on my bed. I was floating above an abyss of darkness. No one else was present. I was alone, wearing a black hoodie. I tried to process where I was, if it was even real. I thought I was trapped in some form of sleep paralysis. I maintained a conscious state of mind. I could look around and feel my presence here. I peered around the empty ongoing void for anyone or anything. Although it was clearly just me here, I still said, loud and questionably, "Hello?"

Right then, I broke free from the void, and found myself back in my room. I felt delusional looking around and realized I was sitting on my bed once again. I switched on the light and firmly planted my shoes on the carpet. For a minute, I sat on the side of my bed with my head resting in my hands.

'What just happened?' I asked myself. 'Where was I?'

I pulled myself together, stood up, and dropped the magnifier in my pocket. I checked the time on my cell phone. My head was heavy. It felt like my room was spinning. The clock on my cell phone read 7:29, so I've been asleep for an hour. My mom should be pulling up any minute if she hasn't already. I walked over to the window and looked outside. Strangely, she's yet to pull up. I unlocked my phone and dialed her number. I raised my window and took in the much cooler air from outside as I waited. I tried to stay focused while listening to the ongoing call until it finally rang out. There was no answer. I dropped my phone on my bed and stepped out of my bedroom. I switched on all the lights, rubbed my eye, and grabbed a random hoodie off the coat rack. I switched on the porch light and headed out the door, leaving it open. I liked to get the car door for my mom after she's worked all day. She's a nurse who works long hours. I walked down the damp pathway and shook out the hoodie. After throwing it over my head, I reached the end of the street. I stepped into it, looked both ways, and saw absolutely nobody. It was just me, alone in the night, under the streetlights. I felt like I was still asleep. Outta nowhere two headlights turned the corner and slowly approached me from down the block. The tires rolled slowly, closer and closer, until the car pulled right up to the curb in front of my house. The vehicle stopped right in front of me. I stood between the headlights, blinded and unable to see who it was. But I could tell it wasn't my mom's car.

CHAPTER 3

ONE SHORE THING

The stereo was cranked and the serene street thumped with rap music. I couldn't tell who was in the car, but I knew it was my boys once I heard someone holler, "Hop in, Ugly." The back door opened. For a moment, I stood glued to the street. I looked back at my house. The front door was still open. I needed to get my things together first. It was cold, even for an October night.

I looked back at my house and saw the lights were shut off. Blackness filled every window. I thought it was strange. I padded my pocket to feel for my phone. I wanted to at least have that on me before hopping in the car. I felt something solid in my pocket and figured it was my phone. The car was cloudy. Smoke rolled in circles under the yellow interior light.

"What's good?" I asked as I climbed in. Once I closed the door, the light shut off and the vape dissipated. I could see my friend's faces clearly.

"You get electrocuted?" 'J' asked me.

I thought he noticed my stunned facial expression after I saw the front door shut.

"What?" I asked. I wasn't sure what he was talking about.

"What's with your hair?" he asked. "It's sticking straight up."

"Oh" I said. I reached for my hair and pulled down all the wild curls I walked out with. I could feel my hair sticking out in every direction. I laughed.

"I took a nap before," I explained. Part of me felt like I was still asleep. We turned onto the turnpike. I threw my hood over the back of my head and rested my head against the window.

"Lower your hood," 'J' told me. "It looks sketchy."

I dropped my hood and lowered my window. I looked up at the full moon shining through the cloudy sky. Something didn't feel right. I could have sworn the house was empty when I left. I didn't hear anyone else on my way down the stairs. Every light was on when I walked out and there wasn't a single car out front except for Jezul's when I left. I wasn't thinking much when I dropped everything and drove out to a place I've never been to before. The hoodie I was wearing wasn't even mine. I stared out my window and looked at the silver stars floating in the dark blue sky. I bumped to the beat of the song as I sat clueless to the lyrics. I thought about the weird things that've been happening lately and thought I'd lose my mind if I didn't let it go.

I looked at my boys and asked "So what's this place like?"

"Don't worry, Jezul knows a nice spot," 'J' said, as he ran his fingers down the line of his fishing rod.

"The place is thirty minutes away," Jezul added.

The light turned green and we were off.

"We out-e," I said.

I looked at the street lights. I tried my best to keep my head together. I was afraid if I blinked my eyes for too long, I'd end up in that dark empty place I saw in my dream. It was only a dream, though it didn't feel like one. I took a deep breath. Right now I'm safe and I'm out. We turned onto the parkway. The time flew once Fronze fired up an old song. After that, we commenced to laughing and reconnecting for the first time in a while. I looked out the window and saw an unfamiliar neighborhood. Each house was decorated with lights, ghosts, and cats. Pumpkins sat on every porch. I was in the Halloween mood. It's one of the best feelings. Jezul turned the wheel onto a small dirt road. I rolled down my window and studied the shadowy woods. The moon vanished over the trees and I could no longer see through the gloom. Usually I'm excited about these kinds of places but something didn't feel right.

Jezul leaned over the steering wheel and looked side to side for anything recognizable. For a moment, he drove slowly until we reached a parking lot in the center of the woods. Once we drove out from under the trees, I could see the stars again. We pulled into a spot and Fronze lowered the music. I closed my window then all was silent. Jezul parked the car and said, "Here."

"This is the place?" Fronze asked.

"Should be," Jezul said.

My friends got their belongings together and closed their jackets.

"You're sure this is the place?" 'J' asked, looking around the woods.

"This is the place," Jezul assured.

The headlights of Jezul's car were the only light in the entire lot. After he shut them off, all was dark. He pulled his keys from the ignition and we all hopped out. The moon was directly above our heads, circled by the silhouettes of sky breaching trees. The trees framed the moon's beauty. I gazed around the outer walls of the woods. I walked with my hands in my sweatshirt pocket and followed my friends towards the woods.

We entered the woods and the air carried the sweet scent of pine trees and sap. The four of us walked in silence. All we heard were the quiet pats of our shoes tapping on the cold powdery dirt. I listened closely to the sounds of the night. I could hear the birds singing their songs high up in the trees. They whistled throughout the grove and brought a peaceful aura.

Around, I could hear the low chirp of crickets echoing through the damp grass. They've yet to be killed by the frost. Occasionally, you'd hear the loud knock of a woodpecker. I looked ahead and noticed the trail growing more obscured with trees. The trees were so tall and thick, they didn't allow any moonlight to shine through. Each of my friends turned on their cell phone flashlights except me.

"Don't worry," 'J' said to me, "I thought this place seemed a little off at first but this *is* a chill ass spot. Plus, we shouldn't get any shit for bein' here. Anything happens, don't say a word. We'll be fine. You got nothin' to worry about."

I nodded my head. I walked ahead and turned around to face the rest of the gang. I walked backwards as I looked around. The woods began to feel more serene. I tucked my hands back in my hoodie pocket and said, "So where are we? This place looks cool." Fronze was wearing a white jacket that matched the color of his shoes and the diamonds in his ears. He had his hair all gelled up. He looked spiffy and insightful. He's one of my main boys.

"This is a small spot Jezul found last summer," Fronze answered.

"It was a few weeks ago," Jezul added, after he looked up from his phone. "Me and a few friends came across this place one night when we were just lookin' for a place to chill. We gotta cut through some woods but we'll be at the spot in just a few minutes."

I turned back around and Fronze turned up the volume. My eyes caught a green spark of light hovering through the trees. Then I saw another flash. Soon, one flash led to the next. I realized it was the luminance of fireflies. That's weird. It's October. I thought it was weird to still see a few out. *Where did they come from?* I wondered.

Right then a firefly flew right past me. It hovered for a second, then flew away. I followed it momentarily until I looked ahead and saw the path coming to a turn. I figured we'd be at the shore by now but a large hill towered. The shadowy hill was covered with trees, shedding their brown leaves.

At the pinnacle stood a large dead tree. Its trunk was crooked and chipped.

"That's the turn up there," Jezul pointed out. "Once we're around that hill, the shore lies straight ahead."

"Bet," all the boys said back.

The trail got lost under the leaves. The boys had their flashlights; if not, it would've been too dark to see where we were walking. I kicked the leaves as we walked around the base of the hill. Suddenly, everyone stopped when we heard a loud, painful, ear-shattering, screech of a bird.

The sound came from the top of the hill. No one said a word. We all stood together and waited. We tried to listen closely for the cry again. After a moment of silence, we just assumed that it was nothing more than a crow. We heard a bird flap its wings and assumed it flew away. We were about to continue when it screeched again. My face fell when I heard the second caw. It was much louder, deeper, and certainly one that I recognized. I looked towards the top of the hill. From out of the shadows, a thick milky mist began to slowly pour down the hill. The mist oozed through the trees and formed pools around the roots. It continued to flow towards us. Once the mist reached flat ground, it broke apart, rolled, and spilled over the dead leaves. It was very similar to the heavy CO_2 that rolls off dry ice. We all stepped away from it. The mist separated 'J' and Fronze from Jezul and I. It was clear that we all wanted to avoid stepping in it.

For a moment we just stared at the fog at our feet, watching it flow past us. The strange mist was harmless; but still, it seemed as though neither of us wanted to touch it. Something about it gave us a weird feeling. I squatted down and blew at it. The mist rolled away like waves on a shore. Jezul didn't intend to waste any more time. His steps made little puffs in the cloud. The fog filled the empty space I disrupted and covered the ground again.

Where was it coming from? I wondered.

I looked towards the top of the hill. Something felt off. I took one step into the dense cloud and watched my sneaker disappear beneath. The mist felt cold. I nestled my hands deeply within my hoodie pockets and continued through. I reached the other side and looked back at 'J' and Fronze who've yet to move. Without any comment, I continued forward and began leading the way. After a minute or so, I noticed a small clearing off the side of the trail. It seemed like the type of thing someone would walk straight past and never even notice. I casually pulled away from the group and approached it. I turned back to my friends one last time before entering. I was curious over what I'd find in it. I had no incentive to be long. I found only a small boulder sitting in the dirt. I stood on top and looked around. I could see something resembling a mansion close by. I looked over the vast terrain. Its tall grass swayed in the breeze. I could see the shore. The ocean reflected the moon's light. It was a breathtaking sight. I was about to step down and head back when I felt compelled to stay for another moment. I glanced up at the blinding moon above. The wind blew and I was hit with its breeze. I stood between the two rocks and looked sharply at the one above me. It had a pearly glow. I found it entrancing. I looked at its craters with fascination. The moon rotates at the same pace it revolves. There's a whole other side of the moon hidden from us. It reminds me to consider the other side of things. The others looked at me, looked up at the moon, then looked back at me. They didn't stop walking. I could hear them whisper as they passed.

"What's that guy doin'?"

"Nevermind. Go on with your story." I hopped down from the rock and hurried after my friends. I suddenly felt afraid alone. I caught up with them and listened in on the conversation, though I didn't say anything. Minutes went by and I began to wonder why we weren't at the shore by now.

I picked up my pace to walk shoulder to shoulder with 'J'. We walked in silence. I haven't seen 'J' in weeks, and we had catching up to do. I just wasn't sure what to say. There was a lot on my mind. He's one of my best friends and he's been a bro for a long time.

Finally I tried, "What's new with you, man?" What I really wanted to say was, *I'm sorry I haven't dropped a word in a few weeks. You know my love and respect for you is always genuine and legitimate, right?* What am I supposed to even tell him? That shit's been difficult? I couldn't. There's no excuse for not seeing the people you love and care about the most. For now, I just kept my mouth shut after my attempt.

"I've jus' been chillin'," 'J' said. "You and I should chill more. I'm always down to fish."

"Same. I'm down for anything," I told him. I looked at everyone and said, "We should hit a club soon." I like dark rooms with bright colored lights. "Not tonight obviously," I added, and everyone laughed.

Being out with my boys made it almost feel like summertime again. I missed those days. I did. The woods were gloomy. I kept my distance from the edge of the trail. I was afraid of something jumping out at me. Here, you're surrounded by shadows. It would make you feel like someone was lurking in every blind spot. I reached back for my hood and gently laid it over my head. The deeper we continued, the cooler the air got. Suddenly, with a howl, a wild breeze blew over our heads. My hood was blown down and I saw stars ahead. I picked up the natural scent of sea salt in the air. A brighter glimmer out in the distance caught my eye.

'J' looked at me and said, "You're gonna like this place 'D'."

I couldn't lie, I already did like this place. Something about it. It was so weird and exciting. The thrill we found here was so grand and enticing. We reached the end of the woods.

The glimmer I caught was the moonlight reflecting on swells. The path led us to a cement ledge, four feet above the shore. I inhaled the breeze and looked out at the endless sea. My head felt clear for the first time today. The horizon was barely visible. The bright stars illuminated the midnight-blue sky. It was a different atmosphere. One that was much more clear. There wasn't a cloud in the sky. The breeze was nice. I like this time of year. We sat down on the edge of the cement platform. 'J' casted his fishing line and his bobber landed far out. You could barely see it. I looked down and noticed graffiti across the entire cement platform. I tried to make out what some of the paint spelled as my friends went on telling stories. I looked up at the universe for a moment before I turned back, threw my hood up, and laid flat on the cement top. The ground felt cold. I placed my hands in my hoodie pocket and gazed at the sky. The stars and fresh air took my mind off things. Stars are constant. With close attention, you can follow them. You're already familiar with the two Ursas, minor and major. (The little dipper and the big dipper.) At the end of the smaller one is the north star Polaris. That star marks the location of the north celestial pole. It's the meeting point of all four quadrants. It's in the third quadrant that you'll find the Libra constellation. In the northern hemisphere, it's best seen in late spring or early summer. It was believed that, together, their stars formed a scale. That's my zodiac sign.

I didn't know what my friends were discussing now. I thought a lot to myself as I tried to quiet my mind. I wondered about life, this Earth, and my place in it. Soon, I began to doze off.

"Im tryna make a move this weekend," I overheard 'J' say. He turned to me and asked, "You comin' out wit' us?"

I wasn't sure what to say for a second. "Yeah man! I'm down." I sat up and faced the row.

"Where' we out to?"

"Anywhere," 'J' responded. "We grab our IDs and bring some heads. It's a move."

I hopped down to the sand and walked down to the water. I looked far out to the horizon for a few minutes. I've been caught up in a lot lately. I'm afraid of people asking how I've been.

Still, why not head out and see everyone again? I'd hit up Player and Baller and see what's good. I'd have to get a haircut. It's been a long time since I've seen all my friends. Some of us played together. I don't know what they're gonna say about me but all I can really tell you is they're some of the best people I've ever surrounded myself with. I have nothing in common with any of them and that's my favorite thing about knowing them. We're all unique and I could never wish for that to change. Some of them have always thrived and they're all bound to aspire. They all carry the name of a saint.

'J's line whipped and his bobber flung across the surface rapidly. He fought with strength the moment his pole bent. He reeled the line in hard. We could see something kicking in the swells. He reeled some more and pulled back on his pole. Next thing, a striped bass was flopping on the sand. I remember catching a Spider Crab and a Sea Robin while fishing with 'J' last summer. Those aren't trophies but I was so proud of myself. It's always fun to reel something in. I looked down at 'J's' fish as the boys walked over. The fish's size was very impressive. 'J' unhooked it and held it up by its tail as I sat down in the sand with joy.

"Beautiful," Fronze told 'J'.

Jezul took his phone and grabbed a quick picture of 'J' with the fish then 'J' tossed the fish back into the sea. Then, with no warning, a brilliant bolt of blue lightning flashed across the sky. There was a loud crash of thunder following it closely. The thunder roared and rumbled. I looked up and saw another bolt, this time the lighting was red. It stretched across the entire sky. The clouds lit up red. For a moment, you could see the line between the sea and the sky. I looked up as cold rain began to splash against my forehead. I closed my eyes and took a deep breath. I threw my hood over my head and a few seconds later, the rain came crashing down so heavy, you could barely see through it. I watched as two lightning bolts, one red and one turquoise, flashed. It was electrifying. I've never seen lightning like it.

My boys had already climbed back up the ledge and were standing on the edge. They were looking down at me like they weren't going to wait another second. I ran from the shore and climbed up. I tried not to slip. Once I got to my feet, I walked ahead and caught up with my boys. My hoodie was soaked. We moved towards the shadowy woods. The stars and moonlight were clouded by the storm. There was no light ahead. We were about to pass through the mouth of the woods when something large and black flew across the path with a roar of wind and completely vanished into the trees. Me and the rest of the guys pulled back and paused. We didn't see what it was but we didn't really want to investigate further. For a moment, the area felt slightly colder. 'J' pulled out his cell phone, switched on its flashlight, and took a step into the woods. Meanwhile, I looked from branch to branch for any stalking eyes or long ragged feathers.

I didn't see anything suspicious. Eventually, we got tired of standing in the torrential downpour. "We're good," I said.

I lead us into the woods. The four of us were soaked. The rainfall echoed throughout the woods. The heavy sound of raindrops could be heard from high above. I dropped my hood, pulled up my sleeves, and continued ahead. Through the hunter green world, we began our way back to the car. Gusts of wind rattled the rustling leaves, mixing with the sound of rainfall. All was peaceful for a short time until, once again, a crow's screech broke through the soothing sounds. I completely forgot about that for a bit. I kept moving straight. It was dark but I analyzed my surroundings.

The branches above continued to drip on the ground. I was calm but I was also curious. I kept hearing vibrations and ongoing echoes throughout the woods. I couldn't tell where they were coming from so I kept it to myself. The wind blew softly and dragged along the ground's foggy mist in a slow, eerie type of way. Soon, the ground was covered in the milky fog. I wasn't fazed by it. My only concern was making it back to the parking lot. The hill shouldn't be far ahead. The seagulls overhead sounded distressed as they flew off in other directions. I felt that was odd behavior for them. Suddenly, every sound, from the shake of the trees, to the howl of the wind, to the crunching of the leaves on the ground, fell silent. All you could hear was the sound of our breathing. I stopped short the moment I felt something was off. The gang stopped moving and exchanged confused looks. I listened carefully. Then from close by, I heard the soft, gentle caw of a bird.

Slowly, I turned my chin. Right then, a brilliant bolt of lightning flashed overhead. In the light, I saw a hooded figure approaching. It wore a black robe and hovered over the ground. In the lightning, I could see it clear as day. I couldn't see its face but I could tell it was looking straight at *me*. The yellow leaves and mist on the ground began to levitate and circulate around the being. It was looking dead-straight into my eyes, and my eyes only. I pulled my eyes away and looked at my boys. Not one of them seemed to have noticed the phantom. By then it had already vanished. I looked back just as the yellow leaves returned to the ground. It was like it was never there.

"Stay close. We should be safe," I said loudly.

"Safe from what?" 'J' asked suspiciously.

I faced my friends with nothing to say. They all looked back at me with confusion. I remained silent and looked around for the figure I knew I just saw.

"I'm not sure," I mumbled back.

Pitch blackness swallowed the path onward. You couldn't see a thing up ahead but the darkness didn't concern me much. My mind was more set on whatever lurks within it. My friends were still oblivious to the potential danger that lay ahead. That's if I'm not entirely out of my goddamn mind that is. I better know what I'm talking about if I speak up. I carefully scoped out each side of the path. The night grew weirder as time went on. The trees danced in the breeze. I looked back at the gang and nodded my head when I saw they were keeping up. Afterwards, all I could do was look straight and hope everything turns out okay. I was in disbelief we were alone in these grim woods. I could see the hill up ahead. I looked over my shoulder and made sure nothing was following us from behind. My friends still had no idea what was going on. I've been quiet this whole time. I'm sure it seemed I was acting strange. I've yet to lose my balance over the situation. When we reached the hill, the air was misty, cooler, and felt strange to breathe in. The leaves on the trees had all fallen. The entire hill just seemed dead and quiet. Once my friends caught up, we slowly started making our way around the hill. From there, things continued to get even stranger. I thought I was hallucinating images of the figure within the fog wherever I looked. The dead trees around began to groan and crackle. I heard distant echoes mixed with the sounds of ghostly moans and whispers close by. The fog began to cluster and pull closer. We moved away from the edges of the trail.

"Screw this, it's cold," 'J' said aloud, and we pushed ahead quickly.

Peculiar noises, sudden shifts in temperature, and catching shadows that wave and wander in the moonlight. Now I felt like it was all beginning to close in. We were met with a massive wall of fog that completely obscured the car lot. 'J' stepped up front and Jezul and Fronze turned on their cell phone flashlights.

All three were about to disappear into the blur. I rushed forward, stopped Jezul and Fronze and yelled out, "Stop!!" to 'J'.

'J' turned around and asked, "Alright man, what's goin' on?"

He approached me as the fog closed in behind him. I remained speechless for a short moment. My boys looked at each other, unsure what the hassle was over, until they all turned to me demanding an explanation.

There, I finally uttered the words, "Something's wrong."

"Whatchu' mean?" 'J' asked. I didn't even know where to start.

"You good?" Jezul asked.

"Yeah," I assured.

"You said, 'Somethings wrong.' So what's wrong?" 'J' asked.

I took a deep breath. I knew they were growing impatient. The wind rushed over our heads. I bit down on my lower lip and rolled my eyes. No matter what, I couldn't find the right words to explain it to them.

"Talk man!" Fronze yelled out.

I looked at them and finally spat out, "There's a-"

Suddenly, we were blinded by the headlights of a car that seemed to have rolled up out of nowhere. I stopped talking and turned towards the bright lights. We shielded our eyes. The next second, the lights flickered blue and red. We could see two car doors open and two men step out of the car. They were both shining flashlights on us.

CHAPTER 4

ALL'S WELL

"What's goin' on in this neck of the woods?" a man asked from behind his flashlight.

"The boys?" Fronze asked in a whisper.

"We're fine," 'J' whispered to us. "Just tryin' out the waters," 'J' said to the officers.

"Whose car is that out in the lot?" the other officer asked.

"Mine," Jezul admitted.

"Can I see your license?" the cop asked. Jezul pulled it out and handed it over.

The first officer turned to me and asked, "Why do you look so nervous?" He shined his light over my eyes before training it on my hands and pockets. "You don't have anything that'd get you into trouble, now do you?"

"Not that I know of," I said, looking down to the ground as he patted me down. I remained still with my hands up. He let go of my empty sweatshirt pocket and checked the pocket of my jeans. My nerves hit as he searched through a hoodie that didn't belong to me. He could have found something that I missed.

"Found a penny," he said to his partner. He dropped the penny back into my jeans pocket then searched through my other pocket. "Hang on, what's this?" he asked me, and pulled out the glass magnifier I took for my cell phone this entire time.

"What's this for?" he asked me.

"I don't know.. how that got in there," I said to him in all honesty.

"You don't know how this got in your pocket?"

"Well I obviously put it in there, I just can't remember when."

I was so lost over all this and the officer seemed to be as well. He pulled the glass apart from its holder, before eyeing me again with suspicion. He showed it to his partner and even he didn't know what it was. My friends were so confused.

"It's empty," the officer confirmed.

He closed the glass up and continued to gaze at me suspiciously. Once he placed the glass back in my hand, I felt relieved. I exhaled deeply and suddenly I saw the specter. I could make out the frame of its ghastly cloak through the glare of the police lights. It hovered over another hill, when suddenly the sky lit up with powerful voltage. The atmospheric dome was filled with bright bolts of blue and white lightning.

In the flash, the unusual being began to lift its arm. It pointed to the large dead tree on the hilltop behind me. There was a loud crash of thunder. Now I was certain it was after *me*. I impetuously broke away from the crowd. I didn't know where I was running to. The only thing following me was the misty fog. I ran until an all-encompassing fog swept the woodlands straight my way. Slowly, it overwhelmed me. The fog condensed and drew closer from every angle. I was surrounded with no sense of direction. My only option was to keep running. I ran blindly through the mist. I may have been running in circles. I ran until I rolled my ankle on a rock and nearly fell to the ground. I looked around for a moment. I couldn't see anything but a nearby hill. I looked around the ghastly land as I climbed up the damp grassy slope. Leafless trees covered the hill. I looked up and saw the large dead tree at the top of the hill. That's when I realized I was heading towards the peak of the sinister hill, exactly where the being pointed me. Like a fountain, the thick fog poured from the hilltop. My shoe slipped on grass and I fell to the ground.

I looked behind me and saw the fog rising, swallowing the hill from the ground up. I ran even further. Suddenly, something from above pushed me down hard. I fell forward and skidded in the mud. I rolled over and sat up in the mist. My jeans were filthy.

I rose from the uprising fog just before it encased me. After I stood up, I ran for the hilltop as fast as possible. As I continued upward, I heard a caw from the left, then heard the same caw from the right. I reached the summit where it was deserted and gloomy. I walked through the trees and glanced up at the tall dead tree. Suddenly, I heard the bird caw soft and gently. It feigned for my attention. I couldn't tell where it was coming from until I heard it again. I walked slowly ahead until I hit a stone well. The strange mist was oozing over its brim. Above the well's mossy shingled roof sat a raven looking back at me through black pearly eyes.

All was quiet as it studied me. It seemed to look at me with fascination until I arched my eyebrows and cringed my nose. Then, the foul cowardly creature disappeared into a poof of feathers before my eyes. *Did that just happen?* I asked myself. I approached the well and placed my hands over the cold wet brim. I looked over the edge and didn't see any water, only mist. I looked down and breathed into the mist, clearing it away to dissipate in the darkness.

After a moment, pin drop silence fell again. I couldn't hear anything. I looked around for any paranormal presence. Suddenly something struck me from the side with enough force to send me flying into a tree. I slammed the back of my head on the bark and crashed to the grass. I landed on my chest and felt the ache as I pushed myself up onto my feet. I was okay, just unprepared for that. I pushed the leaves out of my hair. I moved out from under the trees and stepped into the moonlight. I wanted to face this thing. I don't regularly experience supernatural encounters. The cloaked being dropped out of the sky and pushed me in the chest. Its arms were charged with blue electricity. I was knocked to the ground. Except this time, I felt a powerful shock fire through me. My heart pulsated. I rolled over on the grass and stumbled when returning to my stance. I stood tall before my assailant and looked straight into the hood. I felt cold chills. I rolled my shoulders as a cold breeze trickled down my spine. I bit my lip. I was shocked once I saw the ghost shrink back in fear. I didn't move. I could see my breath while in its presence. Ironically, the phantom appeared to be more afraid of me. I approached it slowly. It cautiously jolted farther away from me with every sudden movement I made. Finally, the phantom spun its cloak and vanished. I wandered around the hilltop, looking over a vast sheet of fog that covered the woods. The fog was too thick to see through. I couldn't see where the forest met the ocean. I was unsure what direction I came up from. I walked through the trees and looked up at the sky. I didn't see a hooded figure, nor a bird. I knew no one would ever believe me if I told them what happened. I still couldn't even believe it. I was nearly halfway down the hill when I began to hear strange noises in the trees overhead. I could hear swooshes and sways like something was flying overhead. I was about to descend into the sea of mist, when suddenly the cloaked being rose from the cloud. For a moment, it looked down on me. The clouds above were stormy. It dove straight at my chest and I leaped at it. The clash resulted in a bright blue electric burst and I was blasted back to the hilltop. The fight wasn't over. I landed on my back and sat up slowly. I felt a cold numbness in my chest like I was just stabbed in the heart with a large icicle. I could hear the phantom coming. I had to get up. I hid behind the well.

The phantom laid its hand over the other and bowed its head. A red star-like energy rained down from the sky in the form of lightning. One of the bolts set fire to the roof of the well and I pressed my back up against the well's side. I could hear the being approach from behind. I looked down at my shoes and controlled my breathing before I peeked over the well. Through the blazing flames, I saw its grim hood hover past in search of me. I threw my hood up, tucked my head between my knees, and tightly wrapped my arms around myself. I tried hard to avoid being seen. I could smell the scent of death approaching as I heard the phantom make a long and cold somber moan beneath its dark cowl. On my toes, I began to maneuver around the perimeter of the well to stay on the opposite side of my attacker. I moved without being seen. It waved its arm over the ground and swept away all the fog within the area. I could feel him tapping on my hourglass. Finally, I fled.

The specter appeared right in front of me. I realized it held a blue spherical orb within its hands. The phantom released the strange glowing orb and the bubble grew larger as it got closer to me. I slowly backed away, then I turned around completely, and booked it. I ran fast in the opposite direction of the bubble but the orb was still catching up. I worried I might explode if it reached me. Hovering high up in the air, the ghost waved its arm and wrapped its cloak around itself like Dracula. The motion caused my footsteps to be pulled back by some invisible force. I fell flat on my chest. I got up and continued to run. The phantom waved its arm outward and this time I flew forward. I firmly planted my hand in the grass and spun around on my fist. Once my feet touched the ground, I charged straight at the being. A part of my leg was pulled into the large blue orb. I broke free and rushed dead ahead. My eyes widened the moment the phantom rose into the air. I didn't know what it was doing. It seemed the ghost was trying to evade me while encasing me in its large glowing blue bubble.

I couldn't escape it; I was finally swallowed by the glowing sapphire-blue bubble. Once I was entrapped, I received a powerful shock and fell to the ground. The bubble started to rise and I began to levitate. I tightly grasped the grass blades between my fingers before they tore out of the ground. The specter rose me up high and brought me forward, observing me. It was mainly focused on my chest. I was suspended in the floating sphere when the phantom raised its hand to the sky and sent a down bolt of lightning that filled the orb. I was struck with another powerful shock. Lightning bounced around the interior of the bubble like a plasma ball. I felt its electricity seep into the blood in my veins. When nothing happened, it looked closely at my chest with dissatisfaction. It was as though he was trying to extract something from me.

The orb changed from blue to a dark crimson color. I was struck with an even stronger bolt that pierced through every inch of my body. The second one was more painful. It was brighter and I could feel it trying to pull something out of me. The phantom wasn't trying to kill me. That wasn't its intention.

But I slowly felt my life slip away from me when the phantom suddenly took me by my neck with a cold hand and pulled me from the bubble. It looked deep into my eyes. Darkness shrouded its face. I was unable to tell who it was, what they looked like, or whether they were even human. I grabbed onto its arm with both hands and investigated its hood. I was sure I'd die if I was shocked again. I could tell the phantom was running out of patience. Whatever it wanted from me, it didn't get it. From high in the air, the being launched me toward the ground. I fell through the burning roof of the well and down I went until ice cold water broke my fall. Chills ran down my spine. Icy water ran down the back of my sweatshirt. I started to kick upward until my head finally broke the surface. I could see up the long stone tunnel. I shouted "Hello!" and my voice echoed and bounced off the stones. I saw stars. I hoped there was someone out there who could hear me but only the hood of the phantom peered over the top of the well. Its torn, ragged cloak blew in the strong breeze. I floated at the surface. The phantom waved its arm over the well and an invisible force pushed me back under the water.

Deep in the dark, I struggled to swim against the current. I ripped and pulled at the water until I surfaced again. Once I got back up, I grabbed some air and looked up at the sky. Dark gray clouds began to gather. The phantom waved its shadowy cloak over the top of the well again and, 'whoosh,' I was sent back down even deeper. I rolled and descended into the endless abyss. Once I was no longer being pushed by the powerful current, I regained control and made my way back to the top. When I returned to the surface, the being held their arm over the top of the well and I was ripped back down. Only this time, I was held under the water. I continued to sink deeper and deeper. Soon, I began to feel light headed and dizzy. My eyes began to tire and my vision started to go. I thought I saw stars appear in the night sky, one by one. I looked up and could see the phantom through the surface. Through the blurry water, I could make out the frame of its cloak against the blaring moon. Its hood gazed down on me as the bubbles from my last breath rose to the top. "Ehhhh."

I saw a great flash.

CHAPTER 5

WELCOME TO OSSYNTHORE

Caught in the water, I felt a gravitational pull so strong I was certain I was literally being dragged from the world. I took off with no warning. I flew through space so quickly, time began to slow down. At least, that's what it felt like. I ran my hands over my hair, it felt soft and feathery. I was all dry now. I noticed that my skin had somewhat of a strange glow to it as well. I pushed up my sleeves and could see the light in my arms and hands. I was still alive. I felt healthy. I could feel it in my face. It felt like I had been cleansed, both physically and spiritually.

I witnessed multiple chapters of space. I watched galactic collisions and saw stars go supernova. I think I glimpsed the birth of the universe. Time worked differently wherever I was. I managed to cross multiple star sectors and superclusters in what felt like a matter of seconds. I traveled to another dimension far beyond our own. It seemed I reached the end of this wormhole when I found myself lying flat on my chest in a long stone tunnel with no recollection of how I got here. There was a light at the end of the tunnel. I stood up and walked toward it. The light at the end grew so vibrant, I eventually had to shield my eyes. I couldn't tell what was at the end of the tunnel, nor guess what I was going to find there. The light ahead began to change to a warm orange glow. I was captivated. The tunnel was filled with yellow rays of daylight. Further, I could start to see clouds in a golden sky. I walked ahead slowly, feeling like all sense of logic was left in the previous world. And I realized I did leave my clothes there. I looked down at my naked body and looked back. The stars within faded. I kept walking. The walls began to close in more and more the further I continued. It wasn't long until I was crawling on all fours under the moss growing out of the stones. The overflow of light blinded my eyes once I reached the end and placed my hand over the rim of the tunnel. There, I immediately pulled back cautiously when I was faced with the perilous drop of a sideways world. The tunnel was an empty well that led out to a crimson forest planted on its side. I sat butt naked and curled up next to the edge like a young kid high up on a playground, afraid to go down the big kid slide. I couldn't understand how or why the hills, the forest, the mountains, everything, was turned sideways. All looked to go on for quite a distance, if not endlessly. I stuck out my legs and sat on the edge of the well. I stared blankly at the clouds as minutes passed. I had no idea what to do. I didn't know where I currently was, or where to go from here.

I looked down at the sideways woodlands below, wondering if I was supposed to jump. I was nearly considering it. "Nothing can happen," I finally told myself.

Suddenly, I rolled back when the world tilted upward and the well stood up straight. I quickly grabbed onto the edge at the last second. I nearly fell down into the darkness. The inner stones were wet and soggy. It was difficult to climb back up. I grabbed onto the top with my other hand and looked down into the bottomless well. No way.

I pulled myself up and climbed over the stone ring. I fell into the flowery grass. I landed on my back with relief and exhaustion. I laid my arms flat in the wild flowers. *This well* was much finer. I'm guessing this was the receiving end of the wormhole.

Butt naked, I sat up and hid against the well. I leaned my back up against the stones. I then heard a 'bloop.. bloop.. bloop..' over my shoulder. I got up off the grass, looked down into the well, and watched water rise until I could see my reflection on its crystal clear surface. I could really use a coin. I looked up from the water and up at the funky clouds high up in the peach colored sky. The wind in the atmosphere was rolling the clouds into little white spirals.

"Where am I?" I asked myself.

"Welcome to Ossynthore," I heard an eerie voice say from the sky.

I looked around. I didn't see anyone or anything. I was alone and naked. My entire body was exposed. I stood at the top of a hill. Behind me were vast valleys of yellow hills. The hills were backed by snowy mountain ranges. Ahead of me stood a red woodland. A small dirt road lined the edge of the woods and served as a barrier between the hills and the woods.

I looked over my back to make sure no one was following me as I walked down the hill. Then, I checked again from side to side when I crossed the trail.

I passed a wooden freight wagon that was left beside the trail. I ran my hand along its edge. The wagon was empty. I found nothing inside but a few sealable glass jars, all empty, and a piece of folded burlap. I was hoping to find some clothing. I walked straight into the woods without a path and hid away in the sticks. It was all I wanted to do. I had thorns at my knees. I tried not to trample as I walked. The trees were short and red. Their branches were curly. They shed their leaves. The falling leaves spun and danced like the type you'd see fall out of a fairytale book. I continued until I noticed a small brook closely ahead. It glimmered under a single ray of sunlight that shone through the trees. I kneeled beside the water and picked up a handful. It was pure and felt cool. It had the look of liquid light. I took a sip. I was too thirsty to care that I was drinking water from another world. I went to dip my hand in for another sip when a strange sparkle began to glisten above the stream. The shimmering spread from where I touched the water to each end of the brook. I looked to the left, then to the right. I backed away from the water and walked away. I was on my way out when a cold dark thought came to mind. The birds sang. The breeze blew over my shoulders. Still, something about it all seemed wrong to me. I walked over to a nearby thornbush. Its roses were ripe and bright. I took hold of a stem and deeply pricked the tip of my finger with one of its thorns. I didn't feel a thing. Not even a pinch. I pulled it out and was devastated when I didn't see a single drop of blood, not even the slightest bit. I clenched my hand into a fist, looked down at the ground and closed my eyes. I wanted to hit my knees. Instead, I just turned around and walked out with a blank face. I walked, feeling the leaf of each plant on my way back. I wanted to make sure they were real and they were. I carried my head in disbelief. I didn't know where to go from here. The sun was setting.

I passed the wagon a second time and noticed it was now filled with all kinds of clothing.

I looked around for anyone, wondering where all the clothes came from.

There wasn't a person in sight. I held up some old red hoodie that looked strangely familiar. Then, I held up a pair of black jeans. They were my size and had tears. I liked them. I'm not a thief, but if I were to be, I'd be a naked one. I reached over and picked up a fresh pair of underwear that were left folded as if someone had courteously left them there for me. I threw them on, ducking behind the wagon. I quickly put on the jeans, while looking around for anyone passing by. I raised the zipper and buttoned them. I was thrilled when I looked over and saw a red thermal. I held it up. Even the shirt, *my size*. I threw it over my head, pushed the sleeves up, then pulled out a few of the top buttons. I threw on some fresh socks and picked up a pair of black boots and began to wonder if someone ran off naked in the woods and left their clothes here. I put on each boot thinking they were nice, but they just weren't right. They fit. They were comfortable. I suppose they'll do. I threw on the red hoodie and pushed each sleeve up. Hopefully it'll be heavy enough to keep me warm through the night.

I looked over and noticed the strap of a black messenger bag hanging from the wagon's shaft tip. I didn't recall it being there a moment ago. Inside the bag held a blank red book and a long black cloth. I grabbed the lengthy cloth and lifted it high. It dropped out to a long dark cloak cut to my length. I didn't recognize it. I didn't recall it ever belonging to me. I lost my red hoodie and placed my arm in each of the cloak's sleeves. The cloak was a bit different from my usual attire but I liked it. It was enough to at least keep me warm and concealed for now. Its tail hung down a little past my knees. I rolled up my hoodie and stuffed it in the bag. I lastly grabbed the folded piece of burlap thinking it'd be useful, and tucked it away in a small inner pocket inside the bag. Over in the corner, I saw a pair of sneakers. I would have considered them earlier if I had noticed them. I felt a weird type of nostalgia when I picked them up. I didn't know where they came from or to who they even belonged, but I was thrilled when I recognized the scratches on the white tips. I pulled them in close and held them tightly with my arms crossed over them.

That's when I realized they were mine, all of this was. The jeans, the shirts, all of this was mine. Not a moment was spent hesitating. I tossed the boots and threw on my sneakers. I stood up and looked around. Still, there was nobody in sight. I wasn't sure if I should be grateful to be alone or not. I closed the bag, picked it up, and laid the strap over my shoulder. After I laid the hood of my cloak over my head, I felt comfortable and confident. I grabbed an empty jar from the wagon and popped back into the woods. I filled the jar with water from the brook then dropped it in one of the bag's side compartments. I wondered what to do next. I wanted to bring the rest of my clothes along with me. I headed out of the woods and filled my bag with as much clothing I could carry. Afterwards, I walked down the path between the woods and the hills. All was in harmony. I was following fate. I couldn't tell you where it was taking me but I felt more comfortable taking the journey in my own shoes, plus I was grateful to be warm. I kept straight. Up ahead, off the side of the trail. I could see a wooden barrel bucket filled with apples. My eyes widened and I clenched my tongue. So far, it must be the first food I've seen in this world. I've been starving since I got here. I walked over and looked down at the bucket. All the apples were ripe and fresh. I looked down the path, in the woods, and in the valley. There wasn't a being in sight. I looked back down at the apples and wondered where they came from. Did they belong to anyone? Were they free? Were they *safe?*

I dropped down next to the bucket and looked around one last time before grabbing a green apple and taking a bite. It was so sweet. It was as though it were to be made from sugar, yet balanced, still retaining its natural flavor. It had to be one the most earthly flourished fruits I've ever come to taste. I loved it so much. I took another bite. Still, I didn't know where they came from. I chewed and wondered why they were left on the grass, alongside the trail. Who left them?

The sky was beginning to darken. I didn't know where I was, nor where I was even going. I grabbed a few more apples and placed them in my bag. I felt guilty about it.

I moved quickly and stopped once I came to a very large grotesque gate. I reached a wall that sealed the rest of the woods. I finished the apple, tossed the core deep into the woods, and approached the gate wings. Each wing was ornamentally strung with metallic leafy vines made of thick iron. The old gate was coated with chipped black paint. Its vines spread across the wings and encompassed a grand 'O' that interlocked the center. Its dense steel bars felt cold under my hands. The doors were very strong and high-standing. Its hinges were old and stale. I messed with the tight steel lock in the center for only a second before I gave up. I faced the sunset, and gave the opposite direction some thought. The cobblestone walls were tall. Its stones were old. I didn't see why I couldn't climb up the stones and hop over the wall. Behind me, the sun was setting between the sticks and the valley. I looked up at the orange sky. Through the gate, I could see stars starting to come out. I clenched my hands around the gate and bowed my head on its bars. Out of nowhere, the inside of the lock gave a small rattle and clink. I let go then, 'EEEEEENNNNNKKKKK.' The 'O' split and the right wing swung out slowly in an eerily welcoming way. I stepped away from the gate and looked up to the clouds in wonder as to how that just happened. I took a deep breath and threw a final glance over my shoulder to make sure there was no one following me. Then, I looked down and passed through the gate feeling like this was going to end badly. I tried to shut the gate as quietly as I could, but of course there still had to be a loud ring once I shut the wing. Its entire frame rattled for a moment. I clenched my hands around the iron to hold the vibration and kill the ringing. Once it went dead, I let go and continued on my path. I carried along trying to cause as little disruption and disturbance as possible. Attention was the last thing I wanted but still, I needed to find someone who would give me theirs. 'O' Who is 'O'? What is this place?

I continued and passed another wooden bucket that was filled with even more brightly colored apples. Apples of red, gold, and sour green. They looked scrumptious. On the right of the trail, sat another bucket. Then down ahead, I saw another bucket. Some of the apples sat in funky straw baskets that were stacked over the top. Some of the apples had even toppled onto the grass. I grabbed a red apple from my bag and sank a bite into it. I felt like I hadn't eaten all day. Night fell softly over the trees. Even though the sky was getting dark, the apple gave me faith. Its skin was smooth. I tasted liveliness in every drop of its juice. The fruit was pure. I didn't know what it was but *something* about it gave me hope. I followed the wooden buckets and trusted they'd lead me somewhere special.

CHAPTER 6

WALKING IN A DREAM

There was a turn down a dark path ahead. I could see a yellow glow in the distance. I didn't care what was ahead of me at this point. I walked slowly to the turn and saw that the yellow glow emanated from a lantern hanging from a post. It wasn't until I approached the post that I saw a short grim-looking being leaning up against it. It dropped its hood and looked up at me. He looked just as miserable as the rest of the place. I followed the trail through the trees and lowered my hood as I approached a small village. I walked slowly. Around, I could see little huts and homes.

Ahead, I noticed a horse stable, passing yet another pair of hoods on the way. One goblin was eating an apple under a dim lantern and another goblin was shucking hay with a pitchfork. The two were about as tall as my waist. Both carried on in silence in the light of the nearby campfire. I didn't want to disturb them, so I smiled softly and continued walking. I took another bite out of my apple. I chewed silently while I passed a group wearing pointy hats and hoods. They were all gathered around the fire. They looked to be near my age, and my size and height, but something felt off. The fire wasn't burning on any type of wood and its flames were white. Each guy and girl had their eyes closed and palms open before the flame, but it didn't seem to emit any heat. I didn't know why they had gathered around it. I called to them, even tapped a few shoulders, and shouted at them. I waved my hand in front of their faces. "Hello? Anyone?" I asked. Not even one of them turned their heads. Their hats and hoods remained still. It was almost as though they were currently being held in some form of trance.

I came across an amazing wagon stationed to the left of the trail. The buggy wasn't hooked up to a horse, but it was painted emerald green and its windows had red curtains. A lustrous purple light shone through its windows. From the grass, I saw a sign: CRYSTAL BALL READINGS. Up on the rein bench sat a short man sleeping under a straw hat. His boots were crossed next to his lute.

Not too far from the wagon rested a sick horse, along with two other women. The horse was wearing a harness and appeared to be miserable. It was laying down in a pile of hay. The other girls were trying to feed the horse a bit of apple, and trying to get her to drink drops of water. They were discussing how the sleeping man had been trying all day to heal the horse using several methods. I could barely comprehend some of the things they were saying. Part of me felt sorry for the horse and I didn't want to disrupt the man so I moved further along and minded my own business. No one looked like they wanted to be disrupted. This place was depressing.

I passed an old woman wearing a long dark gown and a tall pointy hat. She sat alone shivering, but it looked like she was writing musical symphonies on a note sheet. There was a small pile of papers with her. She appeared to be tired and weak. I wanted to offer her my cloak.

I walked over hoping she could shed light on where we were. I approached her and tried a polite, "Hello, madam. Would you like my cloak?" I raised it off my shoulders. She turned the thing away. I figured she would have liked the color. "Could you please tell me where we are?" I asked. She said not a word. She only smiled and looked back at me apparently amused at my confusion. Suddenly she handed me a note sheet from the stack beside her. She had composed a finely written song.

"Lovely," I remarked. "Could you please point me to the shore?"

She didn't seem to know what I was talking about, but she looked at me and silently gestured that I should keep the note sheet.

I decided to move on when one of the hooded beings crossed my path. I stopped short and he snarled at me from under his hood. He couldn't have been taller than my waist. I looked at him with disgust as he continued. He must've been having a worse day than me clearly. I put up my hood and was about to exit the village when I stopped and turned around. I considered if this place could get better.

"Hey," I shouted at the short hooded goblin. I tossed him a red apple, since it was mostly green ones lying around.

I didn't have much but I walked back to the entrance and found the first guy I passed. He remained under the lantern. I reached into my bag and handed him the glass jar I filled with water. I told him about the stream up the road in case he didn't know about it. He took a sip of the water, handed me back the jar, then picked up an empty pail and he was off. Once he was gone, I headed back into the village. I grabbed a lantern off the top of a barrel and carried it back to the two goblins who were working. Above the two was a lantern with an unlit stub. I opened the lantern's glass door, picked up a few strains of straw from the stable, and set them afire with my lantern's flame. The two hooded goblins looked at me, deeply confused. I carefully reached up and held the straw to the unlit candle's wick. Once the candle was lit, the ground lit up orange and the hooded individuals had light to work. The one eating the apple looked momentarily pleased. I shut the door and smiled at them. I passed the group wearing pointy hats and colorful hoods. They were still gathered around the fire. I walked over to the buggy and approached the rider. The rein-man was now awake, playing a soft tune on his lute. His hat was hanging off the footboard of the wagon as he gently strummed chords into a melody. I reached into my bag, unfolded the music note sheet I received from the elderly woman, and passed it up to the strummer in hopes he could decipher its symphony. He nodded proudly. He tuned a few strings on his lute and began to play. The melody brought harmony and joy to all around. People looked up with pleased expressions. The ones gathered around the flame broke out of their little trance and were enlightened by the sound of the strum. I couldn't even read the notes off the stave but the lute player clearly had the affinity. The music brought delight to everyone. I looked over at the horse and picked up the man's hat off the edge of the wagon. I asked if I could borrow it. He didn't mind. I brought the hat over to the horse. The other ladies looked at me askew as I kneeled and focused on the horse's eyes. I placed the man's hat gently on top of his horse's head and within the second, the horse sprung up vigorously on its hind hooves. She neighed strong and proudly. I was amazed by how tall she stood.

I must've scared her, I thought. "Wonderful job," I told both the horseman and the ladies that assisted in healing her. I could see astonished faces around us. They gathered by the horse with fascination. She planted her front hooves and held her chin up high for everyone to capture a glance of her fancy new hat. The ladies began plucking little flowers and colorful herbs. They arranged them nicely around the crown of the hat. The horse turned to me, standing mighty as a palace of bricks, and winked at me under her flowery hat.

I finally reached the elderly lady. She was enjoying the music but still appeared to be shivering. It was clear she was cold. I wanted her to have my black cloak. I was taking it off my shoulders when I remembered the red hoodie I still had. I reached into my bag and pulled it out. I threw it over her shoulders, but the woman turned to me wide eyed and hissed. She shrieked, tearing the hoodie off her back, and threw it on the ground. She looked at me with eyes of rage as I slowly backed away. I looked at the hoodie lying in the dirt between us. I didn't want it either. I put up my dark hood, grabbed another apple, and moved on. The music behind me faded and grew more distant. I continued through the shadowy woods with the lantern. I took a bite out of my apple and kept going until I noticed a pure white light showing on the horizon. I slowed down once I entered a small glade. The glade was centered with a round tree. Its roots were potted in a wooden bucket. A white lantern was twined to one of its branches, shining as I approached. Beside the lantern was a woman on a stool. She was balancing with the heel of her boot in the air, wearing tight pants with a tucked white collared shirt. She wore a vest over her shirt and the hood of a green cloak over her pale gray hair. I walked the inner perimeter to get a better angle of her. She appeared to be picking apples from a bare tree and tossing them down into the baskets and buckets on the ground below. Her only helper was a small troll, or so I presumed, who assisted by carrying the filled buckets away and returning with more empty ones. She finished filling another bucket and away he went. I took another bite out of my apple and figured I might as well try to approach someone again. She might even be able to give me some guidance on where to go from here. I didn't want to interrupt her, but I had no idea where to even sleep. It was getting late. Guessing by the loads of apples, she had been at this all day. Maybe she was almost done. I could wait around for her to finish. Then again, just a quick word was all I needed. Still, I didn't know how to approach her. I wasn't even sure what to say. I made way over to her left. I didn't wanna startle her from behind so I approached her from the side. Her loose green cloak fluttered in the woodland breeze.

"Excuse me, ma'am?" I asked, hand over my heart in hopes I could convey pardon for a moment. I wasn't sure if she heard me. She appeared focused only on what was in front of her. I raised my hand to wave when a bright reddish glow appeared. My words fell. I stepped back and remained aside with a fallen lip. I held my fingers over my eyes to prevent being blinded by the light. I could just make out through my fingers the woman still rendering apples, one after the other. She was whirling her hand in a circular motion. The apples would blossom and continue to grow until they were fully ripened, all from the same stem by nothing more than an odd dance of her fingers. Her apples blossomed in red flashes. What would you think?

She continued pulling each one and dropping them in the bucket. Each apple lushed and flourished in her spontaneous dexterity. She stopped and closed her fingertips when she caught me in her peripheral vision. She turned towards me slowly. I lowered my head and could feel her gaze hard on me. She raised her fingers to the brim of her hood to unveil her face, but by then, I was already gone, leaving the apple I was chewing bouncing on the grass before I could even catch a glimpse of her face.

I felt in a daze, walking in a dream. I tried to put together and rationalize what I just saw. I was starting to think this wasn't a dream. I didn't know where to go. I just kept walking. I eventually slowed and stopped once the trail came to a downward slope. Beyond was just endless woods as far as the eye could see. I noticed a log beside the trail and sat down on it. When I sat down, the log made a loud obnoxious creek and wobbled underneath me so I just sat down on the ground and leaned against it.

Was I stuck here? I didn't want to be lost and alone in this place. Eventually I'd wake up and rise into reality. Reality, a place I can remember dreading, but being *here, now*, I miss it. I would graciously appreciate being back there. I pulled my knee in and tightly wrapped my arms around it. The night fell colder. How do I wake up? I never minded being alone but I really wish I wasn't right now. Everything around me made me think about all the times God had my back. I tried hard to think back on all the things

I ever did. I couldn't remember anything. I tried to think about all the people I made laugh, and all the people I left crying. I wanted to remember all the ones I ever loved and all the ones that ever loved me. Where were they now? I looked down at the dead leaves on the grass. Where was I?

46

CHAPTER 7

A VIOLET NIGHT

"You look lost," I heard a girl's voice say from behind. I turned to see a beautiful young woman very near my age. Her smile was kind. She was wearing my sweatshirt, the red one I left lying on the ground. She tossed me an apple as she approached. This one was pink, much different from all the others. I lowered my hood and pushed my hair from my eyes. I opened my bag, unzipped the small inner pocket, and pulled out the folded piece of burlap to lay down over the log before she sat.

Her hair hung in two long waves of silver underneath the red hood. Her eyes were a palish yellow. She had a blissful smile with teeth the color of winter snow. I patted the burlap, inviting her to sit. She had her hand curled over her mouth. She was trying to hide her smile as she sat down on the dry piece of burlap. The log didn't seem to wobble at all when she sat on it.

She dropped her hood revealing her beautiful face. There was a spark in her eye. A bright one. Her eyes were warm. They gave me faith. They were like two canary diamonds welcoming your gaze. She looked down at me with the tender eyes of a skilled nurse. That was when I realized she was the lady from the tree. I remained silent at first. I was unsure of what to say.

"Did you come from Sunlight Oaks too?" she asked.

I folded my arms over my knee and turned to her, confused. "The Sunlight Oaks?"

"Indeed," she said. "Terrible fire. Mercifully everyone evacuated in time and got out safely. Still, its flames were unlike any I've ever seen."

"No, I'm not from there, but I'm so sorry to hear that. It's good that you and everyone got out. But I'm not from here." I turned back with a flash of desperation. "Where is 'here'?"

"How do you mean?" she asked.

"Where are we?" I asked again, looking up at the planets in space.

"You and I are in the land of Ome, wanderer. It's a small village. We're safe here. After the fire, the creatures that inhabited the forest had to migrate. Many others lost their homes and had to relocate. Chances are, we'll have to move again soon. An eerie mist has been rolling in. It oozes out of the shadows. It's been consuming the woods at its very core. Night after night, day after day. Its noxious fumes won't harm you directly, but I can hear the earth screaming from deep below."

I studied her again. Her hair was gray, but not from age. She didn't look a day older than I. "Why's your hair gray?" I asked respectfully.

She began to twirl it. "My hair turned gray due to an insufficient amount of energy in the earth. It's been that way ever since the mist appeared," she went on to explain, "It not only affected me, but it affected the entire forest as well."

Now taking a closer look at the woods, I could see the picture she was describing. The trees around were black, dry, and leafless. A familiar-looking fog began to roll past.

"There it is again," She pointed out.

"What? The fog?"

"Yes, the fog," she said. "We call it the gloom."

She looked down at the leaves scattered on the ground. "That mist is killing all the greenery and leaving it gray. Before it, we lived in peace. This world's people were safe. There was no controversy, no hunger. We needed nothing. That was, until one day when each field and forest fell under the dark spell of that fog, one by one. There's few ideas of what this is. The woods where the hares used to run are all clouded by fog. The flower gardens and meadows turned gray. Eventually *my* forest became one of the many mysteriously burnt down from a sudden forest fire. Home was good to me for a while."

She looked up at the stars. I felt so sorry for her.

"The endless tree-tops were a gorgeous sight," she said. "The sunlight that shone through the trees is what earned the forest its name. Its gardens were arrayed with the most breathtakingly gorgeous flowers, always. Home was filled with joy and the most extraordinary lifelings."

"Forgive me," I cut in. "You're saying you were born here, in this world?"

"Indeed. I was born long ago in a faraway place. The forest wasn't where I was born, but it's where I spent my time."

"So, is that how you can perform witchcraft?" I wasn't sure if I should have used that word.

"Pardon?" She looked at me fiercely and the color of her eyes changed from yellow to green like two emeralds. I felt that my next words should be chosen wisely. "Witchcraft? Is that what you call it?"

"Wickcraft, do pardon me," I said sincerely. Although, I knew she could still sense that I was being sarcastic. "With all due respect of course, a brief moment ago, you were growing fresh apples repetitively off a single stem. I saw it. I saw you." I mimicked the movement with my hand. "Then you would pluck 'em right off and toss 'em in the bucket."

I turned and looked at her. After her eye color changed back to yellow, she straightened out her fingers and glanced at the back of her hand. "Is that amazing to you?" she asked.

I found it all so confusing. What was even more perplexing was how she kept looking back at me. She seemed to be just as confused by me. It was like we weren't fully understanding each other. She seemed to believe her ability to alter an apple tree to grow ripe succulent apples in seconds, by nothing more than a whirl of her fingers, was natural, nothing out of the ordinary, something I should have always known of. She held a stern gaze and remained still.

"Ok, so if I'm not mistaken, you practice woodland arts? You come from the forest?" I asked.

"Biomancy," she corrected me, "and yes. Somewhat. We just went over this, did we not?"

"I believe so. So how does one ever even learn to-?"

"Learn to.. what?"

"You make things grow?"

She nodded.

I asked, "How does that work exactly?" She only scoffed under her breath.

"Is it like a special power or something? Can you choose it?" I asked.

Her eyes widened brighter but they retained their yellow shade. She seemed to be more and more baffled by every question I asked, and how little I understood. "Never mind," I said finally, giving up. I felt my ignorance was beginning to agitate her so I looked up at the sky, and dropped the conversation.

"No wait," she insisted. "My apologies, but are you honestly asking me that?"

Suddenly, I looked down at my hands. They were becoming translucent, nearly vanished now. I shoved them under my legs and tried to conceal them. I sat back against the log, sank deeper into the leaves, and closed my eyes. I was trying not to freak out.

"Are you ill?" she asked.

"Listen, I'm not from *here,* from wherever this is," I told her. "All of this is new to me, please forgive me." My eyes remained shut. "This might sound crazy, but I think I just died."

At this point, reality was becoming way too much for me. I was processing a lot and I wasn't feeling like my normal self. She continued to study me.

"I'm not sure why, nor do I even know how I came across this world, but I did. All I can remember was a big flash. Then, I climbed out of a well and didn't know where I was when I awoke in this nightmare. I walked alone until twilight. I followed your apples and they led me to the village. I was so grateful when I saw others," I told her. "After I ran into you, I came across this log and sat down. Inside, I felt so lost and alone. Then, within a minute, you showed up."

"All find their way, I suppose," she said, twisting a leaf in her fingers. She didn't seem to possess any insight into my own personal predicament, and I couldn't blame her. I looked back down at my hands and saw they had returned to normal. I probably couldn't have seemed crazier to her. Still, by my side she remained. Against the log, I sat beside her feet. I tried to quiet my mind. Maybe overthinking wasn't the best thing to do right now. The night's breeze blew overhead. Leaves flew by. The two of us sat in silence. I looked up when I heard howls. Bats flew past the crescent moon high in the purple sky. A violet night. I looked down at the dead leaves around my sneakers then rested my head against the log. I turned my head and looked at the girl.

"So this ability of yours," I brought up again.

"Yes?" I had her full attention.

"I'm honestly asking you now, how is it that you can do all the things that you do?"

"All possess their own way of obtaining nature's power," she explained. "Meaning, they all have their very own roots to spread and blossom from freely. I grow things, others can heal, some can even poison. It all depends."

"Depends on what? Where does this power come from?"

"I was born with them."

"Born with them," I repeated back to myself. I looked down at the pink apple and admired its rosé color. "I must say, I find that pretty hardcore."

She looked at me strangely.

"Lovely, I mean. To be able to do what you do, that's extraordinary. Can you show me again?" I asked.

She smiled at me and looked around at the lifeless soil, saddened. I could see dread and sadness in her eyes as she looked at the withering trees. Suddenly, she turned me with tempted eyes and a smirk. She raised her hood over her head and threw me a wicked glare. She had made up her mind about something. Then, she dropped her hood and spat on the dirt. She looked at me seriously this time. Finally, before my very eyes, I watched her raise a small bright yellow orb from the dirt. She raised it like an invisible thread from the ground. The bud continued to grow until it grew so large it curved over. The flower bloomed beautifully into the shape of a rose-gold heart that stood aglow in a cloud of luminous pollen. I looked up into her eyes. I was captivated. The light of the flower shone over her face and I fell into her yellow gaze. I smiled. The person under the hood was becoming more and more visible to me.

"It's called a Heartbell. It's one of my favorites," she told me. "Listen closely, you'll hear it ringing."

I leaned in closely and I could hear a fairy dancing. It sounded like the shimmer of a windchime. "Nature holds a spirit of its own," she continued. "Each life is pure and unique. It's an aspiration that thrives through each seed. All stretch their own roots to bloom from in their own intrinsic ways.

They all grow towards the light. They all hope to reach it one day. Fruit is life's sugar. With a flower, comes a garden. With a tree, comes a forest. Forever and ever, in an endless flow. *That* is Nature and its form. And yes, it is very lovely. It can be quite charming at times. Where I'm from, one is born straight from its heart. It's the type of thing that grows *you*, so you see you have it all mixed up. The practice isn't complex, but very intuitive, I must say. Heart, Desire, Creation, Aspire. Keep it keyed and all can be yours."

With that, we just sat there looking into each other's eyes. I still had so many questions running through my head but there was nothing left for her to explain. I looked at her long silver waves of hair. I was torn between asking more about who she was, or where I was, or where to go from here. I looked down at the pink apple in my hands, then over to the heart-shaped flower that wasn't there a moment ago. My mind was still in space, even after her explanation. I was still under the logical disbelief of one growing flowers and fruit on command; yet somehow, I was still so open and fascinated to learn more. I finally gathered my thoughts together to form one single question, a random question, one that I would never ask anyone.

"Can you help me?" I asked.

There was a blurry moment. She looked at me confused, unsure of what I meant by 'help.'

But she could at least tell I was serious.

"Help you?"

"Please," I nodded.

"Help you how?"

"I'm not sure, but you seem to know quite a lot about this place."

"Oh, and you think what? That this is enough to get your life back and get you home?" I could tell by her tone and her expression that I was still missing a lot.

"You really don't know where you are, do you? There are things about this world you're only beginning to comprehend now."

There was something strange about this place that just didn't feel right. Clearly, I felt out of place, but I felt like I *really* didn't belong here. Like this was all a mistake.

"I have to get out of here," I said. I stood up.

"And how do you expect to do so?" she asked.

"I'm not sure," I said, looking up at the blue night sky. "I gotta try, though." I turned to her. When no words came up, I noticed the heartbell, and sat down on the log.

"I have to try," I repeated.

"This world has its ups and downs. I've been through its twists before," she said.

"Its twists?" I asked.

"You'll see. It's not all fantasy."

I had nothing to say back.

Finally, she offered help. "I know a friend I could take you to. I'm not certain how much she could do, but I'm sure she'd be willing to answer any questions you have, much better than I can. She might even be able to point you in a good direction."

She took a deep breath and looked out into the woods. She nudged me and pointed to something in the distance. At first, I couldn't tell what she was pointing at. It was too dark to see anything. After taking a closer look, I spotted something large and spherical sticking out of the treetops. It wasn't far from where we were.

"I'm just tryna get back home."

"Well it seems like home is a long way from where you are."

I dropped the pink apple in my bag and threw my bag over my shoulder. I laid my hood over my head, picked up the lantern, and placed my other hand in my cloak pocket. Then, I began descending the hill into the misty woods.

"By all means, carry away, but don't forget what I told you about this place. I wouldn't underestimate this world," she called out as she rose from the log.

"C'mon," I said, without any further hesitation. I was getting out of here, with her. We started down the path as a pair of hoods disappearing into a wave of milky mist.

CHAPTER 8

WELCOME TO THE FOREST

We were able to pick up speed once we passed through the mouth of the woods. We walked quietly under the treetops following a lone dusty trail. Heading this way didn't seem like a bad idea at the time, but it's starting to feel pretty daring, especially this late at night. There were multiple turns and crossroads. We were following a complex network of trails around a dead forest. I didn't want to lose her or get lost. She looked at me with intensity in her yellow eyes, and said, "You may call me Atrixia."

I looked ahead down the trail. I could not shake the thought that it'd be best if it was only me out here. If something were to happen to her, I would never forgive myself. In retrospect, I should have just asked for basic directions, simple lefts and rights. Then she would have remained safely at the village. She'd probably be getting ready to go to sleep by now. Still, it was clear that she was determined to help me. She *chose* to accompany me. Still, the way I saw it, her protection was a greater concern. It all made me wonder more about her.

"These paths can twist unexpectedly," she said. But she had a gentle smile. She could tell how strange this place was to me, and she didn't want me to feel stranded. I went along with it. I looked at her beautiful face. She was flawless. She seemed tired, but seemed so sure of herself. I walked by her side and at her pace.

"So, your friend. She 'cool' like you?" I asked.

"What do you mean by 'cool'?

"Can she do interesting tricks?"

"You'll like her," she said.

Time passed. I asked, "Are we close?" hopefully remaining indifferent and relaxed.

"We'll be there soon if we hurry."

The wind began to whip and whistle through the trees. The air was mixed with the odor of ashes and dry sap. A wind kept blowing my hood down. The walk was filled with the subsongs of crows. Their caws began to grow louder and more obnoxious, from all around us. The crows gathered in the trees, one by one. They crowed back and forth on the rickety gray branches curled over the trail. I moved ahead unbothered by the sounds. The howls of wolves could be heard from afar. They sounded malicious and hungry. The wind whispered and the trees rattled. It all synced together and sang danger in its hymn.

The wide yellow eyes of an owl looked down from a tree. We moved deeper into the woods. Soon I could begin to hear twigs crackle and snap. The dead leaves behind us shuffled and crumbled as if someone were tailing us, but nobody was there. The crows flew from the branches closely above our heads, while we ducked under the wet crystalline gossamers that draped them. I threw my hood over my head and looked up at the crescent moon. Its light shone through the trees and set our path aglow. No matter what, we kept straight and followed the moon. This wasn't the place to get lost in. I gazed around and took in the fresh air. The wind eased and the clouds began to clear. A beautiful midnight-blue sky full of stars and planets was unveiled. I could see luminaries between the treetops. I had nothing to say, only a million things to think, and one direction to go in. I took a deep breath and turned to Atrixia. She was my guide.

We came to a cross path and she turned left.

"You okay?" I asked.

She turned around to face me. "I'm fine," she hushed.

"What is it?" I asked.

"The purrs," she whispered.

She smiled at me and turned back around. I listened for the purrs but I couldn't hear anything. I didn't notice much, I suspect, as we focused on our path through the woods. I looked around the base of each tree. I glanced up at the branches and down at the bushes. I didn't notice any activity. All I could see were shadows and starlight.

"I can't see anything. What's out there?" I asked.

"The mooncats. Look closer," she said.

I peered in a bit deeper, then pulled away once I saw multiple pairs of eyes blink each in succession within the bushes. The cats were high up in the trees as well. They were glaring back at us from every direction. All their eyes were different colors. Orange, blue, red, yellow, green. Some of the cats had mixed eye colors. Other cats had two different eye colors. One cat appeared to have only one eye. They began to play and chase each other. Deep in the dark, I saw a creepy white pair that didn't seem to have pupils. Now I couldn't look anywhere and not see cats.

The white-eyed cat slowly began to rise like a small tiger after a deep sleep. I turned towards Atrixia and called for her without breaking eye contact with the cat. Atrixia turned around to reassure that I was keeping up with her, then continued walking. The cat's white eyes formed pupils and turned purple. The rest of the cats dashed away.

Suddenly, the purple eyed cat disappeared and I walked away with my hands in my cloak pockets. I was passing a fallen tree when along came a lone black cat the color of the night sky. She scurried beside me, and walked the whole length of the log. I stopped once I noticed her. Her fur was black like a panther and coated in bluish moonlight, from her ears to the tip of her tail, which whipped around when she sat up to face me.

We studied each other from head to toe. Purple light waxed over her eyes and she gazed at me through sharp vertical pupils. I tried to get Atrixia's attention but when I looked away from the cat, Atrixia was gone. When I looked back over, so was the cat. I hurried, hoping I didn't lose Atrixia somehow. I turned the corner and a phantom appeared out of nowhere. Atrixia was gone.

"Hello?" I asked. Sound seemed to pass around the phantom, but in a strange loop or echo.

The phantom didn't move.

"Who are *you*?" I asked.

Its only response was a bow of its hood.

"What is this place? Where am I?" I demanded an answer.

"This is where your story continues. Your fate lies ahead," the shadowy being finally whispered to me.

"What? My fate? And what would my fate be here?"

"You're in another world. A world that holds a dark future. There's a problem here. You may be the solution. The world awaits. IT'S YOUR TIME," the dark hood thundered. It was hiding something, something menacing.

"Any chance of me continuing my fate in my old world?" I asked.

"Go," it told me.

"You won't be joining me?" I asked finally.

The phantom then pulled back on the sleeve draped over its hand, and I was stunned when I saw no hand there. The being possessed no physical form whatsoever. The hollow cloak blew away with the wind and I started to get chills once I was alone.

The path split into two. I stood between them, uncertain which path Atrixia took.

I stepped left and when it felt off, I backed away. I considered taking the right path and looked down its endless shadowy trail. When that didn't feel right either, I called out Atrixia's name.

"Trix?!"

All was quiet. It was like she completely disappeared. The forest didn't even call back.

Not a chirp, nor a hiss. I was so confused. Suddenly, the ground began to shake, shift, and lift. The earth was changing shape. I didn't know what was happening until the ground beneath the two paths started to rise and twist into a double helix. The two paths spiraled into each other and formed a long singular tunnel. A blue light began to shine from the other end of the tunnel and I began to follow it. The tunnel was filled with its blue glow. It was like looking into a star. I walked, running my fingers through the grass walls. It was so surreal. I looked behind me when I was halfway through. I could barely see out the dark end. Leaves tumbled by the opening. I looked forward and shielded my eyes from the light. The light grew brighter and brighter. I called out Atrixia's name again in hopes I wasn't just walking into deeper trouble. In the light, I saw the silhouette of a girl. She threw her hands over the top of the tunnel and stuck her head in like she was teasing me, before she let go and twirled away.

I wasn't sure if I should trust where I was going. The soft hum of a girl's voice began to echo off the walls. My mind was carried away on a cloud. I passed through the end and entered another world. A different world. I stepped onto the bluegrass of a vast forest land. I looked at the luminescent turquoise trees in amazement. Teal light shone from every leaf and grass blade. Here, there was harmony in the air. I felt a soft tap on my right shoulder. I turned and saw nobody. Suddenly, I was taken by my left hand and spun around by Atrixia. Suddenly we were free. I was caught in the enrapturement of the new atmosphere. We ran quickly. It felt like everything was happening so fast, while at the same time, it felt like the clock was smashed and time didn't exist here. We stopped once we reached a glade filled with bright wisps suspended in midair. She stepped in closer and whispered in my right ear, "Welcome to the forest."

She began to dance with me. I placed the lantern on the glowing blue grass. She twirled around then took me by my hands and pulled me towards her. She placed her palms against mine and looked into my eyes. She gently laid her chin on my chest and when she looked up at me, she smiled. Bioluminescent birds fluttered above our heads. She looked up at the sky and you could see sparks in her eyes.

I barely even knew her. I only just met her but something, no, everything about her, just sang life. A part of me was hit and captivated by her thriving light.

I think I love her.

She threw her hand up and all the white wisps flew toward the stars. The moment was heavenly. She looked at me seriously and I gave her my undivided attention. She gently placed her arms around me and held me close when she asked, "Do you still see my world as a-"

"-Paradise," was the word I used to finish her question. "We could stay here forever," I told her.

She smiled. "Come over here," she said. She waved her hand before two trees twined together and joined at the top. Together, they formed an archway with what appeared to be a blue portal in its window.

"It's time to go," she said sadly.

The two of us approached it together.

"Close your eyes," she told me.

I closed my eyes. Then, I felt her take me by the hand and pull me through.

CHAPTER 9

WHEREVER GOD TAKES ME

I opened my eyes and we were back in the shadowy woods. The portal was gone and I was in a calm state of mind. I had a laid-back feeling. It was as though I just woke up from a dream. Atrixia was up ahead. She was surveying each side of the trees, like she was reading them and navigating her next move. She led us down a path and I walked behind her slowly.

"She isn't much farther," she said. She turned and looked at me. "Hurry along, do you want to be out here all night?" I couldn't help thinking what will happen if we get there, only to find out I'm stuck here.

All I can do right now is hope for the best. I can't remember how I even got to this planet. If Atrixia's friend could at least inform me on how I came to this world, or possibly send me in the right direction, I couldn't really ask for more of her and Atrixia. In fact, I wouldn't be able to thank the two of them enough.

Atrixia seemed to know where to go from here. I caught up and walked beside her.

"So, your friend. Tell me about her. What's she like?"

"What's she like?" She pondered to herself as she slowed down. "Hm. She's a bit - different, a little out there."

"Out there? Like out in the middle of the damn woods, 'Out there'?" I asked.

"You'll see," she said with a smile. "She has one of the kindest hearts you'll ever come across."

"What's she doing all the way out here anyway?" I asked, "Was she one of the foresters?"

"She has her likings for the outdoors. The air, the peace, and the fresh berries and herbs. She and I were friends back home in the forest. We met again in the summer, after the forest went down in flames last spring."

We turned the corner and came to a strange spherical home. The home had an odd roundish shape and its ceiling was caving inward. Its walls were bleak. The home's outer layer had a lifeless moldy gray color. There was a small round glass window above the oval front door.

"Alrighty then," I said, and I approached the walkway that led up to the front door. Out of nowhere I was hit with a strong, foul, nauseating scent. I felt sick. I backed away with my hand clenched over my nose. I turned to Atrixia with teary eyes. I tried not to gag. "Here? Your friend lives here?" I asked.

She just looked at me, before walking to a small purple tree, pulled some pedals off it, and came back. All the other plants appeared to be dead. She looked me in the eye as she placed the pedals in my hand.

"Here, these are Lilacs," she told me.

"Okay." I accepted them, unsure of what I was to do with them. "Thanks."

"They have a *sweet* fragrance, one that won't ever tarnish, ever. Not even in the gloom can they wither. Place them under your nose."

I held them closely to my nose. They smelt flowery and sweet. The scent reminded me of the spring season. I looked at her and smiled once I felt relieved. We walked over to the house and stood before the curvy stone walkway that led up to the front door. I set my eyes on the circular window centered above the front entrance. A yellowish glow shone through the glass.

The lights were on inside. I noticed an odd jar in the window before I turned to Atrixia. "What exactly are we gonna say?"

"I'm not sure," she said. "Just start out small and from the beginning. Tell her about everything that happened after you got here. Tell her where you entered from, and everything that's happened since."

I felt like *all of that* would be impossible to explain. "She'll share any insight she has on how one accidentally stumbles across this place and she'll discuss all the potential possibilities of you returning to your world. And if there's any precautions we should know, she'll share that too." She looked up at me and smiled. "Maybe there's a way to send you back to wherever you came," she said warmly. There was hope in her eyes.

"Back?" I doubt that.

"There's ways."

"And you think it's gonna be easy?"

"It shouldn't be impossible. We'll just talk and hear what she says."

We walked up to the house. I placed the flowers over my nose, took a breath, and knocked on the door with a fist full of lilacs. No answer.

"Maybe she's not home," I said.

"Not home? The lights are on," Atrixia said. She looked up at the window.

I raised my hand to knock again and Atrixia caught my arm before I could.

"Still, I wouldn't wanna catch her at a bad time. Who knows? She might be busy," she said.

"Well, what are we supposed to do?" I asked.

"We could wait," she suggested.

The temperature was dropping. I could see my breath in the air.

"I'll wait," I said, "you should go back."

"What?" She seemed surprised.

"You were kind enough to bring me here. There's no reason for you to have to spend another moment out here."

"What? I wouldn't leave you out here all by yourself."

"I'll be fine. Cut through your little blue forest, you'll be back at the village in an instant."

"I'm not leaving you."

She pulled my red hood over her head, and looked at me. There was a moment of silence between the two of us.

"COME IN!" We finally heard a loud joyful voice say from inside. "Leave the door open," the voice added.

Atrixia smiled at me and we each reached for the doorknob at the same time. Our hands touched. It couldn't have been more awkward when I felt the warmth of her fingers pull out from underneath mine. She gently placed her fingertips over her heart as I opened the door.

Inside was warm and decorated much more vibrantly. I was struck with the strong scent of cinnamon and peppermint the instant I stepped into the room. The home was filled with the sweet air. The ceiling appeared to be higher from inside. It was no longer caving in. A silver chandelier hung from it. The chandelier dangled over padded chairs that were arranged in a circle around a circular table. The table was short, its red wood was polished, and there was a small stack of books sitting on top of it. The bookshelves were crooked and placed circularly around a round red carpet that centered the room. Each shelf held various texts and odd types of flowers. The wallpaper was bright orange with a fancy silver diamond pattern.

I admired it. The other side of the house was divided into two sections. On one side, you'd see a messy kitchen. There were recipe books left open on the countertop with odd types of herbs and flower petals scattered around them. The homeowner had herbs hung across a dryer line in front of an open window. The counter was built along the inner wall, under long cabinets and tall bottle racks. The entire work area was built around a large boiling pot. The pot was releasing orange steam into the air. In the other corner was a crafting station with a small desk covered in tools, cutters, and rotary boards. The section was backed by walls consisting of miniature drawers and compartments storing all sorts of things. The tall shelves held stacks of colorful fabric. One wall held a ribbon rack that dispensed thread off spools and ribbon off wheels. The whole room was silent as if no one was in it. So it seemed until a silver hat covered in white glitter popped up from behind a fold-up curtain. The wearer took off the silver hat and put on a black top hat speckled with white polka dots.

A soft, "Who's there?" echoed across the room. It was a woman's voice. Atrixia stood in front of me, waiting. The lady leaned out from behind the blinds, and screamed with joy when she saw Atrixia. She ecstatically threw the curtain-folds to the side. She was wearing a dress that matched her hat. Black with white polka dots. She rushed over and met Atrixia in the center of the room. There was a tight, long-lasting hug. Her hair was gray like Atrixia's except hers was a little darker.

"I must say, it's great to see you," the lady in the hat said, "I wasn't expecting such a surprise. I would have cleaned." The young woman wandered around the room. "Though, I do love your visits," she added. "They're always so lovely. And you've brought a friend I see, how dashing.

"You have a lovely house," I told her.

I didn't know how else to describe it. I didn't want to touch anything.

"Really? Thank you," she said. "It wasn't like that a second ago."

I looked at her in deep confusion.

She turned back to Atrixia. "How have you been?" she asked gleefully. She held Atrixia's hands in anticipation of good news to share.

"All has been well, for the most part," Atrixia said. "I cannot complain. There hasn't been much to do around here lately. I've just been doing what I can for the village and wandering around. I was able to fill a hundred baskets before the sun set."

"Wonderful. Truly, you're always a great help and so joyful, no matter the color of the day. That's what I love about you," the woman said.

"I thank you. And you, you've been well? You look well."

"Well, thank you," she said, charmed again. "I've been okay. The damn gloom keeps rolling in. I guess the wither season is gonna be much sooner this year. It seems inevitable. Still, I wouldn't mind just a few more of those wildwood berries, but in all this darkness, I wouldn't be surprised to see if they're all dried up raisins by now."

"Very good point. Thank goodness a few dwarfs passed by. They were kind enough to assist me in potting a tree. They ripped up a whole appletree and placed it for me. Otherwise, I never would've been able to grow all those apples."

I waited patiently by the door when I noticed a jar placed within one of the inner ribs of the house. It was like the one in the window. I looked a bit closer. It contained sweet kinds of cinnamon sticks, pinecones, and scented herbs, sealed under a fabric lid. Another jar, filled with the same things, was centered on the table in the middle of the room. I looked around and noticed that the jars surrounded the room. They were air fresheners, I realized. You could find them high up on the shelves and on the window mantels. A few were also tucked under the stair boards. The jars were all different sizes and shapes. Each held a different fragrance. I lowered my hood and looked around the home. Both Atrixia and the lady turned to me. The lady walked over and met me eye to eye by the wall.

She held out her hand to shake mine. "My name is Mint. It was brought to my attention that you're currently caught up in some type of predicament, and it's intellect that you desire."

"I'm just tryna head home," I told her.

"Home is where you make it. At least that's what we used to say, back when Atrixia and I lived in the forest. Could you explain what happened?"

I looked away, unsure where to start.

"You look flushed," she said. She placed her fingers against my cheek. She picked up my chin and looked into my eyes. She walked over to her pot on the other side of the room. She looked excited. She ran her fingers across her counter-top, then spun around towards the pot. She lowered a ring shaped shelf from the ceiling. Once the shelf was positioned over the pot, she brought the water to a simmer. After, she grabbed for multiple jars and canisters from the cabinets. She placed each one on the counter. Without looking, she began knocking ingredients off the drop shelf behind her into the pot. She bumped her elbow back and knocked over a boxed powder, without even taking her eyes off the cabinet. The powder poured into the water and the water turned red. A big red puff of smoke was released from the cauldron. The air smelled citrusy and reminded me of fruit punch before the cloud dissipated. She looked over at me and saw me watching the pot.

"If you're just standing there, why not be of use and grab me those herbs from off the drying rack."

"Sure," I said, without question. I acted immediately. I let my cloak fall off my shoulders and I tossed it to the side. I walked over to the window and began pulling bits of herbs from their strains, hoping they were the correct ones.

"And grab a few of those berries while you're at it. Oh - and some of those pink petals too, if you don't mind."

I dumped some berries from a small jar into my hand then grabbed a handful of pink flower petals from the counter. I walked back to Mint, holding the requested herbs and berries in my hands. Atrixia remained on the red carpet. I looked over at her with no idea what was about to happen next. Atrixia gently lowered her hand, motioning for me to relax. Mint opened a tall cabinet and laid out a variety of bottles. One bottle was small, round, and red. 'Apple a Day,' was written on its label. Another bottle was blue and triangular. Its label read, 'Sweet Dreams.' She added a drop from each at the same time, changing the bubbles below to heliotrope, a bright purplish-blue. She then opened a miniature drawstring sack and pulled out three coal-like rocks. She dropped them in, one by one. "Good (bloop), Nights (bloob), Rest (bloop)," she said, as each one hit the solution.

She asked Atrixia to return the drawstring sack to its place. Ms. Mint seemed to have the recipe for whatever she was making memorized off the top of her head. She tossed some diced fruit over her shoulders and I watched them fall neatly into the pot. I got splashed a bit. She uncorked a labeless purple bottle and poured the whole thing. "Just a little something of my own blend," she laughed. She hipped the drop-shelf and knocked in some green leaves. "Just for flavor," she assured me.

At the same time, she accidentally knocked over a capped bottle that rolled off the edge of the shelf and nearly shattered on the floor. At the last second, she kicked the bottle up with the bottom of her boot, landing it safely back on the shelf, without even having to look at it. She raised the drop-shelf back up to the ceiling as Atrixia walked over and looked down into the pot.

She placed her hands on the edge of the cauldron without it burning her. I was confused until Atrixia swished the steamy liquid around with her hand and told me it was really cold.

Mint continued to add things to the pot, like berries and sugars, when she looked up and smiled at me.

"You got em' all?" she asked.

I arranged the herbs and leaves then held them like matches in a card game.

"I think so," I said. "Hopefully."

"Throw em' in."

I looked down into the pot. The elixir was swirling and bubbling brightly. I looked up at Mint's blue eyes and dropped the leaves and herbs in. The pot hissed. I dropped in the bluish berries. The color of the water changed to ocean blue and began to swell like waves. It was cool to watch.

"Focus," Mint said to me.

I extended my hand over the pot and released the pink flower petals into the center. A massive wine colored cloud arose from the cauldron and we all stood back.

"Wait," Mint said, before she lastly plucked a single herb from the drying line and dropped it into the cauldron. "Adds luck," she said.

She leaned back against the counter and laid her hands flat on the countertop. She turned and faced me.

"It's complete," she declared.

"What's complete?" I asked.

She grabbed a ladle and took a scoop of the rosé colored potion. She blew on it softly and the steam rolled away. Then, she poured it into a wooden cup, passed the cup to me, and made strong eye contact. A part of me was hesitant to drink it but I did. The taste was sweet. For a moment, I felt dizzy though the feeling wasn't too woozy. In fact, I felt refreshed, like I had a weight lifted off me. My thoughts were clear, sort of like the way you feel when you're laying in bed right after you wake up from a good dream. Meditated.

"Wow," I said, looking at both.

My head was a bit more clear now. I didn't realize how drowsy I was feeling until I drank Ms. Mint's 'thing'.

"Are you okay?" Atrixia asked.

"Just fine," I told her. "Whatever this is, it works wonders," I told Mint.

"Some 'Morning Glow' I've always known, if you wanted to remember the name of it. It's a recipe I like to keep around. My mother showed it to me years back when I was small. I've kept it stored away in a book throughout the years but I've known it for so long, I have it memorized like the back of my hand-"

She started sealing the canisters and placing them back into the cabinets. *She needs a coffee maker*, I thought. I jumped at the opportunity to help the woman clear the countertop. I was eager to hear more about Alchemy. I saw a coffee maker I didn't notice before. I thought it was strange. I gathered the droppers and bottles then began placing the petals and herbs we didn't use back into their jars. As we cleaned, she talked. As she talked, I listened. She went on about elixirs and odd complicated chemistry.

"It's a lot of mixing and science. You're working with medicine and plants. Done right, the possibilities are endless. Done wrong, it could-"

'Ah-hem,' Atrixia cleared her throat and Mint suddenly stopped talking before she spoke any further about potions. I held my eyes on Mint and waited for her to continue speaking.

"Yeah?" I questioned, once the silence began to drag on. "Go on," I said.

Atrixia grabbed my cloak off the floor, walked over to me and handed it over. "Well, we must be on our way," Atrixia said to Mint.

"So soon?" Mint replied.

"Thank you," I said to Atrixia when she handed me my cloak. She was acting strange. I realized there was a reason she was trying to pull us outta here and I didn't know what it was. I wasn't reading the room. I took the cloak, folded it like a long pair of jeans, and hung it over my forearm the way a butler holds a drying cloth.

I rested my hand on the cauldron and insisted that the woman continued her lecture. "Go on," I said, very intrigued, except this time, I was slightly more serious. "I'm listening. Done wrong, and it could be what?" I looked at both.

"Oh nothing really," Mint finally replied. "You're fine," she assured me before she excused herself from the conversation and turned back to the cabinets.

There was something the two of them weren't telling me. "What are you hiding?"

Mint looked at Atrixia. Mint tried to explain further but only the word, 'just' came out before she stopped talking and looked down at the floor. It was obvious how cautious she was with her words. I took my hand off the cauldron and stood up straight.

"Just what?!" I finally shouted out.

"...done wrong and it could be disastrous. Catastrophic," Mint finally admitted.

She leaned back up against the counter and crossed her arms. She appeared to be annoyed. She looked back at Atrixia for satisfaction. The room was quiet for a moment. "I wish to hear more about *you*," Mint blurted out. A sudden urge to change the conversation. I closed the last jar and handed it back to her. I didn't know where to start. She stored the jar away and shut the cabinet. She spun around and asked again. "What is it that brings you, darling?" She leaned in, looked at me, and placed her hands in mine.

"Atrixia was kind enough to fill me in on some of the story," she said.

"It's okay if you don't have all the pieces right now. Right now, all you have to do is tell me in the best way you can what you remember before you came to this world."

"I don't know," I told her. "I don't know how or where to even begin."

"Are you saying you don't remember anything at all?"

I looked her in the eyes when not a memory nor recollection came to mind.

"Where you were?" Mint asked, "or what you were doing right before you came here?"

I found it all confusing. Atrixia walked over to me, looked deep into my eyes, and asked, "What's your name?"

I felt a rock sink inside me when she asked that. It was the first time I've been asked for my name. I didn't know how to answer. I was in complete shock.

"So not only can you not remember how you came to this world, but you can't even recall your own name?" A part of her thought this was cute.

I stood between the two of them. I looked at Mint and Atrixia. "Look, I'm sorry," I said. I looked at Atrixia and said, "I never meant to waste your time. I didn't mean to drag you all the way out here." Over Atrixia's shoulder, I saw the door. I looked at Mint and thanked her. "I'm sorry for any bother I may have caused. If only I could tell you more but I have no memory of anything," I said. I began to move towards the door.

I looked at Atrixia. "I'll bring you back first," I assured her.

"Don't part just yet. You've come all this way," Mint said.

"You don't have to leave so soon," Atrixia added. I walked over to Atrixia. "I need you to believe me."

She placed her hand on my chest, and looked at me.

"Where do you plan on going?" Mint asked.

"Wherever God takes me. He brought me here, so this should be an adventure." I stepped away from both of them. "If getting out of here is a journey, I'm willing to take it."

"And do tell me where you plan on journeying to. What's out there waiting?" Mint said.

The wind blew and branches tapped on the window. The solid-core door shook and rattled. I eyed the polish over the bronze doorknob. I could see my own reflection looking back at me.

"I don't know," I said. My face fell. "I don't know what I'm looking for. Let it be an answer, an escape, that's all I'm after. And respectfully, something tells me I'm not going to find that here. Am I?"

She stood up straight and the whole room flashed with a burst of orange light. I ducked behind the closest chair. The light came from her necklace. She lifted her hands off the countertop and crossed the kitchen. She narrowed her eyes, straightened her shoulders, dropped her chin, and looked at me as if she wanted to smack me. Hard. Atrixia covered her eyes while I remained kneeled down, braced behind the chair.

"Listen boy-," Mint said.

Atrixia looked at her, and gently motioned her to ease.

The flare of Mint's necklace softened once she calmed down. She grabbed the gray curls on her shoulder and started to twist them. She walked over to a ceramic jar and pulled off its lid.

She stuck her hand inside and pulled out a handful of black powder. She began to rub the black powder into strands of her hair.

"You speak of the possibility that you were dropped here for some divine reason and there's some marvelous adventure out there awaiting you."

I was seeing a larger picture now.

"Outside that door lies a world. Not only one that you know nothing of, but one that's currently being ripped apart and torn away little by little. You'll see it, and you won't understand it."

"Listen, as I told Trixi, I'm not from here."

"That is very clear," Mint said, "And let me tell you-"

"I wanna see what that does," I cut her off, looking at the gem hanging from her neck.

By that point she was finished rubbing the powder into her hair and all her hair was black. It was pretty. I realized that it was her natural color when the gloom wasn't around. She faced me and surveyed me with curiosity. She held out her arms and her long sleeves dangled from her wrists. She shut her eyes, stuck out her chest, and relaxed her hands. Her necklace began to shine throughout the whole room. It gradually grew brighter and brighter before I heard Atrixia cry out, "STOP!"

Suddenly, the gem dimmed before I could even observe her necklace cause any affect. I looked at Atrixia and I realized sorcery wasn't her thing. None of this was. I was so confused.

"Try this on," Ms. Mint told me.

She unhooked her chain and passed the crystal to me. I took it and placed it around my neck, looking Atrixia in the eye as I did so. Atrixia looked at the two of us furiously. Mint was confused when her gem had no effect on me.

"That's surely sad to see," she said.

"And why would that be?" I asked.

"That's a soul gem around your neck there."

I looked down at the empty lifeless stone in wonder as to why it wouldn't react.

"What does this mean? Am I dead or something?"

She didn't say anything.

"Am I a ghost?" I felt dark and empty.

"I suppose," Mint replied honestly.

"Wait," I said doubtfully. "How could I be a ghost? Ghosts return to express love. I've never been here before, how could I return to it?"

They each looked at me wondering why I knew that off the top of my head.

"I'm not sure," Mint said. "But if it's spirits you wish to discuss, then you'd have to talk to my neighbor Jaxin."

"Where can I find him?" I asked.

"Jaxin? He lives right up the hill," Atrixia affirmed.

"Off we go then," I said. I didn't waste a single second hesitating.

I lifted my cloak off the floor and threw it on.

"Where do you even wish to go in that rag anyway?" Mint asked me, referring to my black cloak.

"To Jaxin's," I told her.

I faced the mirror and raised my hood. It was then I felt something hit me inside. When I looked at myself, I saw a flash of the hooded figure in my memory. I thought I was having de ja vu. I was beginning to remember pieces. Small parts. Flashes. I asked Mint about my memory. "Your old memories will gradually return over time," she explained. "Your most recent ones will be the first ones to come back. Why? Are any returning? Tell me what you see," she insisted.

I was in a forest. I was lost - and I was alone, I recalled. Still, "I can't remember anything," was all I told Mint. The more I thought about it, the odder it seemed and the less I wanted to talk about it. I looked at Atrixia and another memory came to mind.

"I was running, though I wasn't following a path. I could hear loud caws echoing through the trees. I was trampling over yellow leaves. A pale mist began to ooze down a hill. The mist led me to a well." I was starting to get creeped out. "I think I was accidentally misplaced here," I finally said. "It's my first time experiencing this world."

I knew none of it made sense. I caught the two of them exchanging a look, though they weren't the same. Atrixia looked to be both surprised and lost, while Mint looked as though she's seen my case before.

"It's best you go now," Mint said. "But not just yet." She took a part of my cloak and looked at it closely. She draped it over her arm and walked over to a tall wall of miniature drawers. I followed and watched her. I read the labels on some of the drawers. 'Translucent string. Fireproof thread.' I spun the wheel on one of her mechanisms. The wheel continued to spin. I think I activated the machine. I rested my arms on the counter built into it and continued to watch Mint. She ran her fingers over a few knobs before she slid one of the drawers open. Its label read 'Midnight.' The word was written in ink and its letters were written in script, under a round sapphire handle. She reached in and pulled out a small spool of thread the color of the night sky during a fully waxed moon. She pinched some string off the end of the spool and drew out a few feet of line. Then, she placed the end of the string into the machine I was leaning on. I didn't realize it was an old sewing machine until she inserted the thread. She leaned back against her desk and crossed her boot over the other. She was wearing long black and white striped socks that matched her dress.

"So?" she said to Atrixia and I as a long dark blue cloak began to slide out of the machine, inch by inch.

"This world, let me just say, can be strange. It can be dangerous. You better understand that now or you'll learn hard lessons every second you spend here," Mint assured me.

"Well then, I better spend every second here wisely," I said.

I held my eyes on Mint. I showed no fear because I felt no fear. She smiled.

"You'll eventually learn the ways and workings of where you are," she told me. After a moment, the machine finished the cloak and a bell rang. She raised the coat in the air and looked at it with satisfaction. She tossed it over to me and said, "Try it on."

I slid my arm through one sleeve and the length was perfect. I put my other arm through and shrugged my shoulders. It was a nice fit. I turned towards a mirror hanging on the wall and saw that I was still wearing Mints gem around my neck. Although it wasn't lit up, it still looked cool with the rest of my outfit.

"It's better than that dreadful black cloak you had on, wouldn't you say?" Mint asked me.

"I'd say so for sure," I told Mint, "I appreciate it."

I turned around and showed Atrixia. "What do you think," I asked her.

She looked at me and nodded her head yes without saying a word. She concurred. She knew I was ready to embark and there wasn't a person that was going to stop me.

"Do be advised, it's a twisty trip. It may be a short one but still, it could be risky and you could easily get knocked off your path if you're not careful. Stay together as best you can," she told the both of us. She turned to Atrixia and said, "Don't let him out of your sight."

Ms. Mint handed me back the black cloak, and I threw it over my shoulder. I unhooked her gem and placed it back in her hand. "Thank you," I told her.

"For everything," Atrixia added. They shared a tight hug before Atrixia parted and made her way out the door.

"Do be a doll and bring that bowl with you to Jaxin's," Mint requested. "I'd appreciate it a lot."

I looked over at an end table and saw a straw woven bowl filled with cocoa, diced caramel cubes, bags of sugar, and different types of cinnamons.

"With pleasure," I told her. I picked up the bowl and placed it under my arm.

"And one last thing," she said.

"Yeah."

"When you see Jaxin, don't tell him you're a ghost."

"I'll remember to leave that part out. Thanks again."

"Bye now," she said. I grabbed the lamp and walked out the door.

75

CHAPTER 10

FRIENDS IN THE GRAVEYARD

Once out the door, I found myself between two gardens mysteriously grown thoroughly while we were inside. It was a stunning array of flowers. Both beds consisted of red, yellow, and orange mums. Some of the flowers were in flower pots displayed around the garden. I passed a tree with a neat row of pots placed along one of its branches. It was quite the garden. I placed the bowl and lantern on the ground so I could tie my shoe. I smelled the fresh scent of the garden when I kneeled on the pathway. When my shoe was tied, I looked around at all the different types of flowers and wondered how they blossomed so suddenly. I gazed around with much fascination. I stood up, looked over my shoulder, and saw a fully ripened pumpkin standing over me. I turned around and faced it. It was right in front of me. It was enormous. Its skin was now a brilliant orange. It had a touch of blushful red to its tone, like Santa's cheeks. Its twisty stem was full of curly vines. Standing before it, I was amazed.

"Wait, this home, this whole structure, It's a pumpk-" I looked towards Atrixia. "Your friend lives in a pumpkin?"

"Yes of course, who do you think grew it for her?"

Her red hoodie swayed past the fiery flowers as she walked down the pathway. The two nurseries had grown past her knees. I wondered how the gardens grew so fast and how the pumpkin regained its color and size.

"Quick question," I said to Atrixia.

"Keep it for now," she told me. She came back to the trail. "We have to figure out how we'll get where we're going."

"No mystical shortcut for us?" I asked in vain.

"Shhhh," she said softly.

She appeared to be reading the trees again. "This way," she then told me. She was clearly navigating now. The wind blew and I felt energy rush through my cloak fibers like a wave. All the cold and wind was blocked out. I laid the cloak's dark blue hood over my head and the shadowy world around me appeared brighter. The hood allowed its wearer to see in the dark. The leaves and flowers appeared more vibrant. I could see down paths. The night never looked so bright. I had the night vision of a cat.

The cloak was made of good material as well, reflective somehow. It shimmered. My tail caught the glow of the night as I turned in the luminous starlight. For a moment, I just stood between the two gardens, taking a final glance at the house. I was acknowledging and admiring the beauty of it all.

I looked up at the jar sitting in the round window, and reached down to grab the basket. I tucked the basket under my left arm then grabbed the lantern. Atrixia was already down the trail, about to head into the woods.

"Hey! Hold up now," I called out. I hurried down and turned left at the end of Mint's round stone path. I looked back at the house. I didn't wanna forget it. If you placed that thing in a country fair, it'd be the winner of a bar-raising first place blue ribbon for sure.

I rushed ahead and caught up with Atrixia. Once I did, I hopped forward, landed right beside her, and scared her. She turned to me. "Nice of you to join me," she said. She and I walked side by side.

"Listen," I said to her, "you've done plenty for me already."

"Yeah?" She looked at me with a questionable look.

"Thank you for your help. You've given so much guidance and assistance." I placed my hand on her shoulder. "Your heart is composed of pure kindness," I assured her. "I couldn't possibly ask any more of you." I slowly began taking off my cloak. She wasn't sure where I was going with this. I went to hand her the blue cloak in gratitude for her service and saw that she was still wearing my red hoodie.

"Wanna trade?" I asked her.

She refused. I gently laid the hood of the red sweatshirt over her head, then looked deep into her eyes. I didn't want to depart but I had to.

"Whatever this journey ought to be, I'm sure it was given to me, for me to take, *personally*," I said. I closed the zipper of the hoodie halfway and pushed her sleeves up. "Whatever happens to me here will be my own fate. I clearly have to learn to manage myself and hold my own while I'm here and I'll never be able to do that if you continue to carry-"

She cut me off, grabbing the basket of sugars and spices and turning away. I was left standing there by myself before I was done talking.

I followed her as I threw the blue cloak back over me. "Wait!" I called from behind.

I hustled to catch up with her again. "Whatcha' doin'?" I asked.

"Bringing this basket to Jaxin for Ms. Mint. I've done it for her plenty of times. Never during the night though," she mumbled to herself. She looked at me, as I swiped the bowl back from her. "What are you doing?" she asked.

"Ms. Mint pointed me in this direction and asked me to deliver this bowl, so that's exactly what I'm doing."

Atrixia pulled the sweatshirt around her tighter, and continued heading further on the trail.

"You sure you're not cold?" I asked her, partially lifting the blue cloak. I tried offering it to her again.

"I don't get cold," she assured me.

"I wonder what all this could be for," I said to her, referring to all the ingredients in the basket. I was trying to use anything to create a conversation with her. She seemed interesting. Honestly, I wanted to know more about *her* and where she was from. I wanted to know the types of things that interested her, how she felt about her passions, and why? I wished to know the types of things a selfless girl like herself would desire most from this world. I wanted to know what she saw in others. I presented the bowl to her and she seemed curious about its contents as well. She pulled out a tiny sack with the word SUGAR written on it. I pulled out a sealed jar that had 'Corn Syrup' written on its old stained label. Another bottle held honey.

"That's odd," she said, as she returned the bag, "She wants you to bring it to Jaxin?"

"Indeed," I said. "That was her only favor."

"Then we shouldn't waste time."

The scent of the sugar mixed with the woodland air. I looked down at the cocoa powder, chocolate cubes, and cinnamon. *I wouldn't mind a peanut butter cup right now*, I thought to myself. We traveled through the pine trees. The trees were too tall to view the top and too wide to fully wrap your arms around. Aside from the candy, the place smelt of sap and pine trees. The moon vanished over the trees. The sound of our footsteps filled the silence. The pine needles brushed together as the trees blew back and forth in the breeze. I looked at Atrixia. She had her eyes focused on the path ahead. She looked peaceful.

I had the perfect question for her when she stopped and turned to me. "Hey, what's your favorite candy?" I asked, digging through a variety of wrapped candies.

"Pardon?" she replied.

I passed her the lantern and held out the wide straw basket. She dangled the light over a bowl that was now loaded in sweets that reminded me of home. I had no explanation. She clenched her lips at the sight of all the bright colored wrappers. They shimmered and sparkled beneath the glow of the light. She looked up at me with eyes brighter than the candy. I'm pretty sure that it was her first time ever seeing this. She was fascinated and transfixed, while I stood silently in wonder over how they even appeared. I remember thinking about candy when I saw the ingredients. She finally spoke up. "Where did all this just come from?"

"I couldn't tell you," I swore.

Her eyes looked directly at mine. She wanted a further explanation.

"Seriously. I mean it. I was just walking, thinking things through. Who is this guy anyway?" I asked. "What are we gonna say when we see him?"

"Honestly, I'm not sure. I've never actually seen him before. I know he lives in an old mansion on top of a hill deep out in the woods. Occasionally, I'll be asked by Mint to leave things on his steps. I've never actually knocked on the door though. Some say he's crazy. Others say he lives alone."

"I guess we'll find out," I said.

"Here," I said, reaching into the bowl to pull out an orange lollipop with the face of a jack-o-lantern printed on it. "Take this." I passed it to her and she accepted it with joy.

Not only were there lollipops but there were plenty of other choices as well. There were gummies and wrapped chocolates. I recognized all my favorites. I pulled out bubble gum from the mix. I recognized the blue and yellow wrapper. I opened it up and tossed it in my mouth. I closed my eyes and savored its sweetness. It was real.

"Seriously, I wish to know where all this came from," Atrixia said.

The story of how all the spices, syrups, and sugars came to be candy was in messy pieces and I had to grab them all together. Sorcery wasn't even a possibility until I came to this world, let alone a valid explanation. She pulled the lollipop from its wrapper and placed it in her mouth.

She looked at me as her eyes lit up like two fireworks.

"It's good yeah?" I asked.

She didn't say a word. She just continued to walk. But she did look back at me again as we continued in silence. Soon, I spotted an old, rusted high fence. I thought we reached Jaxin's residence but the fence turned out to be around the edge of the cemetery. As we walked along the front, I tried to peer through the fence and get a glimpse of the grounds. They appeared to be abandoned like they were forgotten long ago. There was a mist spread over the damp grass. The grave stones were too weathered and decayed to even see names, or a date on their faces. I was looking from behind the bars. I was too far from the stones. It didn't make any sense to me. None of it did. I was so clueless as to how one can 'die', only to be brought to a world where people still died.

"That's odd," I mumbled to myself.

"I know, who is that?" Atrixia whispered over to me.

"Who?" I asked her.

Suddenly our lantern went out but no wind blew. We took a few more steps until she stopped and pointed. "There, you see?"

I peered deeper and noticed the silhouette of a sharp-hatted stranger sitting alone on a stone outside the cemetery's main entrance. Their chin rested on top of a flameless jack-o-lantern. They appeared to be crying. A part of me was a little freaked out, while another part wanted to rush over and make sure they were okay. Atrixia and I shared a look, unsure what to do.

"Let's go," I said.

I approached the stranger. "Are you okay?" I called out. Their orange hat raised only an inch before it dropped back down again in silence.

Atrixia grabbed my arm and pulled me back. "Wait," she told me. "Not so fast."

I looked over at the poor girl then back at Atrixia. "Trix, It's freezing and they're sitting out here all alone. It's late. Don't you think something's wrong?"

"It certainly is possible," she said. She looked at me and bit her lip. She was trying to hide her smirk and not laugh. She was obviously thinking of me and how lost I was when I first got here. "Still," she said, looking at the girl, "there's no greater temptation than misdirection."

We both looked back at the stranger sitting in the dark. I thought Atrixia was being a bit overly cautious; then again, I still saw her point. Since I've been here, this probably had to be the most serious I'd ever seen her behave. But I knew for sure, something wasn't right. I continued down the trail slowly. We eventually reached a young girl. She was hiding her face.

"What's wrong?" Atrixia asked her, "What are you doing all the way out here?"

She looked up at us. She couldn't have been more than eighteen or nineteen years old. She was wearing an orange skirt with poofed orange sleeves covered in purple polka-dots. Her bodice was black and laced with purple strings.

"One lantern, I wanted to place one lantern," the girl said.

She looked up at Atrixia and wiped the tears from her face. "Just one," she said. She looked down at the jack-o-lantern and shook her head.

Atrixia looked at her dearly and said, "Sugar."

I knelt and sang, "Oh honey, honey," right after. I tried to catch her eyes under her hat.

"Do you wanna tell us why you're crying?" I asked.

"Some dark figure placed a spell over the cemetery," the girl told us. "The spell prevents any flame from entering. The dark spirit has returned to haunt the place but, unlike the other ghosts, it wants the place all to itself. Jack-o-lanterns are known to ward off evil spirits." She looked down at her jack-o-lantern, then up at me. She had taken the time to carve a joyful face, full of stars, speckles, sparkles, and swirls. It was incredible. It would have been a wonder to see it lit. I felt so horrible for her. There was no one else around. Just her. I thought it was dangerous for her to be this far out, alone, in the dark.

"I don't think it's safe out here," I told the girl.

She raised her fist and her hand began to glow with red energy.

"I'm not worried," she said. The sky began to swirl and change colors.

The young girl looked up, looked down, and smiled at the both of us. The clouds began to form a vortex and a blue light flickered on.

"Can you tell me what's happening out here?" I asked the girl. The sky changed from blue to a bright orange and the wind picked up. It looked like daylight. "Why's the sky spinning and changing color?!" I yelled over the wind.

The girl held her smile and remained speechless. My eyes slipped over her shoulder and I caught a glance of the boneyard. My blood iced up as spirits began to rise and wander from their graves. But my curiosity was also rising. I had to slip away and look inside for myself. When I saw the ghosts, I got this weird feeling that there would be some type of clue or answer inside that would shine a light on my current predicament. Something that could sharpen the image.

"You'll catch your death if you sit out here all night," I heard Atrixia tell the girl.

The temperature was dropping. "The groundskeeper should be back in the morning,"

Atrixia informed her.

"I have nowhere to go, so I'll wait until then," said the girl.

"Have you seen anyone pass by lately?" Atrixia asked.

"A few men. They were kind but they didn't seem to know how to help me."

I stopped walking. I didn't drift too far. "You mentioned a dark figure earlier, correct?" I asked the girl.

The girl nodded.

"I'll tell you what," I said to the girl. I reached into my bag, pulled out the black cloak, and dropped it over her shoulders. I looked into her eyes and poured the candy bowl out into her jack-o-lantern. "Give these out to anyone passing by. Share it. Spread it. Don't ever let the light die out," I told her. I stood up and walked away.

"Where are you going?" Atrixia asked.

"To have a chat with whoever's in charge of the household," I said.

Atrixia and the candy girl continued their conversation. Their voices grew more distant behind me. I climbed the stone steps leading to the cemetery. Waves of mist blew away from me as I passed under the entrance's stone archway.

Even though this place bothered me less and less, I still felt like I wasn't living in reality. I felt like I was dead, like I was living in a dream. My memory and thoughts were blurry. I pulled my arm from my cloak pocket and spread my hand. *Is this a Ghost?* I asked myself, while studying the back of it. I looked up at the other spirits. I didn't seem to resemble the rest of them. Nothing seemed to make sense. Each ghost appeared to have a different age, gender, and place of origin. They were completely translucent, yet still so energetic and filled with… *life*. They carried nothing but the spiritual remains of who they once were. Some chatted on a bench. Some were just out enjoying the evening air. A few could even be seen dancing with one another. I walked along and passed multiple statues of saints and phantoms. They were gothic and composed of stone. Up ahead, an eerie statue faced me. It had a large ghastly cloak that looked strangely familiar. It towered over me and had a skeletal facial structure that seemed to only infer doom and despair under its stone hood. All the ghosts in the graveyard looked at me with cold expressions. I watched them slowly disperse as if they were to have seen their own ghastly reflections in the mirror for the first time. Impossible, but still. Some began to wander away while others dropped back down into their graves. I turned around to see that the stone phantom had vanished, leaving only an empty stone mantle.

Suddenly, I felt an icy chill on the back of my neck, straight down to my core. I turned around and saw that the stone phantom was now transparent, and drowsily moping around the yard. It turned its hood and looked at me with cold eyes. The dark gray figure began to circle me slowly without taking its eyes off me.

"Why have *you* come?" the ghost moaned out.

"Forgive me. I tend to wander. I was just checkin' out the place. Nice brib." I blew and snapped a sweet bubble with my gum. It was clear the ghost didn't like me. It moved in closer and breathed deeply through its nostril holes as if it were to be smelling me.

"I sense life," the phantom said.

"No, I'm pretty sure I've lost that," I joked.

"Death? Is that what you claim to be a victim of?"

"Victim?" I questioned the word. I didn't like the sound of it. Never did.

"Tell me, have you ever felt the essence of your spirit be pulled from your body."

"Ehh," I said back. It felt relatable.

"Have you ever taken your last breath and surrendered to your fate?"

I wanted to laugh but something told me now wasn't a good time.

"No you haven't-," it told me, "-but soon you will."

My face fell stern.

"Eventually, you and everyone you know will disappear. That is once the gloom has all Ossynthore completely enwrapped. No one can escape the darkness. Not you, not anyone," said the ghost in a cold hoarse voice. The spirit then vanished. I looked around. There was no trace of the specter. I took a few steps before a dead voice sounded right over my shoulder: "Soon it'll have *you*."

By the next moment, I was rushing out of there. I trampled over the gravel and nearly tripped racing down the stairs of the entrance. I ran past the girls and heard Atrixia ask, "You make any friends in the graveyard?"

I disappeared into the shadowy woods.

CHAPTER 11

STAY AWAY

I trampled through the unceasing darkness. "Wait," I heard from behind. I could tell it was Atrixia by the sound of her voice. I looked over my shoulder. She was keeping up, but stumbling. The wind blew and shook the dead leaves. I slowed down but continued to walk a few more feet before I stopped completely, turned around, and faced Atrixia. I wanted to get as far away from the cemetery as possible. I tried to catch my breath. After a moment, I walked to Atrixia. She had been tripping and rolling all over the place just to keep up with me. I felt bad. I looked up to the sky and felt like this was my wake up call. It was time for me to get out of here and head home. "What's the matter with you?" she asked, once we were face-to-face.

For some reason, I just took her in my arms and held her for a moment. It was all I wanted to do. She didn't judge me. She knew I was freaking out and understood me. "I just met a phantom," I said.

"I see."

"It said we're all gonna disappear."

"Did it?"

"I gotta get outta here," I told her. We each caught our breath and I looked around. I was unable to remember the direction I came from. I let go and turned away. We were lost. "I'm sorry," I said. "I didn't mean for this to happen."

"Mean for what?" She was confused.

For a moment, I was speechless. I didn't know how to elaborate anything. "Everything," I told her.

"Come," she said. "We can talk."

I wasn't in the mood but I looked at her and moved along.

"Could we finally talk about you?" she asked.

"If you wish."

"There's still so many things you haven't told me. I don't even have a name to call you by."

"I can't remember it."

"I have only one question."

"Ask me." I was open to hear it.

She looked at me and stopped walking. "Why are you so desperate to get out of here?" She asked softly. "This world truly is a wonderful place. If you remain, you might see a different side of it."

I had no response. She looked down at the ground and carried on feeling let down.

"C'mon," she said.

Time went by and I saw a light in the distance. I looked at her, wondering if she noticed it too. She walked, appearing to be deep within her own thoughts. I tapped her on the shoulder and pointed the light out to her. Once she saw it too, she looked at me with nothing to say. She just continued in its direction like she already knew what it was. "Hey," I said. She slowed down and looked at me. "You can call me 'D'," I told her. "That isn't my whole name, but it feels right."

She smiled like it was another step forward in our friendship. She smiled at me and said, "Okay 'D'."

"You know where we are?" I asked.

"They do," she told me.

"Who's they?" I asked.

She nodded her head at the light. I held my questions until we reached it. We came to a lit jack-o-lantern with a questioning look on its face. I concentrated on the roundish eyes carved into the pumpkin. An old pair of glasses had been placed over the jack-o-lantern's eyes. The lantern looked back at us with its stern mouth and held the look of wisdom and intellect, as if jack-o-lanterns might possess a brain. We noticed another light over to the left, up ahead. At that moment, the candle in the jack-o-lantern before us blew out. "C'mon," Atrixia said.

She and I began to move towards the second light. The candles were the only form of light in the woods. They made the lanterns identifiable and easy to spot in the night. We walked through the leaves. The area was filled with trees and thick bushes. We reached the second jack-o-lantern and its eyes were fixed on the third lantern. We could already see its light ahead. Once we noticed the third lantern, the candle in the second pumpkin blew out.

"Let's go," I said, "Where are these things leading us anyway?" I asked on the way to the next pumpkin.

"Oh you'll see," she said excitedly. She wanted it to be a surprise. "Keep going."

We reached the next one, sitting centered between two other lanterns in the distance. One light could be seen to the left, and another to the right. The light in the one before us blew out.

"Your turn," I said. I didn't have a clue which direction to go in now. She considered each one.

She, herself, was unsure of which direction to choose.

"How 'bout I take left, and you take right," I suggested.

" I don't know. I think we should stay together," she said.

"We'll stick by each other," I assured. "We'll each remain within eye distance of the other." At first, we kept an eye on each other without increasing distance from one another. We remained parallel for as long as we could. Eventually we had to break off. She headed to the right, and I to the left. After a minute, I saw my target. It sat on a rocky top, carved with a frightened face as though something had spooked it. I knelt before the rock and studied the lantern's eyes. I couldn't tell what they were looking at. It was creepy. I didn't know whether they were looking up at me, or behind my back. I looked over my shoulder. There was nothing eerie present, yet, the jack-o-lantern's mouth was dropped with terror. I searched for the following lantern. No other light was present or visible. I looked over to Atrixia's position just as both lanterns blew out at once. After that, I could no longer see her and she could no longer see me. I heard her call out my name: "D!"

"Atrixia!" I yelled back. I looked around for her. I couldn't see her but I could see the light of the next jack-o-lantern in the distance. It shone ahead between the two of us. I hurried, hoping we both saw it. I wouldn't stop running, not until I was reunited with Atrixia. Once I got closer to the light, I called out her name again. "Trixie!" I was close enough to the lantern to make out its face.

I turned around to search for Atrixia. The moment I did, I heard her say, "Over here." She approached with her eyes fixed on the jack-o-lantern's. She looked at its face curiously as the light within it began to slowly die out. "To the next," Atrixia said.

Eventually we got the hang of it and the two of us tried to turn it into a game. I gazed around. "Where' we headin' now?" I asked, "See anything?"

"There." Atrixia pointed to a tiny light in the distance.

"That is a fine eye you got there," I told her, "C'mon."

We came to a lantern that didn't even have a face; instead, it was speckled with carvings of autumn leaves. I politely asked, "These are at least taking us *somewhere*, aren't they?"

"I can assure you, they're leading us down a path. The question is, a path to where?" We were signaled by another lantern.

"Well there's only one way to find out," I said, "let's hurry, I can see the next one." We reached the light. Then that lantern brought us to the next one. The woods were starting to feel warmer. I was eager to discover where the lanterns were leading us. They were such strange findings. What awaited was all I could think about at this point. "How many of these jack-o-lanterns are we gonna come across?" I asked Trixie.

"Oh we're in for a light show," she said.

"Show?" I questioned back.

"He tends to do it big."

"Who's he? You've yet to elaborate."

She leaned in closer and whispered the name. "Jaxin."

Suddenly a thousand jack-o-lanterns sparked on and flickered at the saying of his name. The woodlands lit up in multiple colors. There had to have been well over a thousand. I moved closer towards Atrixia's side. Together, we stood in what looked like a sky of red, orange, and yellow stars.

"Ahh," I said. I found the warm glow soothing.

"Breathtaking, isn't it?" Atrixia asked.

"Yes, I have to say." There were so many flames, it provided heat. "Does it feel warmer out here?" I asked.

A trail had been revealed and we moved along through the vast display of lanterns. Their colors began to shift from blue to purple then to green.

"He has quite a passion for jack-o-lanterns," I commented.

"No, I hear he has an obsessive hatred for ghosts."

"Oh." I remembered Ms. Mint advising me to leave out any parts about me potentially being one. Atrixia and I each pointed out the lanterns we found remarkable. We admired their faces, their designs, their patterns, everything. One would appeal to her, then another would strike me. Each conveyed an expression.

" I love the fall season, don't you?" she asked me.

"Yes. It's a wonderful time of year."

"It's delightful to see one making use of its harvest."

I had to concur as I gazed at each jack-o-lantern. I was amazed by how many there were.

That, and the fact that one individual pulled all this off. I didn't care if we were far or close. I had Trixie and I knew I was alive. Some of the lanterns began to levitate. I looked at Atrixia in question over how that could even be possible. Yet again, her soft smirk reassured me that all was normal and well in logical reality here.

"Did he carve all of these himself?" I asked.

"He certainly did. He keeps 'em out year round too."

"Year round? Why?"

"He can be a little precautious."

I looked at her and huffed. I could already tell that meeting him wasn't going to go well. I didn't need to ask what he was trying to keep away. The wind hushed and every light in the woods went dim. I looked at the jack-o-lanterns. They were now all looking back at us with sour faces. Then, they all slowly began to rise and draw closer. Their eyes flared up with red flames. "That's a touch," I said. "Uh, Trix."

She stepped ahead and looked at all of them with disappointment, as if they were her own children. I stepped between her and them to protect her. I examined them closer and saw that their eyes weren't fixed on us. Instead, they were looking over at something behind us.

Everything then went silent, pin drop silent. I turned around and guarded Atrixia's back. I looked around but there was nothing there. I remained in position until each lantern lowered and returned to the ground. The fires in their eyes went out and their faces changed back to their previous expressions.

"Was something following us?" Atrixia asked.

I gazed around. No one was present, at least not anymore.

"I'm not sure," I told her.

"Perhaps you were followed by a graveyard ghost, or better yet, a ghoul, a phantom, something just delightful," she said humorously. I didn't laugh. "We should be fine now," she said. We continued ahead even though I was still suspicious. I wasn't convinced we were alone. She led while I followed closely making sure that no one was following us. A dark bird began to circle our heads.

I took her by the hand and picked up the pace. The bird cawed and I hid the two of us under a tree. *This isn't good. I shouldn't have brought Atrixia*, I thought. "Don't let it see you," I said. The bird flew away and she looked at me like I was crazy. She carried on unbothered. The jack-o-lanterns switched back on. We were surrounded by lights and colors again. She turned around and looked at me. She looked gorgeous.

"You coming?" she asked.

I rose and followed her. After a minute, I began to hear the low sound of twigs snapping, as though someone or something were walking nearby. I quietly slowed my steps then finally paused. Atrixia walked ahead a bit more until I stopped her. "Something troubling you?" she asked.

"Stay there," I told her. "Don't move." Suddenly, all the lanterns blew out again. I stepped out under a thin ray of moonlight and gazed around. Nothing lurked in the mist nor loomed in the trees. I observed a tiny person wearing a pink hood run past and slip into a large jack-o-lantern. They giggled in a young girl's voice as they did. The moment the lid closed, a magenta gleam shone through the jack-o-lantern's face and then the pumpkin was as empty as it was before. "Maybe *they* were the cause of all the ruckus," Atrixia said.

I considered the possibility but I still had doubts. Whatever had been tailing us clearly didn't wanna show itself. I gestured once I felt that it was safe for us to continue. The leaves ahead of us began to brush towards us as though they were being kicked up by someone approaching. But there was nobody there.

Danger was lurking within the darkness of these woods. I reached for Atrixia's hand and pulled us in the opposite direction. Once she saw a rabbit jump out of the leaves and hop away, she stopped and pulled her hand away from mine. She looked at me like I was being ridiculous. We heard the branches crackle. Then, the leaves on the ground began to blow by without making a sound. And then it all went silent.

"Darling, if I say run, I want you to run. Don't ask why, and don't stop for me."

Atrixia moved closer to me. "What's happening?" she asked. She sounded scared.

Other than her voice, there wasn't a sound heard, yet the branches continued to shake and the leaves on the ground continued to roll by. "I'm so sorry," I said. I held her. "You're fine," I assured her. The poor girl was so confused. I don't attach myself to people. I don't invest in them.

This was why. This was my mess. Not a light could be seen. I myself wasn't sure what was happening so I just held her hands to calm her. She remained silent. I quieted my breathing so I could listen carefully.

The jack-o-lanterns arched their shadowy eyes at us in anger. Their mouths grinned with evil. Atrixia knew something was wrong once she saw that all the jack-o-lanterns had, once again, adopted their horrific facial expressions. *I knew* something was wrong when they all started looking at us.

"What's going on?" she asked.

"Nothing yet," I said.

The eyes in the nearby jack-o-lanterns blared up with flames of blue.

"That's new," I said.

They rose from the mist and formed a ring around Atrixia and I. We looked at each one as they began to close in. None seemed to be backing down this time. Suddenly, one by one, they each started to hurl themselves at us.

I grabbed her hand and ran away. The pumpkins clashed together and formed bright collisions of fiery sparks. We ducked and dodged them. I saw the face of one flying straight towards us. I stopped short and pulled Atrixia down with me. Its flames soared right over our heads.

"Let's move now," I said. We rushed ahead and evaded most of them. Eventually, we made it to safety. My cloak was on fire and she had sparks in her hair. She looked good with them, frankly. I shook them out quickly, then she shook the tail of my cloak until the flames went out. "You okay?" I asked.

She nodded. "You're okay?" she asked.

Immediately, I felt an icy chill strike the back of my neck. There was a sudden drop in temperature and I didn't move a muscle. I could see my own breath. Clouds started to fill the sky, masking the moonlight. Blue lightning flashed above our heads instantaneously. I still wasn't sure what was happening but something felt familiar. The wind blew through the twisty branches until its soft whistle was hushed, yet the trees continued to shake. I moved only my eyes over my right shoulder. Then I quietly knelt to gather a clump of leaves. Although I couldn't see it, I could still sense the energy of something standing behind me. Atrixia knelt and squinted her eyes at me. She didn't know what I intended to do with the leaves. I looked her in the eye and nodded my head. I assured her to bear with me. I just wanted her to remain quiet. I knew what I was doing. I looked down, closed my eyes, and although there wasn't any sound, I still listened over both my shoulders for anything to break the silence. Suddenly, I heard a loud caw overhead. Quickly, I turned around, threw the leaves, and in the flutter stood the outline of a tall ghastly humanoid figure. The sight of it stunned me. The spirit was standing directly in front of me. It was completely invisible. Some of the leaves ricocheted against it while other leaves rolled off its shoulders. Its form was solid.

I was so frightened, I felt a spark in my heart and it caused two red flares to fire up in each of my hands. I heard Atrixia softly gasp in horror behind me. I looked over at her. She was terrified, except she wasn't looking at the ghost. She didn't even notice the ghost. She couldn't see it. Neither of us could. She was looking at me.

The leaves flew away and I stood my ground. I called Atrixia's name and heard nothing back. When I looked over at her, she was slowly backing away from me. I remained where I stood with the expectancy of something rising to rival me. She didn't see it. The flares in my hands vanished. The appearing and disappearing of the flames weren't done on command. The temperature returned to normal and it was warm again, not cold. The tension was gone. I turned around and saw Atrixia waiting for me. Her arms were crossed. The jack-o-lanterns had formed and illuminated a single lane.

"Come with me," she said.

I passed her and she placed her hand in mine. She made sure I wasn't going anywhere. I could tell by the way she looked at me that something was bothering her.

The jack-o-lanterns gave off a warm orange glow. We followed them down a small path to a short mountain with a cliff edge. I couldn't see what lies at the top. We passed a jack-o-lantern at the base of the mountain. The trail continued up the mountain in the form of an escalating spiral that led us to the pinnacle. Her and I continued upwards. Around and around we went. We were halfway to the top when we came across another jack-o-lantern. Its eyes were looking towards the summit. She and I looked at it, looked at each other, turned the corner, and kept walking until we reached the top.

Once we reached the top we oversaw the entire woodlands. I pointed out Mint's pumpkin. Far across on the other side of the woods stood a tall hill with a large mansion built on top. The mansion was surrounded by green grass. At our feet sat the final lantern. Carved into it were the words:

STAY AWAY

CHAPTER 12

A WHOLE NEW WORLD

I needed rest. No matter how hard I tried, I couldn't fall asleep. I reached into the black bag and pulled out the blank red book. Starting on the first page, I wrote down everything that happened since I arrived. The well, the woods, the forest, the jack-o-lantern path… I even sketched Mint's pumpkin so I didn't forget it. Eventually, my eyes started to get heavy and I shut the book. I laid back, rolled over, and closed my eyes. Soon, I fell into a deep sleep. I awoke in the morning to the sound of a loud scream.

The sun shone brightly above. It was a gorgeous day. Atrixia was thrilled. I sat up and saw her skip and spin around me in excitement. "Do come," she told me.

I stood up under a clear blue sky. It was a completely different atmosphere. I walked to the edge of the cliff and looked out over a different world. It was the same place except the woods, the air, the *vibe*, everything was just enhanced. The vibrancy of the world was more radiant. The trees were now covered in the most beautiful leaves. They were no longer black with gray leaves. The endless orange and yellow forests were breathtaking. You could see mountaintops breaking through the clouds, waterfalls in the distance, animals playing in meadows, and more. Strange looking birds flew in packs.

It was a whole new world. The land was permeated in flowers and sunlight. Atrixia playfully ran and I chased after her. "Wait up!" I yelled out. She ran down the path and I slid down a grassy part of the cliff. We both met each other at the bottom at the same time. The cardinals sang with the blue jays. I walked in wonder over how the trees regained color. This part of the woods was gray last night. Atrixia walked over to a tree and felt the delicacy of its leaves.

"Magnificent," she said.

She was so fascinated by the red and orange colors. She looked at me with enticement in her smile. She quickly took off the red hoodie and hung it on the tree. She took off her boots and told me to turn around. Then, with our backs turned to each other, she let her pants fall to the floor. She took off her vest and unbuttoned her shirt.

Once she was completely naked, she put the red hoodie back on. Her upper body was covered but her bare butt was showing. It was cute. She walked barefoot into the woods. She didn't go far before disappearing behind a red maple tree. *What could she possibly be doing?* I asked myself. A rose-gold light flashed behind the tree. After, she stepped out on the other side and when she did, she was wearing the most breathtaking dress. It was mainly composed of leaves, bright red maple leaves. Together, they formed a skirt. Her hair was no longer gray, it was blonde and curly with streaks of red and orange. Leaves were peeking out of it. Her eyes were beautiful. They were green like two emeralds. They were no longer yellow. I was mesmerized by her once again.

"You look stunning," I told her. "I like your dress."

She tossed me the red sweatshirt and stretched her arms out over her head. After, she looked at me, smiled, and thanked me. When I was younger, I watched a girl make a dandelion chain in the field behind my house. When she was done, she threw it on her wrist like a bracelet.

Atrixia's dress reminded me of that.

I let my cloak roll off my shoulders. Then, I placed the blue cloak, the red hoodie, Atrixia's boots, and the rest of her clothes in my bag. The day was warm. We didn't need our coats and she preferred to continue without shoes. Atrixia walked across a log with her arms out.

We headed in the direction of the mysterious mansion.

"What happened to all the gray trees?" I asked. "When did all the gloom clear?"

"I don't know. It must've strangely vanished overnight. It usually comes and goes but not that quickly."

She reached the end of the log and hopped down. She was happy I was finally seeing what this world looks like on a good day.

"So, what do you think of this world now?" she asked me. She twirled around and looked up at the sky.

I wasn't sure what to say or think. I felt lost, but strangely at peace with it. I didn't know what the two of us were to expect and I liked it. Also, she made me happy.

"I love it," I told her.

Her green eyes lit up with joy. "Well that's certainly delightful to hear," she said with happiness in her voice.

"I want to know. What can you tell me that you haven't told me already?" I asked.

"I've already told you nearly everything within my knowledge."

"I want to hear more about your forest, no, the creatures that live in the gardens, everything."

She just didn't know where to start. She thought as we carried on through the sunny woods. Sunlight poured through the gaps in the trees. That was when she laid eyes on a small funky shaped tree. Its branches were oddly bent. I had no idea what she saw in it but she approached it. She grasped onto one of its long curvy branches, shut her eyes, and concentrated. The tree began to shake slowly. Vines began to grow out of the branches and the tree began to curve and bend. Leafy vines twisted and twined until the whole tree transformed into a vine strung harp. She held an instrument by the time the transformation was complete. She sat down in the tall grass, crossed her legs, and began to strum. Birds of all colors gathered around to listen. Even the birds would hum along to her symphony. I sat down across from her. I was amazed by her harp. Its sound was gentle and it just pulled you towards her. But I wasn't astounded until I heard her sing. In her song she sang about her home life and what it was like growing up.

"From a forest we grew. Our lives were anew.

We grew to sizes no one knew. Under a sky always blue.

We shared love, me and you. We shared love, me and you."

I looked around at all the cardinals and blue jays. They all had quieted. A lot of birds have gathered since the start of the song.

"How was that?" she asked.

"I think the birds adored it," I laughed.

"Thank you," she said. "It's called 'Anew.'"

"Where'd you learn that?"

"Home."

I rested my hand on my cheek and strummed a few strings.

"I wish you could take me there," I said.

She looked at me and thought about it. "Maybe I will one day."

I smiled. She looked at me and in that girl's eye was a spark. A hidden one, the type of light that finds *you*. She saw me. She talked about pixies and pumpkins. Back in her forest, flowers were her specialty, she informed me. She explained this complex process of how she makes them grow. Now matter how much she told me, I still wanted to know more and more about this place and hear more about her. I couldn't hear enough of her stories about the forest.

We were far from the mansion but we didn't care. We both enjoyed each other's presence. It could rain and we wouldn't care.

"How old are you?" I asked.

"Uh, around your age," she said, oddly put off by the question. It was awkward. "How old are *you*?"

"I don't remember," I said honestly. I was so confused. I could remember everything that happened since I've arrived here, but only pieces of the moments before.

"Doesn't matter, I suppose," she said.

I looked up at the two planets in the daytime sky. The larger one was accompanied by a turquoise moon, its surface appeared to be aglow, even in the daylight. "Those planets," I pointed out.

"Yes?"

"What are their names?"

"Lya, Dorias, and the small moon revolving Lya is Xyra, though many have their own name for Xyra. Xyra is the source of power to many. Dorias is futuristic," she told me. "It's home to many advanced civilizations. The next planet is Lya, I don't know too much about it, and the planet you and I are standing on is called Galaxius. We're in the lands of Ossynthore. This planet might be a long way from where you're from."

"I guessed that."

"You still can't remember where you're from?"

I nodded my head no. "I'm far from it, that's all I can tell you."

"It's okay," she told me. "I'm far from my home too."

We smiled at each other. We walked until the afternoon. The sun was setting over the hills when I heard light footsteps running through the woods. I moved behind the closest tree and hid. I leaned over and looked to see who it could be. I saw a small child-sized individual wearing a pink cloak wandering close by. They were giggling in a high-pitch under a long hood. They were running over the hills then began heading straight in my direction. I shuffled my position to remain out of sight.

"What's going on?" Atrixia asked.

"I don't know," I replied.

The small individual stopped in the middle of the trail and raised their hand like they were motioning for something in the sky to stop moving. They reached into their pocket and pulled out what looked like a pink glowstick. They began using it like chalk to create indecipherable markings that lit up on the dirt. I couldn't tell what they were doing. I moved away from the tree and crouched down behind a bush that was nearer. I looked closer at the markings and could make out shapes like diamonds and loops. All the shapes were confined within a circle and lit up as the individual drew them. Next thing, sparkling dust popped out of the drawing, and then 'Kapow.'

Flowers began to spring up from the ground. They continued to grow until they were as tall as the trees. Afterwards, the valley was a vast forest of giant sunflowers, tulips, roses, and daisies. I even noticed a large dandelion. Its seeds blew away with the wind. *I wish to stay here forever*, I thought. Flower petals opened out right above our heads. The child flicked the tip of the marker and changed its color from pink to blue. They began to illustrate a different pattern and once it was completed, a massive vibrant rainbow appeared in the sky. I was amazed when coins started to hit me on the head. I looked up and saw them all raining down from pink clouds that formed in the sky instantaneously. A unicorn appeared and dashed away. Then, a rocket ship appeared and blasted off toward Dorias.

Soon, the whole trail was nearly covered in spectacular lit up designs.

I picked up a coin that fell from the sky and read its place of origin, Ossynthore. I could tell the coin was made of something precious. I looked up at the sky and wondered how all of this was happening. Time went on and the sun remained in position. I wasn't sure how. The shadows casted by the sun didn't move. The little artist drew on, holding the sunset for what felt like an hour. Finally, I heard a woman yell out from within the woods, "Come along now, Googin-hyme." The woman walked over to us and said, "No, I'm not cleaning up another one."

"Oh c'mon ma, can't I play for a little longer?" the child asked.

"Tomorrow you can play. Right now, we need to get back home," said the mother.

The young one waved their hand at the sun and the sun continued to set. The tall flowers were sucked back into the ground and the pink clouds cleared away. The sky returned to normal; yet, the rainbow remained as did its coins. I threw a bunch of the coins in my cloak pockets and wondered what use they'll bring.

We were heading up a grassy slope when Atrixia said, "I think this is the place." We approached a shady turn. Leaves rained down from a yellow sky lit with what was left of daylight. Around the corner stood a grand mansion. Its walls were coated in dark paint. Its central tower was tall and composed of bricks. The tower had an orange light flickering through the windows of its crow's nest. The patio wrapped around the entire house. The backdoor had a walkway that led through a garden. There was a row of fountains on each side of the walkway. In the middle of the walkway was a fountain as tall as the house and at the end of the walkway was a large pond with lily pads scattered across its surface. Toads and turtles were hanging around it.

I looked up at the orange light pulsating within the top of the tower then looked down at the front door.

"This the right place?" I asked.

"Indeed."

"I aint going in there," I laughed. "The place looks like a haunted house."

"We must," Atrixia urged.

"What if he ain't home?" I asked. I looked at the heavy jade door knocker.

"It's worth a shot," she told me.

We ascended the stairs side by side. The floorboards creaked as we walked across the deck and approached the door. I looked at Atrixia, then loudly banged on the door three times with the jade knocker, eager to meet whoever was inside. They say jade releases your negative energy and replaces it with good. When no one answered, Atrixia reached for a long rope that hung from the deck ceiling. She yanked on its large knot and rang an old bell that rang throughout the house. Suddenly, every window shade dropped down at once. When there was no answer the second time, we both turned around and headed down the steps. A long slow creak was then heard behind us. The door slowly opened with a mysterious jack-o-lantern now suddenly at the foot of it.

"Do enter," we heard a voice say from within.

We entered a large living room with fabric walls. The walls displayed actual stars that lit up and shone against their dark blue cloth. There were millions. I noticed a cherry red piano in the corner of the room. I looked down a hall of great length. It was dark. There was a row of candleholders mounted to the wall on each side of the hallway. Two claps were heard from the end of it and suddenly, the wick of each candle lit up.

"It's him," I heard Atrixia whisper.

We followed a red carpet down the hall. Through an ornate doorway, we noticed a large dining room. I glanced at a long clothed dining table surrounded by twenty chairs. Every fine glass, dish, and utensil was made entirely out of crystal. Candles were prepared and arranged across the table as well, as if many were about to gather around for a formal gathering. We carried on and passed the stairs that led to the top of the tower. Finally, we stepped into a study area. That was where we found Jaxin. The first thing I noticed was a fireplace shaped like a lion's mouth. Inside was a fire blazing brightly. Its flames flickered and casted a glare that shone halfway across the room. Jaxin was sitting in the corner of the room. He was studying in a chair, before a wide wall of books. He was a dark skinned man who exuded wisdom and intellect. He wore glasses that made him resemble the jack-o-lantern we found in the woods. I knew then that we'd found him. He was wearing a white vintage button down shirt under a black vest. *Paranormal and Supernatural Encounters* was the title he was currently reading. Beside him on a small hand-carved wooden table sat a stack of books on similar topics and subjects. I turned to Jaxin, whose attention was on the book in his hands. I sharply read his name off the spine of the book and realized he was the writer of it. I then remembered Mint advising me not to mention anything ghastly about myself. I tried to be choosy with my words.

"A quick word sir?" I asked politely.

"I'm listening," he said, with his eyes flowing from side to side across the pages of his book.

"I'd introduce myself but I can't remember my name. Matter of fact, I can't remember anything. I seem to have stumbled into your world."

"It seems you've stumbled into some deep sh-"

"That's why I'm here," I cut him off.

"What do you want?" Jaxin asked me.

"I wish to go home," I said simply.

"It says here that passages work both ways," Atrixia pointed out in a book she carried.

"'You need a map?" Jaxin asked. "I keep plenty of Atlases."

He motioned his eyes over towards a circular room. I looked back at the two of them and walked over. I wasn't wasting any time. I entered the round room and looked up at the glowing calcite crystals on the ceiling above. The inner walls were lined with bookshelves. The shelves were built floor to ceiling. Each was loaded with maps, atlases, and scrolls. Centered on the floor was a massive brown globe. The globe displayed continents with no similarity to Earth. I walked around the room and studied the books. None of them seemed to be useful. I've never even heard of the places labeled on their spines. I passed a chair and a tall rolling ladder. I ascended the ladder and began browsing books that mapped out the stars. Jaxin entered with a cane and Atrixia followed.

"Can I help you find something?" Jaxin asked.

"I don't even know what I'm looking for," I told him sadly.

"Please," Jaxin insisted.

He tapped the top of the globe, the library disappeared, and a billion stars were projected in midair all around us.

"The stars map out the entire universe. They provide a common link between you and your ancestors," Jaxin said. "Again, can I help you find something?"

I slid down the ladder in amazement. He could locate any star by a simple search. Yet, I wasn't sure what to tell him. He knew I was lost.

"First, tell me the name of your star," he started with. I was so confused. This had to be the first time I ever had to think about it. "You mean to tell me you don't know?" he asked.

I looked at him not knowing what to say. "You mean Earth's?" I asked. "If I remember correctly, my planet has only one star. It's neighborly, I never had to know it by name. It was always just referred to as the sun."

"Earth's," he said aloud. Nothing happened.

"The Milky Way galaxy," I then said aloud.

Yet again, the globe didn't project anything different. The stars didn't shift to display my home sector.

"That's bizarre," Jaxin said.

"What's bizarre?" I asked.

"Your home star doesn't appear to be *anywhere* within this dimension."

My mouth dropped.

"You give it a try," he told me. He sat down in the small chair. "It's easy. Close your eyes, then place your palm on the globe. Real simple."

Atrixia leaned on the ladder and observed me as I closed my eyes, took a deep breath, and placed my hand flat on the globe's cold surface. The globe and I exchanged energy. I felt a force, yet I remained concentrated. I heard Jaxin say, "Ah."

I opened my eyes hoping to see Earth's sun, but instead, the globe displayed a different star above. A brighter star, one that was small and young. Its light was shifting from red to turquoise. The room was filled with its light.

"Ain't that something?" Jaxin asked. He placed his walking stick between his knees.

Atrixia kicked off the ladder in amazement.

"That doesn't *look* like my home star," I told Jaxin.

"Oh it's your star alright. It's young like yourself," Jaxin said to me. "It's still developing. Through all my years of studying and reading, I've never come across a star like *that one*." He seemed to be an expert on everything.

"Well, what do I do now?" I asked.

"Find that star. That star will take you home. That star will take you *anywhere* you wanna go."

"I'll take him home," Atrixia said, pulling me away.

He turned to Atrixia. "Now if you wouldn't mind Miss, I'd like to have a moment for just him and I to have a word."

Atrixia didn't like where this was going but still, she nodded and politely stepped out of the room.

"I'll see you in a minute, " I said to her.

"We won't be long," Jaxin told her. I slid the ladder over to Jaxin's chair and sat down on its steps.

He waited until Atrixia was completely gone before he turned to me stern as a ghost, and whispered, "You weren't followed into this world were you?"

I wasn't sure. I wanted to say no.

"You can't lie to me," he told me. "I know why you've come."

"How?"

He looked over at a glistening sphere sitting on a table just outside the room.

Immediately, my eyes were locked into it. I was in a daze. Imagine being under a trance. It was the first time in my life I've ever seen an actual crystal ball.

"I've been watching the two of you since you've left Mint's pumpkin," he said.

"You keep a crystal ball in your study?" I asked him.

"She does." He motioned over to a portrait of a gorgeous woman, sitting elegantly in a blue and white vintage gown. "She does readings and healings. We'll just say she's currently away on a business trip. She'll be back in a few months." He looked at my eyes and smiled. "She would have loved you."

"She seems nice," I told him.

"Indeed she is. Now on the other hand, you've clearly sparked the interest of an evil spirit. A very dark force, I must say."

"What could it possibly want from me?"

"I'm not sure, but it's been on your tail for quite some time now. It tried to follow you through my front door, but I wouldn't let it. You're safe now. This house, its gardens, and its woodlands are blessed and free of evil energy. You're welcome to stay the night if you wish. You and your delightful friend. Please, I have a small pond house out in the gardens. Take it. I keep it locked during the cold season, but it's prepared and ready. It could serve you well. As long as you don't mind spiders that is."

"I won't sleep," I stood up. "Not until I've returned home."

"Son, you're a long way from home. The only way to go back to your world is to go forward in this one. You're in another dimension, a dimension far outside your universe."

"My universe," I repeated to myself. I sat back down and tried to remember it. "Can you show me Earth?"

"Not easily, but come," he told me.

I passed him his cane and we both rose. I followed him out of the map room and he motioned for Atrixia to join us. She had changed back into her boots and pants. She was wearing her shirt and vest, except she wasn't wearing her green cloak, but my red hoodie. It was hers now. She was again studying a bookshelf, admiring its variety of antiques, treasures, and books.

There were gems and jewelry. When Jaxin called her over to the crystal ball, she looked at me wondering what was going on. I wasn't sure either. Jaxin sat down at the square red table set before the ball. I sat down in the chair right beside him and Atrixia sat down across from me.

He held out both his hands for each of us to take.

"This is more my wife's thing," he said. "But we'll give it a shot." He shut his eyes then Atrixia and I did the same. "Show me Earth," he said to the ball. The ball filled with a white cloud and when the smoke dissipated, the sphere revealed planet Earth, its atmosphere, and all its oceans. It was a breathtaking sight. I watched it rotate within the glass. I reached out my fingers to touch it. I felt so far away from it.

"My wife hates fingerprints," he told me.

"Oh," I pulled my hand back, and just watched in amazement. The oceans made me miss home. I remembered more now.

Suddenly the room went dark. The ball turned blue and there was a hooded figure sitting in the empty chair across from Jaxin. Atrixia shrieked. I remained still. Jaxin rose and stared down the cloaked being, until it just disappeared.

"KEEP OUT, YOU FORCE OF DARKNESS!" Jaxin yelled once it had left.

"What was that?" Atrixia asked.

No one said a word. I thought I was safe here, but none of us were. Jaxin looked at me and could see my misery.

"Come," he told me with a smile. There was something he wanted to show me. He led us out of the room and down the hallway. When we reached the stairs of the tower, Jaxin ascended them slowly. I looked up at the crystal chandelier dangling above the stairwell then looked down at my black and white sneakers as I began to walk up the red stair runner.

Where were we going? I wondered.

He had many fine paintings. I slowed down to admire each and everyone that we passed. One was of an old ship on a stormy sea. I climbed a few more steps and came to another painting. It showed a tulip garden with glistening fountains and hummingbirds. I looked forward to passing the next portrait and wondered what it might be. But we came to a window showing a sky full of stars. There had to be a billion scattered across it.

Jaxin stopped and faced Atrixia and I. He pushed open the window and said, "Feel free to gander. I think you'll find the view very soothing."

The arch window split then he stepped back and waited patiently for us to observe. I placed both my hands on the sill and felt like I was in a royal palace. The window overlooked his whole mansion. You could see his entire estate from up here. The sight was a portrait.

"You see your star?" Atrixia asked me out of humor.

"It's out there," Jaxin said seriously.

Atrixia came over to my side and looked out the window. Right then, a shooting star zoomed across the sky. She placed her hand over mine and the two of us watched it fly by.

"Wish for something," I told both of them, "anything," I told Atrixia.

I closed my eyes and wished for guidance. For someone to always be out there watching over me. That was it. The shooting star was there and gone in a flash. We then heard a thump from the top of the tower. Jaxin placed his hand on the banister, leaned over the edge of the railing, and looked up. The diamond chandelier above the staircase was shaking.

"Come along now," Jaxin said from the front.

I remembered the orange light shining through the windows of the crow's nest. I didn't know what we were in for but I looked at Atrixia and smiled. She smiled back at me. We locked eyes. I smiled and bit my lower lip. She was the first to look away but she looked back and looked beautiful when she rolled her eyes. "It's a bit of a trip," Jaxin said as we ascended higher.

We continued past a few more paintings and windows. The windows overlooked the entire woodlands and each one showed a different view. We eventually reached the top and came to a door with a glittering orange light slipping through the door frame. It was the same light we saw shining through the windows. I wondered what was creating it. Jaxin banged his cane on the base of the door twice and the door opened on its own.

He entered a bedroom occupied by two young girls. One was cleaning the room while the younger one sat on the floor before a complexly drawn out pattern. The pattern was a variation of circles and triangles spread across the floorboards. The shapes were drawn out in orange light. The young girl waved her hands over the pattern then twisted her wrists around each other. As she lifted her hands, out of the floor came the tail of a mermaid. It kicked around for a moment. Its purple scales glittered from every angle before it swam back down into the floor. It was so real.

"Focus, my child," Jaxin said.

He flicked the frame of his glasses, sending all the books on the shelves whirling around the room. Each book displayed their texts. She closed her eyes and channeled her attention on the pattern. The pattern began to grow brighter. The young girl clearly possessed some form of inner charm and the pattern was charged by her power. Suddenly, all of us were blinded by a yellow glow. Afterwards, I felt somewhat refreshed. The air in the room felt more pure. Jaxin and Atrixia appeared to be soothed by the aftereffect as well. I felt lighter than Peter Pan. Sort of how I felt after I drank the cauldron tea. Except this time, I felt more healthy and restored, in both spirit and strength. All my negative energy was gone. Atrixia stepped over and took me by the hand. She looked into my eyes with harmony in hers. She smiled. I assumed she was familiar with restoration spells.

"Simple alleviation spell, it'll aid you in combat," Jaxin said.

"It's a blessing," Atrixia said. "I remember performing healings. Mainly on animals. The spell can even readjust your fate. That's more of a fortune teller's thing though." Atrixia looked at Jaxin and said, "You're raising her right."

"Thank you," Jaxin said proudly. "Ever see a six year old complete a major level healing spell? She's the only descendent to possess the gift. She's gonna be the first in her family to go to school."

The floor was covered in books and stuffed tigers. A few rainbow specs remained floating around in the air.

"The older one is my eyes and ears just like the woman who gave them to her. Get some rest, girls," Jaxin said.

The older one snapped her fingers and anything out of place flew back to its proper position. The room was cleaned instantaneously.

"Really?" Jaxin asked, annoyed.

"Daddy, you can't even snap the lights on with your fingertips. I have to do it. Why is it that every time I zap a mess clean, I gotta hear lip?" the older one asked.

Atrixia and I stepped out of the room and Jaxin followed.

He closed the door, turned to me, and said, "You must be brave, child. Everything you think you know is about to change. Believe me, it will happen right before your eyes."

"What's about to change?" I asked.

"Time will tell. Give time, time."

I followed Jaxin down the stairs. Atrixia walked beside me. Every one of Jaxin's words danced around my mind. 'Find your star. Be brave. Everything's about to change.'

Atrixia took my hand. For a moment, she and I locked eyes again and in her eyes, I saw a spark. It gave me hope. Her light assured me everything was going to be fine and it kept me going on.

CHAPTER 13

HER SIDE

Jaxin led us out to his back patio and lit a porch lamp. "Go straight. The house is to the right of the main fountain. You'll need the key." He took out a large key ring and pulled off a golden key. "You'll find the house not too far from the pond, don't get lost, or do."

"Thank you very much for your help," I said. "You've provided a lot of insight." I was grateful. He placed his hand over his chest and nodded. He stepped inside, shut the back door, and turned out the interior lights. Atrixia and I stood on the back terrace under a single porch light. We looked over the garden. The night was dark and quiet. I looked up at the stars. The sky was clear. Atrixia and I shared a glance. She stepped forward and waved her hand over the garden. As if on cue, all sorts of flowers and exotic plants began to arise. Many grew out of the plant beds. Others bloomed out of the lawn vases and looked incredible. The ceramic flower pots had all sprouted strawberries. Vines grew up the stone walls and roses bloomed one after the other around the statues. With class, I raised my left elbow and once Atrixia took hold of it, I escorted her down the stone steps. The fountains were activated by motion. They turned on as we passed. They were gorgeous and I loved their splashy sounds.

We walked by flower planters. They were taller than me. We also noticed an arrangement of bird baths.

We passed through a gate. Once I closed it behind us, we continued and found the central fountain. Above it were four wide circular basins. The fountain towered over the entire garden.

Its water showered down and glistened in the moonlight. It was even more ginormous up close.

"I think this is where we turn right," Atrixia said. Straight ahead stood a white wooden archway that led to the large lily-pad pond.

To the left was a hedge garden covered in blue roses. I wanted to explore both and get lost. To the right stood a cabin with a beautifully playful design. Its tall roof was curvy and twisted like the top of an ice cream cone. Its glass windows were shaped like moons and stars. They were speckled all around the roof. Before we made our way towards the cabin door, I reached into my pocket and pulled out two sky coins. I laid a coin in Atrixia's hand and walked over to the fountain. I was glad I kept a few. The fountain glistened like the stars.

"What's this for?" she asked me.

"You'll see," I told her.

"I don't even recognize this coin," she told me.

I laughed and smiled. "Now shut your eyes and imagine something that only the bottom of your heart would desire. Don't tell me what you're thinking of; better yet, don't ever tell anyone. Think of something you truly desire or wish to see in the world and then think of it until your coin hits the surface. She closed both eyes and dreamed for a moment. Then, she tossed her coin. It was my turn. I looked at the fountain and thought for a moment. Sometimes your heart knows more than your mind. I looked at her and threw my coin. She had yet to move.

"Ready to go?" I asked.

She remained kneeled in front of the fountain with her eyes held on her coin.

"You okay?" I asked.

"Now what?" she asked me. "I'm so confused."

"It's all yours," I told her.

She jumped up with joy. "You mean what I wished for is going to happen?"

"Hopefully," I said. I reached into my pocket, pulled out the small golden key, and held it out in front me.

She grabbed the key from me and headed towards the cabin. Once she walked away, I kissed my fingers and placed them on the fountain. I followed her over to the cabin. We reached the door and stood side by side. She turned and faced me. In that moment I thought of Einstein, who once asked himself, *If I could ride a beam of light, what would I see?*

I looked at her and regained focus. She looked at me and when our eyes locked, she dropped the key. We both kneeled to pick it up and I beat her to it by a second. This time, her hand was laid over mine. Except this time, she didn't pull away like I did at Mint's front door; Instead, she looked into my eyes and stared. Her hand was a lot warmer than mine. There was a part of me she wanted to keep here in this moment. I turned towards her, gently laid my other hand down on top of hers, and gave her my full attention.

"Yes?" I said.

She wanted to say something but instead, she looked away. "Never mind," she told me.

"What is it?" I asked. "You can tell me what you wanna say."

"The first time we met, at the apple tree-"

"Yeah?"

"Remember it," she told me. "Don't forget it."

I was expecting a bit more but I could tell how serious she was being. She meant it.

"Why?" I asked.

"Just don't," she replied.

"I won't. I'm sorry," I said in a flash of guilt.

"For what?" she asked.

"For running away from that tree - before we knew each other."

"I understand. My powers freaked you out. It's okay."

I ran my fingers along the zipper line of her red hoodie. "Hang onto this. Keep it. It's all yours. I want you to have it."

She smiled and said, "Thank you."

I opened the door for Atrixia and said, "After you."

Atrixia and I stepped into a beautiful room with aqua walls. Dream catchers hung from the ceiling. The roof looked so groovy from inside. Sky lights were all over the place. Two large twin beds sat against each wall, opposite from each other. A fine pair of diving flippers hung over one bed and flowers dangled over the other. I dropped my bag on the bed below the diving flippers. After, I took off my cloak, rolled it into a ball, and tossed it on the corner of my bed.

I sat down on the edge of my bed and dug through my bag for a different set of clothes. In the corner of my eye, I watched Atrixia slowly remove the red hoodie and neatly fold it into a perfect square. She placed it in a small dresser. Afterwards, she asked for my cloak. I tossed it to her, and again, she folded it into a perfect square and tucked it away. I didn't bring any pajamas or sweatpants so, while her back was turned, I changed into a pair of dark blue jeans and a dark red t-shirt. It was the first time I changed since I arrived. I felt slightly more fresh after.

I looked at her vest and pants and wondered what had happened to her leafy red dress from earlier. I missed it. She shut off the lamp that hung from the ceiling and all was dark for a moment. Suddenly, glowing blue orbs began to grow from a flower pot on the windowsill. The room was lit by their light. What happened next was something fantastic. She turned and looked at me as she walked past her bed and made her way across the room. In a dark corner, she stepped out of her clothes and let them fall to the floor. The moonlight entered the room through one of the moon shaped windows in the ceiling. The crescent moon lined up directly with the window. She stepped over to the other window with the plant on its sill and shook out her hair.

The light from above shone over her. She was wearing only her underwear. She took hold of one of the plant's leaves and closed her eyes. A luminous translucent blue nightgown began to form around her. The fiber was the same shade as the blue forest she took me to, a radiant turquoise. The gown grew past her shoulders, down her back, and around her knees. She was now the most brilliant light in the room.

"Outstanding," I told her.

"Are you saying I stand out?" She felt insecure about it.

"I am, it's a good thing."

"You're not alone," she told me. She picked up her clothes and grabbed her boots. She dropped her boots under her bed and folded the last of her clothing.

After tucking them in the drawer, she laid down in her bed and pulled the blue covers over her. We laid with our eyes open. Together, we stayed awake. I wasn't sure what to think, let alone say to her. She rolled to the side. Her back was facing me after.

"Thank you," I said.

She rolled back over and faced me. She looked at me like she wanted to hear me say it again. I've thanked her plenty of times but now I was just thanking her for being her.

"Thanks for staying with me," I added. I could say it a thousand more times, a million, I couldn't thank her enough. I'd be totally screwed if it wasn't for her. "I have to say, I really love your nightgown." I smiled as her face lit up from the compliment. "It's so lovely," I told her.

Her mouth dropped into one of those shocked smiles. The kind that one makes when they're flattered, but don't know what to say back. "Why thank you," she said. She held out her arms and looked at each sleeve. She made sure that everything was on point. She flicked the cuff of her sleeve and blue sparks flew out.

"Well, I wish you a good night," she told me.

"You too. I wish you a better one."

I threw my shoes under my bed and sat back against the wall. When I looked back at Atrixia, her eyes were closed. I laid down, rested my head on my pillow, and looked up at the ceiling. I placed my hands under my head and thought. I had no desire to sleep. I remembered the red book I used to log everything. I pulled it out of my bag and wrote in the moonlight that shone through the window, until I was all caught up.

CHAPTER 14

YOU'RE NOT ALONE

I stared into the night sky through two star-shaped windows above my bed. Time went by and I remained awake. After an hour, a ray of moonlight shined through another moon window.

In the beam, I saw a violet spider dangling from the ceiling. The spider minded its own business. It climbed up and began to spin a web. A spider dreams. It imagines and creates. It's all intuitive to the spider. I sat up and wondered how it can do the things it can do. It isn't afraid of the fall. It's always holding on and it's always holding its own. I sat up on my bed, rubbed my eyes, and rested my head in my hands for a moment. I slid down to the end of the bed and grabbed my sneakers. I quietly put on each of my shoes and made sure Atrixia was still asleep. I tiptoed over to the dresser and was careful not to make much noise. I rolled out the drawer and reached for my cloak. She had it folded so nicely. I turned to her again. She was still sound asleep. I put on my cloak and gently stepped over to the door. I looked at Atrixia; she looked gorgeous while asleep. I was mesmerized by her beauty every time I looked at her. I kissed my fingers and placed them on the door frame before I stepped outside and shut the door. Then, I was all alone in the night. The area was quiet. I wasn't going far. I just needed to step outside. My head wasn't clear. The pond was nearby, I could see the moon reflecting off its surface. I walked over to the water and sat down on a large rock. I looked up at the sky and down at the water. I could see my own reflection on its surface. I looked up and began to wonder where I was, what this world is, and what I am to it. I looked at the stars and wondered where my star would be or how far I'd have to go to find it.

117

I stargazed a while longer. Time passed and I found myself in a state of balance. Jaxin mentioned something about my relatives sharing the same stars. 'A common link,' was the term.

I wondered if my blood was linked to any other visitors to this realm. I felt lost. I closed my eyes. *What lies beyond the atmosphere? How many other universes and dimensions have I yet to see? I'll cross every galaxy till I find my star, even if I have to travel light years to find it. I'll return home. Cross my heart*, I thought to myself.

I opened my eyes and right then, I saw a red flash across the water. I stood up, looked deep into the woods, and waited for the blast again. After a moment, it appeared a second time. I chased after it. It didn't seem like the type of thing I should involve myself in, but I had to know what it was. I threw my hood up and ran. Once nearer, I saw the blast a third time. Still, I wasn't close enough to tell who was responsible. I just hoped no one was hurt. I pulled my hood lower over my face and moved through the trees surreptitiously. I was now standing exactly where I saw the first blast. I didn't see anything but trees. The woods were serene and still. No one was around except for me. At least so I thought. Ahead stood a peculiar looking tree. Its bark had something carved into it. I approached the tree slowly, it gave me the creeps. The words *You're not alone* had been scratched into it in an eerie way. They were the same words Trixi said to me earlier.

Suddenly, the temperature fell and everything went silent. I pulled my hood off and sighed. "Is it you again? Now?" I said in an exhausted and annoyed tone. "Listen, I ain't for your games. I'm not for your hatred or your little obsession so whatever it is you want from me, make it clear because you and I…" I was interrupted by something shuffling deep within a cave close by. I set my eyes on the mouth of the cave.

And then there was a tall knight armored in steel plates darker than the night sky, stepping out of the cave. The Knight walked into the moonlight. I was expecting a ghost. "Oh, you've brought a friend," I said aloud, under the impression the phantom was listening. I pushed my hair to the side to look presentable. I wondered what Atrixia was doing right now. Hopefully she's still asleep. The knight's helmet had two long sharp horns, one on each side. The knight looked at me with two glowing blue eyes and froze. I remained in the shadows. We had to have been fifty yards away from each other and still, I was certain that its eyes were looking down on *me*. Nextly, all sound was obliterated. The knight carried a triple ball flail. The rattling of its chains ceased and the balls continued to clack without sound.

"Oh," I said.

The temperature around me had dropped so low my fingertips started to feel numb and frostbitten. The sky flashed with blue lightning. At that exact moment, the knight charged me using superspeed and used its chest to slam into me.

I flew back and landed in the dirt. Sound returned and the first thing I heard was the loud crash of thunder. I had been knocked flat on my back. My old football coach would have told me to "put some syrup on that." The knight clenched his gauntlet tightly around my shirt, and lifted me off the ground. Clouds of jade began to gather in the sky. I looked the knight straight in the eyes. It had eyes like two fiery sapphires that wanted to swallow you.

"The other guy was a lot friendlier," I told the knight. I was still certain the phantom and knight were pals. The knight turned and threw me. I landed in the dirt on my stomach. When I looked up, I saw the knight charging straight towards me. I got up and ran as hard as I could at it. The knight suddenly stopped short and stood tall. I stopped charging as well once I wasn't sure what it was doing. The knight stood battle ready and didn't move from its stance. I slowly began to approach it. Its eyes gazed down on me as if they were determining my worth and questioning my courage. I tossed my cloak in the leaves and continued. My heart was pounding beneath my shirt.

I'm gonna rip that helmet off by its horns, I told myself.

I ran at the knight. I was gradually increasing speed while the knight had yet to break from its position, indicating that it was a very territorial fighter. I lunged at the knight. It attempted to counterattack when I threw my arms at its horns. Somehow, I managed to grab onto one. I clenched it with every ounce of strength I had in me. The knight's helmet was fastened to its shoulder guards, tugging was no use. The knight took me by the neck with a powerful static electrical charge pulsating through its gauntlet. I couldn't breathe, nor feel. The knight readjusted its grip and threw me away by the neck, like a football. I crashed on the ground hard and roughly. I heard its heavy boots approaching slowly from behind. The knight reached me before I could recover. It picked me up off the ground, lifted me high, and then body slammed me hard into the dirt by my neck. That one I felt. The knight unfastened its flail from its holster and raised it high. The three spiked stars clacked in the air. The knight thrust straight down at me. I stopped the force of the swing with my left hand, then using both I was able to pull the flail from the knight's grasp. After I confiscated the knight's flail, I tossed it to the bottom of the black pond.

"Sorry, we won't be having any of that here," I said from the ground.

The knight looked down on me with confusion. I needed to get up.

I pushed on the knight's chest plate and shoved it back. In that exact moment, a blue blast of light fired out of my chest. I felt a shock in each of my arms. It scared me. I couldn't see anything in the flash. I thought the knight was still on top of me. I sat up and saw that the blast had blown the knight back twenty feet. I was in a daze. I felt dizzy and woozy as I slowly got up off the ground. The knight began to do the same. I got up and entered a battle-ready stance before the knight even stood up straight.

The knight nodded at me, indicating a truce. I was *beyond* confused. It looked at me with satisfaction, like it didn't need to see anything more from me. There was so much to configure. I watched the knight turn around and walk in the opposite direction. It walked back into the cave. I stood and gazed as the knight's cape disappeared into the darkness. It's about time I headed back myself. I found my cloak lying in the leaves. I grabbed it, shook it out, and began to walk back to Atrixia.

I had so many things on my mind. What just happened? I was just in a brawl. My heart just fired some force of energy. I thought I was better off keeping it to myself. I reached the pond house, and opened the door quietly. Luckly, Atrixia was still asleep. I closed the door behind me and made my way over to the dresser. The room was dark. I took off my cloak and folded it as best I could. I rolled out the drawer and placed my cloak neatly inside. The drawer made a loud creak as I closed it. Once I was in bed, I lay back and shut my eyes. I felt cold. I looked at Atrixia.

CHAPTER 15
ON THE WAY TO ANYWHERE

I awoke alone in the house the next morning. A sunray shone through the star-shaped window. Atrixia wasn't in bed, but she made her side. The pillows were placed straight and the sheets were spread flat. The blue blanket hung neatly off the side of her bed. I checked in the drawer and her clothes were gone.

Only my cloak and the red hoodie remained. I lifted the bed skirt and saw that her boots were gone as well. From the window I could see her sitting beside the pond. I grabbed my shoes, threw 'em on quickly, then grabbed my cloak from the drawer. I headed out the door and looked around. The morning was gorgeous. I heard the songs of birds. The air smelt fresh. I put on my cloak as I walked to the pond. Atrixia was sitting on the same rock I sat on last night. She looked at me, looked down, then looked out to the water. She looked crestfallen.

Neither of us said a word at first. I leaned back against a tree trunk.

"You slept well?" I asked.

She turned to me with little expression in her face and looked back at the water.

"I *was* sleeping well last night-" she said.

"That's good."

"-that was until I woke up in the middle of the night to a loud crash. I saw blue flashes shining through the window. They shone over your bed and you weren't in it!"

"I'm sorry," I said sincerely.

"Sorry? I was alone last night. I woke up and I was all by myself. The room was empty. Where were *you*?" she asked.

"I went for a walk."

"A walk? When? When the sky turned green?" She thought it was asinine. "Where did you go?"

"I walked around the pond. I couldn't sleep and I just needed to step outside for some air and clear my head, that's all."

"Well, while your head was clearing, mine was growing more and more tangled with every minute you were gone."

I felt guilty over leaving. "I'm sorry I left so suddenly," I told her. "I would never want you to feel like I would just ditch you. I'm sorry. It won't happen again."

She looked at me and nodded. She forgave me. The moment was quiet and I couldn't hold back for another second. "So I'm aware there's some form of 'supernatural power,' I'll call it-" Her eyes shot to meet mine. "-that seems to be possessed and practiced by every inhabitant of this world. Is that the correct way to put it?"

"What did you see last night?" she asked.

"Enough."

I looked over the water, remembering the red blast I saw last night.

"At least enough to know that this world is a mysterious place. One of secrets, and sorcerers, and heaven knows what else," I said.

"No, what did you see last night?" She sounded really concerned.

I looked at her. Memories of the knight began to return.

"I met a knight. This world is home to some powerful individuals," I told her. I looked down at the grass. I wanted to explain what happened. 'How can I elucidate?' I wondered. I didn't want to lie so, with pleasure, I told her everything. I told her how I couldn't sleep, how I saw a strange red flash in the woods while out stargazing. I told her about the knight and how it had struck me. Then, I told her about the brawl that followed. Her eyes gradually widened in shock the more I spoke. It was almost as though I was making it up. I didn't know how to explain the blue star burst that fired out of my chest and she was waiting to hear how the story ended.

I looked up at the bright sky that held the stars the night before. I looked over at the rock Atrixia was sitting on and remembered sitting on it myself. "So..." I said smiling, "I may have found my star."

"Your star?" she asked.

"Mhm," I mumbled. I tried to hide my smirk.

"Where in the heavens did you find that?"

"Somewhere. Somewhere deep within, really deep."

"I don't understand what you're saying."

"Last night, I was saved by this sudden spark. I felt my body release it. There was a bright flash. How I wish you could have seen it. That one moment of light."

"I heard a storm that ended with a really loud crash," she said.

"The knight charged at me and the green storm followed shortly after."

"Is that what woke me up in the middle of the night?"

"Most likely," I told her. "The light from my chest was like a star bursting. A great blue flame."

"Blue? If I remember correctly, your power was red when you first got here," she reminded me. "That's strange. Most don't have two colors. Sorcerers and magicians often possess red. Blue is usually owned by knights and warriors. It's something you're born with. Of course you can always adopt different forms of power and learn new traits. It's not easy and it takes a long time, but it's possible."

"Could you explain the process?" I asked.

"Oh firstly, affinity and devotion begins with you and it comes from deep within.

Secondly, it's about how much of yourself you attribute to whatever it is you're doing."

I grabbed a stick, rested my cheek in my hand, and began making little circles on the surface of the pond water.

"Listen to me; matter of fact, watch," Atrixia said.

Using two fingers, she gently grabbed a nearly matured caterpillar cocoon off the leaf of a nearby plant, then placed her other hand over it. She encased the frail being warmly while still giving it space.

She waited a moment, opened her hands, and out popped a blue butterfly. I watched its colorful wings flutter over the pond. Its wings were a sharp blue color. They flapped over the lily-pads and into the woods. I wondered how all of this could be real.

After the flare I felt in my heart last night, I was seeing the world in a whole new way. I saw all these new opportunities and possibilities. I felt like I was thinking straight. My head was more clear. I looked at all these new horizons with optimism. I saw an infinite amount of directions to go in, an infinite amount of roads to take. I felt like I had unlocked every door and gate in the universe. The secret key, it's yours as well. Hold onto it tightly.

"You can achieve all that you desire," Atrixia told me. "Stay consistent, confident, and encouraged. You can make anything become possible."

"I don't suppose it'd be like pulling a rabbit from a hat?" I asked.

I smiled at her softly. She gave me a smirk back. I could see temptation in her jade eyes. She raised a single finger to her lips and hushed me. Once all was quiet, she placed two fingers in her mouth and gave out a quiet high pitched whistle. The whistle was so quiet that it was more like a whisper. After that, the two of us sat patiently in silence. I was unsure over what was supposed to happen next. She sat, expecting the arrival of something. I looked at her wondering when it would be okay to talk again. She insisted on remaining quiet for a few more moments so I did. The very next second, a gorgeous maple colored rabbit hopped out of the bushes. He leaped in circles around Atrixia then plopped down on its back in front of me. I scratched and rubbed its belly. The rabbit looked at me and I looked at Atrixia with fascination.

I looked at her. "I thought of you last night. I don't know why, but you crossed my mind right before the trouble hit." I looked at her flawless face. "I'm happy to see you again." It may have sounded silly, but I meant it. It completely changed the direction of the conversation. She could tell how honest I was and admired it. On top of that, she forgave me. She and I shared a smile and watched the sunrise. The morning was delightful. I moved beside her and sat up against the rock. She looked over me blissfully from the top of the rock. I felt graced by her kind eyes. I took her by the hand and she held mine tighter. Her hand was warm, I never wanted to let go of it. She opened my hand and held her palm against mine. We each closed our hands around the other. Our hands matched like piano keys.

I looked up at the miraculous neighboring planets orbiting above. The daylight sky was quite a sight. One planet had rings that stretched across the entire sky.

"The sky looked amazing last night. The luminaries, the stars, everything," I told her. She nodded her head in agreement. "If we ever get another chance to visit that log we chilled on the first night we met, I'd love to sit out there with you all night and just stargaze."

"That sounds wonderful," she told me.

Life couldn't be better. All we had to do was run away. I thought for a moment and said, "Let's run away together," in a low tone. I rubbed the back of her hand with my thumb. I wasn't sure what I was even saying.

"Pardon?" she asked.

"Never mind," I said after a sudden change of mind. I looked at her and a part of me feared for her. I kissed her hand and apologized.

"No, you wanted to say something. Say what you wanted to say. You mumbled the first time. I didn't hear a word."

"You wanna come along with me?" I asked. "I want you to tell me more about this world and devotion on the way. I wanna hear about you and all your affinities. Everything you're willing to tell me."

"On the way to where?"

"On the way to anywhere," I said.

I stood up on my feet. I took her by her hands and she pressed her palms against mine. I looked her deep in the eyes. She stood up from the rock, without breaking eye contact.

Something was on.

I could fall in love with this girl, I thought. I just felt happy to feel that way. We let go of all the what-ifs. I looked up at the powder blue sky and ran off into the woods with her hand in mine.

CHAPTER 16

NEW BEGINNING

Away we went. "Wait, what about our stuff?" I asked. She reached into a hollow tree knot, pulled out the red hoodie, then reached in deeper and lastly pulled out the black bag. She handed me both. We were set.

"How did you do that?" I asked. I helped her put her hoodie on.

"You picked a fine forest," she said.

I didn't intend to pick a forest. I looked up and saw sunlight shining through the yellow tree tops.

"I just wanted to run off in a random direction. We're in the forest again?"

She clapped and a glowing ring of light expanded from her position. The ring of light swept over the ground and everything glistened after.

"Oh, we're back," she said.

Once the light spread throughout the trees, the whole forest came alive and active.

The leaves on the yellow trees popped yellow pollen and the leaves on the red trees popped red pollen. Their branches began to move around. The pollen sprinkled over the ground and flowers began to grow around our feet. I was careful not to step on them.

'What a place,' I thought as the leaves began to glow one by one. Even in the daylight, they were so luminant. There was a single green tree. Atrixia told me to wait on the trail. She slipped behind it and she was wearing a leafy dress when she stepped out on the other side, except this time, her dress was green.

Her hair was changed and it showed her eyes more. She used yellow pollen as an eye shadow. She wasn't kidding when she told me to give this place a chance.

She took my hands and pulled me away. We took off through the forest and man we were flying. The grass began to grow around her footsteps. She held onto my hand tightly. We were free. She led me to a small wooden bridge. I slowed down at the sight of it. Asters and yellow mums the color of the sunset were grown all around its posts. The railings and balusters were wrapped in vines. The bridge was only a small step, but on the other side, I saw a new beginning.

I thought it was a gorgeous sight. A painter would love to capture this.

"Over this brook," Atrixia said.

We stepped onto the small bridge and it creaked as we passed over it. The stones in the shimmering water reflected the sunlight. We stepped back onto the grassy path and Atrixia asked, "Where are we going?"

I turned to her and said, "I intend to discover the same thing."

Eventually, we came to a hedge garden with only one entrance. We stood side by side, debating on whether to walk *through* the garden or around it.

"Let's go through," Atrixia said.

We entered the garden and followed a short path until that path was intersected by another path. Her and I stood in the middle of the cross road unsure of which direction to go in.

I looked both ways before Atrixia said, "You take left, and I'll take right."

"Be safe," I told her, and went off. I followed the path all the way down and the only direction to take after was another left. I turned left and then made a right. After, I came to another cross path. I turned right, followed that path down, made a left, and came to a dead end. It wasn't long until I realized we were navigating through a maze.

I turned around to turn right and the way I came was blocked off. Another path had been revealed.

"ATRIXIA!" I screamed out.

"D!"" I heard her scream back.

We were both scared. The maze was changing. I thought it was going to encase us. The hedge walls were too tall to see over.

"It's trying to trap us in," she yelled.

"Stay put, we'll get out of here eventually."

I began to run through the maze. I continued talking to Atrixia. I tried using the sound of her voice to find her. She was trying to find me too. She sounded stressed. More paths continued to open. I couldn't tell if the garden was trying to trap or guide us. I was pretty sure the hedges were steering us in a specific direction.

An entry way opened and I raced through it. Atrixia and I found each other on the other side. We held onto each other tightly. We looked into each other's eyes as the surrounding hedges closed us in. We were completely engulfed until, lastly, a final path opened. The path led us to a mossy wooden door that sealed a dark rocky cave in the middle of the garden. We followed the path and approached the mossy door.

I knocked three times, took a step back, and stood beside Atrixia. The door opened on its own. We entered the cave only to find a shadowy lair of nothing but dirt, cobwebs, and some moss hanging down from the rifts in the cold damp ceiling.

"Hello?" Atrixia asked loudly.

The two of us looked around the silent room. I waited a moment before sarcastically saying, "Well, this place was a good investment of our time."

I turned around and headed towards the creaky worn-out door. I was reaching for the knob, when suddenly Atrixia and I were knocked off balance by a forceful, booming voice that had yelled, "STOP." The voice came from the darker end of the cave. At the same time, we were blinded by a light that shone from the center of the room. The light reflected off the cave walls. For a second, I remained in place shielding my eyes. Through my fingers, I peeked at the light. Although the light was tremendously bright, I pulled my hand away and stared directly into it. I was caught in a trance. I felt like I was looking into another world. The light eventually softened and my eyes adjusted to the dark. I could see a crystal ball sitting high on a tall stone pedestal centered perfectly on the floor of the cave. The ball is what drew my attention. Imagine bottling a sunset. I had already broken free from its trance, and still, I stood gazing at its yellowishorange colors.

Once I had fully regained my vision, I was able to see what was occurring in front of me. I could make out the dark frame of a figure peering back at me from the shadows on the opposite side of the light. They seemed to be seated in a crisscross position on what appeared to be a bed. The figure rose slowly and made its way on to our side of the room. Atrixia moved away from the shadows and stood next to me as the being approached. Atrixia looked puzzled and worried, while I was still trying to put together what just happened a moment ago.

From out of the darkness came a young woman. She stepped into the light, right where Atrixia had just been standing. She looked to be around our age and her hair was gray. The mysterious girl had pale blue eyes and wore a tightly-fitted nightgown. She looked tired, dirty, and her face was beautiful. She stood silently as if waiting for someone to speak.

"Hello," I said.

She just stared back at me. I looked at the Crystal ball. "Care to tell us what it was we just felt a moment ago?" I asked.

"I had you both hypnotized," the girl said. "Any reason the two of you wandered into my hedge garden?"

"We didn't mean to intrude," Atrixia said. "What are you doin' out here?"

"I was about to ask you the same thing," the girl laughed.

"We just wanted to cross through the hedges, we didn't mean to trespass," Atrixia said.

"You picked the wrong garden," said the girl.

"Forgive us," I said. "We'll be on our way now."

I nodded at Atrixia and we each began to walk towards the door.

"Wait," the woman said.

Suddenly, Atrixia and I were frozen in place. She and I were unable to move the moment the girl spoke. I moved only my eyes over at Atrixia. There seemed to be a red energy radiating around our bodies. Suddenly, the red energy vanished and Atrixia and I were able to move again.

I turned around and faced the girl. She had a necklace like Mint's, except hers was red.

"That's quite the charm you got there," I said. "Where'd you get it?"

"I made it myself. I can take you where I got the pieces for it if you want."

"Could you?" I asked. I wanted one.

"That won't be necessary," Atrixia said.

"Where do you intend to go, once you leave?" the girl asked me.

"We ain't too sure," I said to the girl honestly.

"You two are the first to enter here since I found this place eight years ago, or was it nine? I'm not sure. I don't receive much company."

"Well maybe if you got rid of all the cobwebs and got a hookah up in here, this place would be bumpin'," I suggested.

"Or better yet, move out of your cave and go see the world," Atrixia said. "It's changing out there. The dark curse is slowly being lifted and the gloom is clearing," she added.

"Well I guess that would explain how your hair is blonde," the girl said to Atrixia. "I was wondering why that was."

The girl smiled at me, waved her hand over the floor, and all the dust blew off her stone floor. She snapped her fingers and the cobwebs on her books and furniture disappeared. Her bed covers flew up and landed on her mattress perfectly. She clapped her hands and the moss hanging from the ceiling was obliterated. Once the hanging moss cleared, the cave was clean and spotless.

"Where'd this come from?" the girl asked, as she picked up the hose to an actively burning hookah. She took a pull and exhaled. She turned to me with fascination and smiled again. "There's an old Observatory once owned by a wizard," the girl said, "That's where I got the parts to make my necklace. If you were to go there, you would need my guidance and assistance."

"He already has guidance and assistance," Atrixia assured her.

"Oh really, and what is your presence good for?"

"I carry my insight, intellect, wisdom, and experience."

The girl smirked and replied in amusement, "You're a forester, you grew up in a garden."

"Oh by all means, please tell us all about the intellect that one picks up while spending the last half of their life hidden away in a cave," Atrixia snapped.

The girl said, "I've spent sol cycles devoted to my studies. Reading, conjuring, practicing, mastering. Just give me a moment to grab a few things." She turned away and walked over to her sleeping area.

"We need to rethink this," Atrixia suggested.

"Rethink what?" I asked her.

"She's clearly a witch."

"So?" I asked her.

"So?"

I began to play with the crystal ball. The colors would respond to my hand gestures. For a moment, I pretended to be a mad wizard. I wanted a crystal ball in *my room*.

Atrixia crossed her arms. She wasn't amused. In fact, she was appalled. She walked over to the other side of the ball and looked deep into my eyes.

"Do you see a bright future?" she asked.

I took her by the hands. "I see you. My future is bright and promising as long as you're in it. I don't need a glass ball to see that."

I walked over to the mysterious girl.

"Can I assist you with anything?" I asked the girl.

She turned to me, gently slid her fingers on my cheek, and smiled like she already had a few things in mind.

"You can pass me that rag," she said.

Close by was a rag hanging on the wall. I grabbed it from its ring and handed it to her.

"Thank you," she told me.

She wet the rag with fresh water dripping down from the ceiling then used it to wipe her forehead clean. Then, she fixed her hair in a mirror lit by candle on each side. She had a row of spell books up on a shelf. Each book was a different color. I pulled a heavy black one off the shelf. *Spirits of Darkness* was the title.

I skimmed through the pages and saw diagrams of molecules and disturbing pictures of ghouls. I closed the book and stashed it back on the shelf. The girl turned around and faced us.

She snapped her fingers and zapped into a midnight blue dress. She looked down at it, decided against it, and zapped into a bright red dress. It was shorter and tighter than the blue one.

"My name's Caydia," she said.

After, she covered herself with a dark red cloak with a long hood. She laid the hood over her hair and looked up at us.

"This is Atrixia," I told her. "You can call me 'D'."

"It's a pleasure," she said, as she handed me a small black box.

"What's this for?" I asked.

"I want you to accept this as a token of my friendship," she said to me.

I opened its lid and inside was a bright glare. Casting this glare was another crystal ball, fit for a ring. I took it out. The ball was the size of a large pearl and underneath was a silver band.

"Try it on," she told me. "It has a one size fits all feature."

I slid the band down my finger and it fit me perfectly. I was fascinated by the activity of the ball. I didn't even know mystical crystal balls existed until last night and now I wore one on my finger. I investigated it and saw collisions of lights and colors. It was totally me. The colors were warm and trapped in a glossy sphere of infinite secrets.

"That ball should keep you safe and show you wonders," Caydia promised. "You'll learn how to read it."

The ball shined a bright red. "What does that indicate?" I asked.

"That would be your power shade," Caydia said.

"My power shade?"

"Indeed. Your spirit is what powers your soul and your soul is what powers your body. The color of whatever power your spirit possesses will appear in every soul gem. That ball will display your color as well."

"That can't be right. The first night I was here, I tried a soul gem on and nothing happened. Shortly after, I was freaked out by something and two red flares fired out of my palms. The night after that, I released a large shock blast and its fire was blue."

"No, red's definitely your color," she said, "you're just like me."

"I don't know about that," Atrixia said.

"Yeah?" Caydia questioned. She looked at me and said, "Tell me, are you disastrous? Maybe even a little rageful?" she asked with a smirk. "There are different forms of power. In time, one can learn them. It takes a lot of time and commitment but it's possible. But then again, why change what you were put here for? Don't ever neglect what you were born to do."

She grabbed a bag and slid her arm down the bookshelf, knocking each book into her satchel except for one. A black one that sat on the end. She went to hand it to Atrixia.

"I don't need it," Atrixia said.

"Okay, I'll just hang onto it then."

The three of us set out the door together. The hedge maze was gone and there was a trail covered in orange leaves to the left of the cave. When I asked why the garden had mysteriously disappeared, Caydia explained that the garden served as a security system and the maze only came and went as it was needed.

We were walking to the leafy trail when Caydia said, "One last thing."

She reached into her bag and tossed me over a spare cloak. It was red like hers, except *this one* was fiercer and had a darker tone. I placed my dark blue cloak in the bag then tried on the fiery red cloak. The crystal ball on my finger glistened white when I put my hand through the cloak's sleeve. The cloak was a fine fit and it had some form of connection with the crystal ball.

"It looks good on you," Caydia said.

Caydia wore a bright red cloak, I wore a dark red cloak, and Atrixia wore the red hoodie.

Caydia silently read a passage from one of her books then whispered some words as she shut it. The ground caved in and a hole formed. Suddenly, a white horse charged out of the hole and galloped around in a circle. Caydia tossed the small book in her bag, then hopped the horse's back.

"Welcome back, Majesty," she said to the horse.

CHAPTER 17
ENJOYING THE JOURNEY

"This way," Caydia told us. She led us through the woods.

"Where are we going?" I asked.

"The observatory," Caydia said.

"You know where you're goin'?" Atrixia asked.

"Surely," Caydia said.

I didn't care where we ended up. We walked most of the day. The color of the trees changed from orange to green. We adventured through a jungle. Atrixia and I followed Majesty on foot through a wide world of endless green. We were surrounded by vines and ivy. The environment was peaceful and serene. We were enjoying the journey.

"Stay together," Caydia said from the front.

"So we're just gonna pop in?" I asked

"And pop out. We'll be in and out, one, two, three," Caydia said.

"Aren't you worried about running into some random home?" Atrixia asked.

"Don't worry. This place was abandoned long ago," Caydia assured.

Suddenly, the ground began to rumble. "What's happening?" I asked.

They both shrugged their shoulders. None of us knew what was going on. Sunlight shone down from above. I looked around as the trees began to shake. Caydia hopped down from her horse. The three of us gathered as a monstrous beast ferociously engaged the scene. The beast roared and tore down the trees in a ferocious manner. It walked on four legs and possessed reptilian traits. It had dinosaur-like scales and long horns. Atrixia and I both looked to Caydia once the beast noticed us and began to charge.

Atrixia placed her palm on the ground and tried to calm the beast through some form of spiritual communication.

"I have no hold on it," Atrixia said. "what do we do?"

"I believe we're supposed to stand still and not move," I suggested.

A red flare appeared from both of Caydia's hands. I looked at her and, in the heat of the moment, I charged a blue fire bolt in my right hand without complaining or having to think about it. I knew what I needed to do. I stood ready with my fist cocked. The beast lowered its chin and positioned its head to ram us like a giant bull. Suddenly, at the last second, something swooped down by a rope and laid a trap that unrolled and tripped the beast. The beast rolled forward and landed on its back. From out of the sky came a young red haired man. He dropped down and landed on his feet. His hair was tied back in a ponytail and his entire outfit was forest green. He wore a sleeveless shirt and had gold necklaces that hung over his bare chest. His pants were green and he wore brown leather boots.

"I'm Thatcher. You should know that forest stompers are very territorial creatures."

He looked at Caydia's fire bolts and asked her, "How would you feel if someone were to intrude *your* yard?"

Her eyes widened and her jaw dropped. Her face was priceless. She laughed sarcastically like she knew the feeling. Thatcher was accompanied by a girl of the same age and hair color.

She was even wearing a dress the same exact color as Thatcher's outfit. She approached on foot. Her hair was curly and she had light blue eyes. Once she stood beside Thatcher, the resemblance was clear. They were twins. The beast moaned and squirmed around until it broke free from the trap, rolled over, and stood up on its flat, heavy feet.

I stepped forward to help defend against the beast.

"Stand down," Thatcher told me, "Deliah care to assist me?" he asked in a cocky wiseguy type of way. She seemed annoyed with him but she knew she had to help. She threw her hair back, tied her curls in a ponytail, pulled an arrow from a quiver, and drew it back with her bow all in a single motion. I was impressed. She fired the arrow into a tree. The arrow was attached to a long rope. Once the line was secured to the tree, she fastened the rope around her waist. Thatcher fired an arrow and did the same. After, she and Thatcher began to run. The two circled the beast while maintaining their distance from it.

"Step one, be aware of your situation," Deliah said. She looked at her brother.

"Step two, take account of your allies," Thatcher said.

"Step three, have a plan," Deliah said as she rolled out a spring loaded trap.

"Step four, remember your plan," Thatcher said, annoyed as he began to drive stakes into the ground.

"Step *four,* channel your power," Deliah whispered with her eyes shut.

"Step five, let it embrace you," they each said at the same time.

Their lines retracted and the two of them flew upward. They began to swing around the ferocious being, entangling it with their lines. I watched Thatcher cut his rope, spin around, fire an arrow, and grab onto its rope. I was impressed.

At the same time, Deliah's spring loaded trap unleashed two web-like nets. The nets flew into the air and intertwined with Thatcher and Deliah's cords. The twins landed on the ground, cut their lines, then found two ropes that had been dangling. They flew up into the air and swung circles around the beast. Their weight and momentum is what made the nets rotate and close. They trapped the monster, restraining it without harm. They continued to circle until their ropes had no more slack. They finished off by swirling around each other and tying a knot. It didn't look easy to do. Thatcher and Deliah touched down on the ground at the same time and secured the ropes to the stakes. The beast fought. Although the beast was strong, it wasn't strong enough to break free.

"Thank you," I said to the siblings.

Atrixia and Caydia were still in shock over what just happened.

"We should be going now," Thatcher said. "be sure to be clear of that monster before those nets dissolve."

"We'll see you around," Deliah said.

"I hope so. That was hardcore," I said.

They each fired a rope into the trees. Both had a mechanical reel attached to their waist.

Their lines retracted and the two flew off.

Caydia hopped back onto her horse and said, "That monster isn't gonna stay trapped forever."

The stakes in the ground began to loosen. We hurried away until the beast's roars could no longer be heard. We walked through the afternoon. After some time, night began to fall and Caydia said, "This should be far enough." She hopped down from her horse and lowered her hood.

"Far enough for what?" Atrixia asked.

"For us to stop and get some rest."

"You mean to tell us that we aren't reaching the observatory tonight?" Atrixia asked.

"You didn't think it was close, did you?" Caydia asked.

Atrixia didn't complain and neither did I. Atrixia was all for getting some rest and was the first one to fall asleep shortly after. I laid near her. Caydia laid down a few feet away with her back turned to us. The ground was cold. I rolled over countless times trying to get comfortable. After some time, I looked over at Atrixia and wished that I was laying with her. I looked the other way and saw that Caydia wasn't lying in her spot anymore. I sat up and saw her sitting alone on the edge of a cliff, staring up at the moon. Caydia seemed to be distant and detached from Atrixia and I. She didn't say much during the walk. I understood her. She only just met us today. I'm just as shy sometimes. I quietly sat up and walked over to her.

"Hey girl," I said with a smile. I sat down beside her and looked into her blue eyes. The moonlight reflected off them. "I like your cloak," I told her, referring to the red one she gave me.

She smiled back. "I'm glad," she said. She looked back out at the sky.

"Do you ever feel guarded sometimes?" I asked, hoping I wasn't being intrusive.

"All the time," she said.

"It's okay. Sometimes I feel like I'm living in a bubble."

"Life's been a pretty rough ride for me. I always tried to keep my life filled with positivity while the world around me consisted of sad things like death, fighting, and people addicted to dark energies. They're not things that make up my life, but the things that circle around it like a storm while I stand alone in its eye." She looked at me and asked, "You know what that's like?"

"Yeah. They're like thorns in your climb. Clouds in your sky you never asked for."

"Well one day you eventually reach a point where you can't carry any more of the weight of the world because you're already carrying so much of your own. You cut what's not yours loose and just carry on by yourself."

"Is that what you've been doing?" I asked her.

"I ran away, found a cave, and that's where I've been living for the last nine years."

"You ran away as a child?"

She nodded. "That cave was home to me. There, I was able to study."

"Study what?"

"Anything and everything," she said happily.

Man, I was so happy to be with her. I felt sorry for her. I was happy to pull her out of that cave even though she seemed like someone who gets out often. She was exciting and fun. I wanted her to feel comfortable with Atrixia and I. I wanted to learn everything she knew. She seemed just as lost as me.

"I'm happy I found you, really happy. You don't have to be alone anymore," I promised.

"I love your spirit. I love your world," I added.

"Are you not from here?" she asked.

"No I'm from another … universe, I suppose."

"How sure are you about that?"

"I'm pretty sure. I still can't remember much of it. I know people don't have powers where I'm from. I ran away the first time I saw Atrixia's and she was only growing apples. When it's reality and it's right there in front of you, it hits you differently."

I looked over at Atrixia and made sure she was still asleep, "I saw Atrixia's face clearly afterwards. That was even more amazing."

"I can't grow an apple," Caydia admitted.

"Have you ever tried?"

"I can give it a shot."

She slightly curled her fingers and twisted her wrist while focusing on a tree, just like Atrixia would. She even managed to grow a fat green apple. She picked it and passed it to me. It looked and felt alive. A single leaf hung off its stem.

"It looks perfect," I told her.

"That doesn't mean you should bite into it. Don't be deceived by looks. It *looks* efficient but the apple was conjured. Its process was rushed. It wasn't formed by the earth, therefore it holds no nutrients, making it toxic. Noxious. A poison apple." I looked at it and placed it on the ground.

"Well I'm sure Atrixia would be happy to help you out with the rest," I told her. "It would be a good way for the two of you to bond in the time we have together."

She rolled her eyes.

"It was only a suggestion," I said.

Our conversation was interrupted when we saw a red flash in the woods.

"Did you see that?" I asked.

"I did," she said.

"What was that?"

"I don't know. You wanna go investigate," Caydia said eagerly.

"We can't just leave Atrixia out in the open."

"She's a forester, she lives outside," Caydia informed me.

"I promised to never neglect her."

Caydia rolled her eyes and clapped her hands. After, a ring of fire appeared around Atrixia. The ring had Atrixia completely circled.

"It'll explode if anyone dares to cross it," Caydia assured me.

"A fire trap? Really?" I asked.

"C'mon," Caydia said.

I followed her and made sure I didn't lose her. It was dark out and the woods were twisty. She and I began to run. She turned the corner and I lost sight of her for one second. When I spotted her again, she was already so far ahead of me. I ran after her and caught up.

When she turned around, it wasn't her. I was alone with another girl that I had mistaken for Caydia. She wore tight black clothes under a red cloak that resembled Caydia's. Her hair was white and her eyes were red. They intrigued you. I found them entrancing. Her skin was pale as if she only went out in the sun once a year. Her lips were red and her smile was daring. Right away, you could tell she was a total baddie.

"My name's Shadow," she said. We heard a howl and she said, "Come, it isn't safe out here."

"I have to find my friend," I said.

"She'll be safe as long as she remains out of sight."

Shadow brought me back to her cave. For a cave, the place was well furnished. There were other members who lived in the household. They had no front door. They didn't seem to be worried about an intruder entering. I walked with Shadow down a candle lit hallway. Their home decor was very gothic. Their hallway carpets were bright red. Shadow seemed to be grateful to have me as her guest. We passed a room with walls that held a variety of sharp weapons. I found them a little disturbing. There were old daggers locked in display cases. We stopped in front of a room that held multiple opened, empty coffins. I looked inside the room and realized they were beds.

I heard a loud clap from behind. I turned around and saw Caydia standing over Shadow. She had just hit Shadow in the face. The ground shook when Shadow hit the floor. Caydia must have hit her pretty hard. After, Caydia got right up in my face and screamed, "ARE YOU CRAZY?" at the top of her lungs. I looked back over at Shadow. She looked up at me and showed her sharp fangs for the first time. Her eyes were glowing red. Caydia grabbed my arm and we ran for the exit. Shadow began to get up and Caydia threw a fireball at her. It only held her back for an extra moment. Two more vampires attacked us from the front. Caydia froze one with a spell that temporarily makes one stand still. All I wanted was a handful of garlic powder. Suddenly, one appeared in my hand. I dashed some on Caydia then blew the rest into the face of the other vampire while his mouth was open. He choked and coughed while he held his eyes. They had to sting. The other vamps were so dizzy from the scent of the garlic that they all transformed into bats before our eyes, and fled their cave. Caydia and I shook the garlic powder off our cloaks and followed the bats out. Atrixia was still sound asleep when we returned and I sat down beside her. Caydia could tell that I liked Atrixia by the way I looked at her. Caydia walked over to me and pulled the lid off a box that contained a black dagger. A large clear gem was held within the center of the dagger.

"What's this?" I asked.

"A little souvenir I found in the vampire cave. Its gem is used for storing souls. Could be a clean way to end a fight."

"Let's keep all of this a secret for now," I whispered to Caydia.

§

We woke up early. The day was bright and we got an early start on our hike. We wanted to get to the Observatory *today.* Later that morning, we passed some villagers chatting about a strange house up ahead.

"It's changed again," I overheard one of them say.

We came to the house and found it looked exactly like my house on Earth. I was able to remember the instant I saw it. Only difference was that this house appeared to be old and gray. It was dusty, and ran down. Caydia lived in a cave, and Atrixia never specified where she was from, but this house looked like the one I grew up in.

"I've passed this house before," Caydia said. "A witch who lived here long ago put a spell on the place so that its appearance would change to look like the home of whoever walked by it. It's meant to lure those who pass. Why? I don't know."

"I'm confused. Is this a haunted house? Or a witch's house?" I asked.

"I don't know. Let's head in and find out," Atrixia said jokingly.

"All for it," Caydia said.

"Whoa, I was only kidding," Atrixia said.

I just stood back, taking a long and hard look at the house as they talked. Memories were coming back to me. Not all of them were positive.

"I think the place would be worth checking out," Caydia said. "The witch who lived here died and she cursed the place right before she did so. I don't think it would be under new ownership."

"What do you expect to find in that place?" Atrixia asked.

"Anything," Caydia said, "It's not my house and I don't think it's yours." Caydia turned and looked at me. Atrixia realized the house was mine and suddenly wanted to rush in. She was hoping to find a thrill inside. "C'mon," she said, and ran up the pathway.

I wasn't afraid. I followed her. Atrixia stepped in and Caydia yelled 'BOO' once Atrixia entered. Caydia teleported inside before Atrixia and I even reached the door. The door slammed shut behind the three of us on its own. The loud slam made the girls jump.

"It's okay," I told them.

I looked around and the place was covered in dusty cobwebs. There were dead bugs all over the floor. The furniture was laid out the same except all the couches were stained, ripped, and torn. The place was gray. The walls were light gray. The floors were dark gray. Furniture, gray.

"Looks like anything that crawls into this place dies," I laughed.

The girls didn't find it funny. Everything looked like it hadn't been touched in years. There was one thing that had color and looked out of place. A long sleek black box that was sitting on a shelf. I walked over to it. Atrixia headed up the stairs to search the other rooms. I picked up the box and watched Atrixia walk up the stairs. Once she was gone, I opened the box and saw a wand light up inside. Immediately, I dropped the box out of fear. The tip of the wand hit the gray floor and, instantly, the color of the floor changed to purple. All the dead bugs came alive and crawled under the green groovy shaped furniture. The place still looked odd and old fashioned except now, its walls were red, its floor had a different pattern, and the furniture had character. Spell books appeared on the walls. Caydia looked over each of their labels. I don't know what made me drop the wand. It was the first time I've ever seen one in this world. I was unsure of what it was going to do when it lit up. The end of the wand was blinking red. I picked it up, placed it back in its box, and left it on the shelf like I never touched it.

"We should probably go," I suggested. "This place is dark."

I saw my reflection in a mirror on a vanity table. I walked over to it and looked into my own eyes. *That's a good sign I'm not a ghost*, I thought.

The previous owner had a lot of colorful powdery makeup on the table, along with a music box, a bottle of perfume with an apple as its bottle. I noticed a necklace holding a gem like Caydia's. I picked up the gem and felt a strong temptation to put it on.

I unfastened its chain and laid it around my neck. Suddenly, the gem and both my eyes lit up red. An unrecognizable voice of a woman was heard throughout the house. "Perfect," the voice said, "I have you trapped. You're mine now."

Atrixia ran down the stairs and saw me wearing the necklace. She sighed and said, "I leave the two of you alone for one second and-"

"Ah, the flower child," the voice said. She cut off Atrixia, deeply unsettling her.

"The three of you are now locked in my domain and I won't release *a single one* of you until that boy submits his power to me."

I remained calm even though I didn't know what to do.

"Wearer of the gem, who are you?" the voice asked me.

"I can't remember," I said back. "It's coming back to me."

"Your power is unseizable, I'd already have it if it wasn't. It's one I've never seen before. I want it."

"Let's go," I told the gang.

"That necklace will kill you if you try to leave the house," the voice informed me.

Atrixia stepped in and said, "I will tear this place down if you don't release him now. I may not show it but I am the last person in this room you wanna mess with."

"You don't believe in possessing power," the voice said to Atrixia. "You think what you do is simply done through nature. I have you locked in my house, would you like to see the power I possess?"

Atrixia stepped back.

"I believe in possessing power," Caydia said, as blue electricity bolts appeared in both her hands.

"Possessing power?" I questioned. "Power, power, power," I repeated, like it's already been said a million times. I looked into the vanity mirror and looked at the necklace. "Is that what this is about?" I asked. "Clearly, if your power was strong enough, you wouldn't feel the endless need to take it from others."

The necklace compelled me to my knees.

"Hand over your power or else," the voice said.

"Or else what?" I asked.

The walls cracked and the house began to rumble and shake.

"Okay," I shouted. I didn't want anyone to get hurt. I knew what the voice wanted. I just didn't know what I had to do. I closed my eyes and concentrated my energy. I focused my attention and activated my power. It was submitted into the necklace slowly once I did so. *I never even got to see what my true power was*, I thought to myself sadly.

A light began to grow inside the red gem. I could feel it. In the mirror, I could see the necklace glowing. A tiny crack formed in the gem. I realized the gem couldn't contain all of me and laughed. I looked up and said, "Careful what you wish for, sweetie."

I charged the gem with a fire so bright that it made the gem burst. Both Atrixia and Caydia hid as a massive uncontrolled explosion went off in the room. After, I was left standing with the gem lifeless and in pieces on the floor. The mirror had cracked. I was free from the necklace's trap. We heard the woman's voice scream until it faded away. Afterwards, the door slipped open and sunlight shone through the house.

"Let's go," Atrixia said. We walked out and I shut the door behind us.

"We done trick-or-treating?" I asked.

"What's Trick-or-treating?" Caydia asked.

Chapter 18

A MATTER OF TRUST

Later that day, the three of us continued through the woodlands when the trees started to release an odd smoke. At first, none of us knew what was going on, until Atrixia screamed and clutched her chest in pain. She fell to the floor and held her heart. "Oh no," she said, as she turned to me. "It's happening again."

I rushed over to her. "What is?" I asked. The bark of each tree began to crack and glow red from within. Suddenly, every nearby tree ignited with fire. Flaming sparks flew everywhere. The jungle was crumbling apart and the area was no longer safe. Atrixia appeared to literally feel the destruction around her. In a heartbeat, I lifted her up and rushed her out of the woods. Caydia followed on her horse. I saw sunlight on the horizon as we neared the end of the jungle. I pushed aside the wild leaves and stepped onto a vast deserted landscape. We left the jungle and entered a new environment. The ground was cracked and entirely dried out clay. Once we were free, Atrixia regained her energy and health. She was able to stand and walk again. I gave her a hug and held her tightly once I knew she was okay. While she was in my arms, I looked back at the forest. I saw the figure of a woman apparently consumed in fire twirling around what was left of the woods. She hovered in the wind. Atrixia had tears in her eyes. She took one look at the woman composed of flames and recognized her immediately.

"That's her," Atrixia said, "the one behind all the mysterious fires. My forest was immune to the gloom so it had been burnt down."

Caydia was smart. She could sense that I was the one the woman made of flames was really after and why.

"Let's go," Caydia said. "She's not the one we need to stop if you wanna end all this," she told me. "I can undo the destruction she caused to the woods but we have to keep going," she told Atrixia.

A massive blue glass sphere with four brick towers built in a spiral around it was all that stood in the distance.

"We're close," Caydia said. "We gotta get to that orb."

"That's where we're going?" I asked.

"That would be the observatory," Caydia confirmed. She hopped down from Majesty and gently pet the side of Majesty's face. "I'll be back soon, girl," Caydia whispered.

She clapped her hands twice and the white horse disappeared in a puff of pink and purple smoke. Through the desert we walked. The ball served as the building's core and the network of towers and tunnels made the place look like a freak of architecture. Atrixia and I walked side by side behind Caydia. We walked over the cracks in the ground until we reached the entrance. We climbed up the stone steps. Caydia pushed on both doors and the three of us stepped inside the massive blue orb. The ceiling was made of glass. Everything looked like it hadn't been touched in years. All the telescopes, monoculars, and sundials were covered in cobwebs. Even the astronomy and astrology books had a thin layer of dust over them. Atrixia looked around in fascination. Caydia was nowhere to be found.

"Where'd she go?" Atrixia asked.

"I don't know," I said. "Uhh Cayde?" I called out.

There was a railway built around the interior of the glass bubble. It allowed the rider access to every level of the facility. Caydia had raced down it in a cart as the lights switched on, one after the other. The laboratory was an incredible sight. Seeing it all lit up was an exciting surprise. The ceiling was high. Above, I saw floors of book chambers and doorways. Caydia reached the bottom and hopped out of the cart. She was excited to be here. So was I. There were four stairways. Each one led to the top of their tower. Atrixia walked over to another part of the Observatory and explored. Caydia noticed an enchanting table against the wall on the opposite side of the room. We walked across the room and passed a large circular disc on the floor. The disc was made of stone and it held four stones on top. Each stone was arranged across from each other. Two were round and two were cubes. Each stone was marked with its own symbol. I didn't understand them. They lit up when we walked past. I didn't know what the device was, nor could I even guess what it was used for.

I walked over to the enchantment table. The enchanter was a round table with a ring of candles placed around the edge. She asked me to empty my bag. I pulled out some clothes and found some apples. I found a red beanie in a pocket I've never checked before and lastly, I pulled out the blank red book I've been using to log everything.

"Hand me an apple," Caydia said.

I handed her a light green granny smith apple. She placed the apple on the center of the table and the candles ignited. Then she reached into her bag and pulled out a dark blue book. She skimmed through it until she landed on a particular page then whispered a few words from it.

The candles lit up brightly, then blew out. After, the apple glistened every color of the rainbow.

Caydia picked it up and looked at it closely then tossed it over to me.

"What does it do now?" I asked.

"Take a bite and find out."

I eyed her as I placed the apple down. After, she requested my bag. I handed her my empty messenger bag and, like the apple, she placed the bag in the center of the table and the surrounding candles lit up. She flipped through her book, then I heard her whisper the words,

"No bottom, no weight, carry good fate."

The candles lit up even brighter, then all blew out at once. She lifted the bag up by its strap. It appeared the same.

"Now it's bottomless and weightless," she told me.

"That's amazing," I said to her. She passed me back the bag. "Incredible," I added.

"It works on water bottles too. I've tried the same enchantment on my favorite bottle of wine once."

"How'd that work out?"

"Greatly," she told me as she pulled a wine bottle out of her bag. 'Angel Kiss,' its label read. Its substance was turquoise. It was my first time ever seeing blue wine.

She passed me the book and said, "You try."

The book had a thousand pages. Each page held a hundred different enchantments. When I found one I liked, I untied my shoes and threw them in the center of the table. I whispered a few words from the book and my sneakers lit up. Afterwards, they still retained a yellow lightning-like glow. If I did the enchantment correctly, the shoes should now provide its wearer with super speed. I threw 'em back on, laced them up, and handed her back the book. I dashed around the Observatory in an instant. The enchantment and test run were both a success.

This world is awesome, I thought.

She took a sip of her wine and offered me some.

"Are you even old enough to drink?" I asked politely.

She laughed and said, "The drinking age here is eighteen."

"And are you eighteen?"

"I'll be nineteen this Halloween. How old are *you*?"

"I can't remember."

I took a swig and its taste was unlike any other. The substance was delicious. I could see why she wanted an endless amount of it. I passed her back the bottle and she took another sip.

"I can't recall anything," I went on to explain. "I crawled out of a well and can only remember the events that followed."

"You don't even remember the day you were born?"

"Nope."

"Hmm." She didn't find it strange. She knew all about the process of newcomers adjusting to this world I assumed. "So. You and Atrixia, you guys a thing?" she asked.

"What's a 'thing'?" I asked back.

"Let's play a game," she said as she passed me back the bottle. I took a sip and followed her. She walked over to the center of the room and stood in front of the circular stone disc we passed earlier.

"What's this?" I asked.

"This would be an arcane table. One uses it to create new spells and learn new powers. With this, you can practice different arts and combine spells. First we choose an element."

"You mean like earth, air, fire, and water?" I passed her the bottle.

"Those would be elements of nature. I'm thinking something more," she took a sip and said, "expressive." She set the bottle down.

"Like *what?*" I asked.

"Love," she said out loud. The arcane table began to light up and spin. The markings and symbols carved into the stones lit up.

"How do you win?" I asked.

"You have three turns to create a stronger force."

"This is ridiculous." I backed away.

"Whoever creates the stronger force by the end of the last round wins." She took another sip of her wine and looked at me.

"What do I do on my turn?"

"When a stone passes, speak to the stone, one energetic word, and its essence will appear above in light form, understand?"

"Not really, but let's go."

A stone slid by her and she said the word, "Lust." A red light appeared above the table.

"Your turn," she said as a stone came my way.

"Devotion," I said aloud.

The light turned blue and grew brighter. Caydia picked up the wine bottle, took a sip, and eyed me as she said the word, "Amorous."

Then the color of the light changed from blue to red. She walked over to my side and said, "Your turn," as she passed me the bottle.

I took a sip, swished it around my mouth, and thought for a second.

"Passionate," I then said. The light remained red but grew larger and brighter.

"We matched colors," Caydia pointed out.

I passed her the bottle. I wasn't keeping score.

"Next round wins it, I suppose," I heard her say.

She took a large sip then thought long and hard for a moment. "Spontaneous," she said.

The light expanded and softened to a warmer color. After her turn, the light shone orange. She slipped me the bottle and stood back to watch the final turn. I took a long sip right before a stone passed by. I knelt, closed my eyes, and whispered the word "everlasting," as though it were to be a wish. A blue light formed and collided with Caydia's orange light. There was a bright purple star-like light above.

"That's something I've never seen before," Caydia said.

"Who won?" I asked.

"I'm not sure," she said.

I stood up and looked at her. "That was fun," I said. "Next sips yours."

I passed her the bottle when I heard Atrixia say, "Pardon me, I don't mean to interrupt."

She had been standing there the entire time.

"Trixi? Sup Gorgis?" I asked. I meant to say gorgeous.

"Gorgis?!" She questioned back. I was buzzed and she could tell. I looked around and thought the place looked so cool. I totally forgot where we were for a moment.

"You.. Are.. A Rockstar," I said to Atrixia impulsively.

She looked at Caydia furiously. Even when Atrixia was angry, I still thought she was *the* most gorgeous girl in the world - in any world. It didn't matter which one we were in. I smiled at her. Atrixia came up to the both of us.

"Having fun?" she asked.

I looked up and saw a million stars through the glass ceiling. Night fell. "Yes," I said excitedly, "let's go outside."

"Am I the only one who remembers why we came here?" Atrixia asked.

"To carry on," Caydia said.

"Pardon me?" Atrixia asked.

"To carry on," Caydia said again. "That's why the three of us came here." She sounded emotional. A tear nearly came to Atrixia's eye. I looked at Caydia speechlessly. She was right. All of us were constrained by some part of our past. I knew one thing, she and I just became best friends.

"We'll just grab what we need for the necklace and go," Caydia said to Atrixia.

"No rush," Atrixia said back.

"Good, cause I don't remember where I found them last time."

"That's okay," I said, "we'll just look around and check each room." All I wanted to do was wander around this place. "Let's get lost," I said. Caydia was with it.

"Okay," Atrixia said. She held her eyes on me.

"We'll each choose a tower and search through it," I said to them.

I picked a tower and ascended its stairs. A blue carpet adorned the floor and books of all kinds lined shelves built into the tower walls. I grabbed a torch from the wall and continued upward. I reached the top and entered a clear glass dome with a large telescope in the middle. The large end of the telescope protruded the glass ceiling. I could see breathtakingly gorgeous stars all around. It was out of a sci-fi movie. I looked through the telescope and saw a strange distant planet with rings and moons. *I would love to go there*, I thought. I headed back down the stairs, returned the torch, and entered the blue glass sphere. I walked across the floor. The sphere was empty. Atrixia and Caydia were searching in other towers. I approached the tower opposite of the one I just came out of. It was sealed with a wooden door. I tried twisting the knob and it was locked. I turned away and I heard the lock 'click' behind me. Like the gate at Ome, the door had mysteriously unlocked shortly after I touched it. The tower's carpet was purple and its walls held fancy jewelry. I ascended the stairs and entered a room that held a large collection of rocks and stone fragments. There was a large stone locked in a display case. The gem lit up purple when I walked past it. I walked back over to the gem and stood in front of its case after I noticed its light. I was so fascinated by its bright purple glow.

"That sure is something," Caydia said. She had been searching through this tower.

"How long have you been up here?" I asked.

"A few minutes before you came in."

"Did you let me in?"

"No. The door to this tower was open when I first found it. I was alone. I left it open just in case I ever wanted to return. This time, I locked it behind me but I didn't unlock it."

"You won that game," she told me. "I think that stone in the display case might be the one for you."

"It was a tie," I told her, "and that rock looks priceless. We're not taking it."

She looked at me annoyed.

"We're not even sure if this is going to work," I told her, "let's just find a simple gem."

"If you don't take it, somebody else will." Atrixia walked in and I dropped the conversation.

"What'd you see in *your* tower?" I asked Atrixia.

"I found two bedrooms built below a single patio garden," Atrixia said, "You said this place was abandoned long ago, right?" she asked Caydia.

"Indeed," Caydia confirmed.

"What's in the remaining tower?" I asked.

"I explored it the last time I was here," Caydia said. "I found an alchemy laboratory and a library. I could stay here forever."

Atrixia nodded her head in agreement. I walked over to a cabinet. Behind two glass doors were shelves of different stones. I opened it and started examining the different rocks and crystals. Atrixia walked over to me.

"Do you even know what you're looking for?" she laughed.

"No, not really," I told her.

"Those are charge crystals. They're meant for enhancing enchantments."

"Oh." I placed a few in my bag, thinking they'd be convenient. Atrixia looked at me confused by all this.

"What do you need a soul gem for?" she asked me.

"I'm not sure. I don't even know what their main purpose is."

"They're meant to concentrate and channel power, power you've yet to even discover. Inside you is a spirit. Your spirit is attached to your soul and your soul is connected to your body. The stone links the three and enhances your power. The stone will only make you stronger. They're optional."

I was confused by why she knew all this. I wondered what her history with these stones was. She didn't seem to like them.

"This gem should suit you well," Caydia said to me. She held up a small rock. The rock was good enough for me.

"Let's find a chain," I said.

Atrixia began to search little drawers and small wooden boxes. I looked in the jewelry cabinets. Caydia slipped away for a moment.

I opened a fancy-looking jewelry cabinet and found amulets, rings, and golden cuff links. We weren't here to rob the place so I shut the cabinet doors and walked back over to Atrixia. I didn't wanna take anything we didn't need. Atrixia held a chain around my neck and imagined how it would look on me. When she felt it didn't suit me, she put it away and tried another.

"I love this one," she finally said.

The chain was silver with helix-like links. Caydia walked in with a pendant holder, saw the chain, and admired it as well.

"Do we have everything we need?" I asked Caydia.

"We do," she said.

"Let's do this," I said.

"I think it'd be best to do it outside," Caydia suggested.

Atrixia held the chain and Caydia held the stone. I followed them down the stairs and out the door. I wasn't sure if this was even gonna work.

What if it does work? What would my power be? I wondered.

We stepped into the night. I was eager but nervous. Once we were clear from the observatory, I said, "All right. Let's give it a shot."

"You may have a power that's yet to be introduced to this world. Out in the open may not be the best place to attempt this spell," Caydia advised. "It's night time," I pointed out. "Who's gonna see us?"

"You never know," Caydia said.

Far off to the side, we saw woodlands and decided it was safer to test the spell there. We entered the woods and Caydia pulled out a book. "The book says to set the stone, its chain, and its pendant holder on the ground and get clear of it," she said.

Caydia placed the gem and its holder on the grass and Atrixia set the chain down right beside them. They seemed to know what they were doing. I was clueless.

"Perhaps we should take a few steps back," Caydia suggested.

"A good mile," Atrixia added, "who knows what the blast radius of this stone will be if something goes wrong?"

Although the gem wasn't impressive in size, Atrixia didn't underestimate it. I could tell Caydia was excited. I looked at both, looked down at the necklace, then looked up at the stars.

"I'm ready," I said.

Caydia questioned the stone with her eyes and recited a passage from the book. The stone shined red, but only slightly.

"I'm not sure if I'm strong enough to do this," Caydia said. "I can craft one for myself but to make one for another person is a bit more complicated. It requires more strength. You should be strong enough," she said to me.

"You can do this," I told her. I had faith in her.

Caydia shut her eyes and held her arm out over the necklace. She wasn't afraid. The sky lit up with lightning. A cloud had mysteriously appeared above. A bolt of lightning flashed and the stone was gone after.

"I didn't mean to do that," Caydia said. She felt guilty. Suddenly, a caw was heard from above.

"I doubt it was your fault," I assured Caydia the moment I heard the familiar caw. I looked around for a floating cloak.

"I don't like this," Atrixia said.

I walked over to her and held her. "You're okay," I promised.

We heard another caw overhead. I looked at Caydia and she looked back at me. Even though she had no idea what was going on, she looked at me like she was ready for anything. I loved her.

"Let's go back," Atrixia proposed.

"Not yet," Caydia said.

I watched a raven flee the scene.

"The gem is gone," I reminded Caydia.

I figured this was a lost cause until Caydia said, "'D,' a quick word?"

"I'll be right back," I told Atrixia.

I walked over to Caydia and asked, "What's up?"

She reached into her bag and held out the large soul gem from the display case. My first instinct was to hold it down and keep it out of sight.

"Caydia, this isn't ours," I whispered. "I told you, don't ever take something that isn't yours."

"I told you, if you don't take it, somebody else will."

"What do you wish to find in something that doesn't belong to you?"

"I want you to look at this… Things like these… they don't just come by. Even the most ancient books have never referred to anything like this. Things like these are just legends and myths, like fairy tales that have been long forgotten. Yet, here in my hand, I hold not only a soul gem but a powerful one, one that seems to only react around you," and the rock shimmered with purple light, "it's irrefutable that it belongs to you." She looked down at it and said, "I've certainly never seen one do that before. Its capabilities are unknown. Many would love to get their hands on this or at least prevent you from ever discovering its true power. Don't even try to tell *me,* or *yourself* especially, that it's not yours." She passed me the rock and held it firmly in my hands. "You're keeping it."

I wanted it more than anything. I wanted to discover its power and capabilities. "Okay," I said, "but only under one condition, nobody is to know, nobody. If this ever got out and word blew up, there's no telling what it could lead to. It needs to be kept concealed and controlled. Is that understood?"

"Oh believe me, I understand. The less who know, the better," Caydia said, motioning to Atrixia.

"You're saying we should keep it from *her*?" I asked. "No, I'm not worried about her."

"She's a little, eh, off. Trust me, I would know."

"I barely know her and still, I would trust her with my life. It's a matter of trust."

"Did she trust you with knowing all of her capabilities at first?"

"Yes."

"*All* of them?"

I looked at Atrixia and back at Caydia. "That girl has nothing to hide," I said. "She was the first friend I made in this world."

"That girl's holding you back."

"That girl makes it a fairy tale," I said, and by my tone Caydia could tell it was the end of discussion.

I walked back over to Atrixia and said, "Hi." I looked into her kind light eyes and took her by the hands. I forgot what I wanted to say and laughed.

"If this wasn't my form, would that bother you?" she asked randomly out of nowhere.

"What do you mean?"

"I mean if I didn't look this way, would you still see me the same?"

"Always."

"Even if I wasn't a 5' 10", green eyed, blonde girl?"

"You found me. I will always see you as the girl who found me."

She looked up at me and said, "I'll never forget you." She placed a silver chain in my hand. "You were wearing this the night you were brought here. It appeared next to you one night while you were asleep. I meant to give it back to you but I forgot I had it. You know how your memories are coming back to you over time? Well your belongings work the same way. They aren't gone forever. They'll all eventually be returned to you one way or another. You'll find each one in a random place at random time."

I looked down at the chain and remembered it. Back on earth, I received it as a gift from my oldest brother. I looked at Atrixia and said, "I'll never forget you."

"If only," she said. "You know once you return to your world, you'll have no memory of me or this place whatsoever?"

I won't lie, I felt a part of my heart shatter when she said that. "Well I'm here now and you'll always remember me. We're gonna be alright." We held each other tightly and looked into each other's eyes. We both smiled.

"You found *me*," Atrixia added.

"Let's give that necklace another try," I suggested.

Suddenly, she was excited. We walked over to Caydia.

"Ready to do this?" I asked Caydia.

"Are you?" she questioned back.

She placed the larger stone on the ground with a pendant holder slightly larger than the last. I laid down the chain I just received from Atrixia, and Caydia handed me the book. I saw its texts were written in another language. I looked at each word with doubt. I had no faith in myself. I didn't think this was gonna work.

"I don't even know what I'm doing," I admitted.

"You're using your soul to bind the gem to its chain," Caydia explained.

"Was that supposed to be the simple version?" I exclaimed.

"You know how to control your power, you've done it before," Caydia said, "Just concentrate and use it on the gem."

I barely know how to use my powers on command. It's only when a situation demands it.

I read the book's instructions repeatedly.

"Just channel your power," Caydia advised.

I wasn't sure how, but I was willing to attempt it. Fiery red and electric blue, if I can do this correctly, we'll uncover what happens when the two collide?

'What's the effect of an individual conjoining the two?' I wondered.

I placed the book on the grass and the two took a step back. I laid my hood over my head and opened my palms towards the stone. I closed my eyes, and focused. My hands began to feel hot.

"Is it working?" I asked.

"Not quite," Caydia told me.

I concentrated harder and tried something else. I could feel the attraction of the surrounding magnetic field and it allowed me to create electrical sparks. I was behaving like a star. My hands felt tingly and numb. I peeked at the stone, still unchanged. I tried concentrating half my power towards warming my left hand and the other half on charging my right. The two girls gasped once they saw the stone light up and glow purple.

"What are you doing? How are you doing that?" Caydia asked.

I opened my eyes and saw that I was holding two violet solar flares. I looked up at the stone as it began to levitate off the ground. A wind picked up. I was controlling my power.

"Whatever happens, this'll be kept concealed," I assured Atrixia. She liked the sound of it.

"-and secret," I said to Caydia. Caydia nodded her head like she understood.

Her face was serious. She just looked at me like she wanted to see the spell be performed already. I closed my eyes and felt a part of me become one with the gem. I just imagined what I wanted. There was a blinding flash once the additional pieces were added. They came together and finally conformed the necklace. Once the gem and chain were in one piece, the necklace fell to the ground and shimmered in the grass. I felt lethargic afterwards. I was excited, but very tired. I knelt on the ground and felt like I was going to fall asleep. Atrixia came over and knelt beside me.

"Are you okay?" she asked.

I nodded. I looked at the necklace and saw it blinking back at me. I turned to Atrixia, took her by the hands, and the two of us rose from the ground.

"Go on," she said.

I walked over to the necklace and looked down over it. The clouds cleared. The silver chain glistened in the moonlight. The soul gem shined brightly. A bright purple, my favorite color. I held it. Then, like last time, I made strong eye contact with Atrixia as I put it on.

Something about wearing one in front of her made me feel weird. Then again, she was a lot cooler about it this time. I fastened its latch slowly and carefully. Nextly, I felt an energetic rush throughout my soul. My whole body tingled. I closed my eyes, took a deep breath, and became one with the charm. The gem made me feel alive and ecstatic.

"How does it look?" I asked Atrixia.

"Flashy?" she asked.

"Really? I'm never flashy."

I thought it was a change. I showed it to Caydia and asked her what she thought.

"Like you were born to wear it," she told me.

Atrixia straightened my cloak. Suddenly, green storm clouds gathered in the sky. Lightning flashed and thunder rolled. It began to rain. Suddenly, a blue portal appeared and the tall black knight passed through on a dark horse. I stepped forward and made sure both Atrixia and Caydia were behind me. A smaller portal appeared on the left side of the knight and a larger portal appeared on its right. The female figure, made almost entirely out of flames, exploded from the smaller portal. A massive barbarian with a monstrous face stepped out of the larger one. The barbarian had one eye, sharp teeth, and long horns. I could see the Flamedame trying to avoid the rain. It appeared to be stinging her.

Suddenly, the temperature dropped and all sound was obliterated. I could feel the presence of the phantom. The knight's blue eyes beamed down on me.

I turned to Caydia and said, "Take Atrixia back to the Observatory."

Flares appeared in each of the Flamedame's hands and I screamed, "Now!"

I looked at Atrixia and Caydia and calmly said, "The both of you, please stay safe."

This battle was mine. The two of them provided me with so much. This mess of mine is for me to clean. It isn't anyone else's to get dragged into. My wish is for both to stay safe. "Where's your little phantom buddy?" I yelled at the Knight.

The Knight didn't seem to know who I was referring to. The question seemed to annoy them.

'How many people are after me in this world?' I wondered. I'm sure the knight was now wondering the same thing.

"What do they want from you?" Atrixia asked me.

"That," Caydia said, pointing at my necklace.

Its purple light pulsated. I buried it under my cloak. It was mine. I entered a defensive position. Instead of fleeing as I asked, Atrixia and Caydia stood by my side. I stood between my allies and the knight did the same. The knight's accomplices engaged. Atrixia brought down thick thorny vines that snatched the brute and entangled him. The brute dangled as he struggled to break free. I was impressed. The knight stepped forward with its sights set on me. Its glowing blue eyes were focused solely on my stone. The knight seemed to be sure of me this time. It pointed its glove at my necklace.

Caydia fired up a red flare within each of her hands and began to launch firebolts at the knight. The Flamedame caught both of Caydia's fireballs and threw them back at her. I threw my arm out and yelled, "No!"

I wanted to extinguish the fire and a great burst of water shot out of my hand. Both fire bolts were put out as Caydia ducked. I looked at my hand not knowing how I just did that. I held my stone tightly in my hand. Then with my own eyes, I watched the Knight back away in terror. It was bewildering. Atrixia and Caydia were just as confused as the dark trio retreated through their portals. The sky cleared and the stars were visible.

"What...just... happened?" Caydia asked.

"I don't know but something tells me they'll be back," Atrixia said.

"We should go," Caydia said. "You okay 'D'?"

"I'm fine."

That was a lie. I stood in place unaware of the power I held around my neck. I felt scared. All I knew was others feared my gem and wanted it more than I did.

"That was incredible what you girls did there. The way you rose up. They're after me. I'm so sorry you were pulled into this."

"They're not after you," Caydia said. "They're after your power and I will defend it as I would my home."

"Who knows what they'll use it for?" Atrixia asked.

I concealed the purple gem under my cloak. "It's best we head back," I said.

We reached the observatory but I didn't wanna go inside. I just wanted the girls to get some rest. I sat down on the front steps and the two of them went inside. They ascended the stairs to their bedrooms. Once they were far enough, I whispered the words "thank you" to them.

CHAPTER 19

WE COULD BE HEROES

Alone, I sat on the stone steps. It started to drizzle. Tiny raindrops began to softly fall on the steps one by one. The dry cracked ground began to soak up the rain. The clay turned to mud. I sat outside for a while. Eventually, I reached into my bag, grabbed my red book, and logged the events since I last wrote. I drew pictures and wrote marginal notes. Later in the night, I heard someone leave out a side door. They were wearing a red hood. I couldn't tell if it was Caydia or Atrixia. They were heading towards the woods. I followed quietly. We reached the woods and I managed to remain unnoticed. The girl began to shed her clothes. She was under the impression she was alone. Her back was turned to me and it was dark out. Deep in the woods, she sat down on the ground, crossed her legs, and softly began to sing. I knew who it was then. I approached from behind. Right when I was about to call out Atrixia's name, the girl held out her hands and two roaring flames fired out of her palms.

"Caydia," I yelled out.

She didn't seem to be startled. She reached out her arm and her red cloak flew into her hand.

I covered my eyes and asked, "Why are you naked?"

"It's more energetic when your body's in direct contact with the earth," she explained, "not wearing clothing is therapeutic."

"What are you doing out here?" I asked.

She put on her cloak and stood. She began to get dressed. I looked away.

"I've sent the call," Caydia said.

"Who did you call?" I asked.

She smiled at me. "Everyone."

Once she had her clothing on, she threw her cloak over them, and began to walk further into the woods. There was something different about her. She was much more confident tonight.

"Tomorrow, there will be a large gathering," she said. She stopped and looked at me seriously. "Are you prepared for it?"

"I've yet to know what it's even for. It's not going to attract the wrong kinds of attention is it?"

"It's going to attract all kinds of attention."

"How's this gonna sit with Atrixia?" I asked.

Caydia eyed me. "I don't know, how's this gonna sit with Atrixia?"

The question hit me weird but she thought it was mine to figure out. I guess it didn't matter. She held her eyes on me as I thought. She walked over to me, took me by the hands, and pressed her palms against mine. We shared an energy, I could feel it. I just couldn't tell what kind it was. I looked directly into her eyes. I wanted to tell her how nice they were the first time I saw them. They were a pale blue.

"You have crazy eyes," I told her.

She looked back at me and said, "Okay?"

She wasn't sure if it was a compliment or not. She stepped away from me and took off at supersonic speed. I was complimenting her, not hitting on her. There's a huge difference. I ran after her. She was fast but so were my super-shoes. She finally stopped running and I caught up.

I met her in the moonlight on the edge of a cliff. "I see the shoes work well," she said. "Good job."

"I love them," I told her.

"You can do more. We could *be* more," she said.

"What do you mean, *Be more?*"

She turned and looked at me. Her smile was tempting as usual. She leaped backwards off the edge of the cliff and fell. I screamed out her name and ran to the edge of the cliff.

The instant I looked down over the drop, she flew back up. When she returned, her hood was up and her head was bowed. She looked menacing.

She lowered her hood and looked at me. "We have a chance to be something great. We could be-"

"Heroes?" I asked humorously. *We could hide away in daylight*, I sang in my head.

"Whatever you wanted," she said, clueless. "*Anything.*" She flew up and did a backflip.

"Okay, show me how to do that right now," I said anxiously. "What's it take? Happy thoughts? Faith, trust, and fairy dust?"

"What?" She laughed. "It doesn't need to be taught. There's nothing for me to show you.

Just fly," she said. "I'll catch you if you fall."

"You're crazy."

I tried to lift off the ground and nothing happened.

"Humans aren't meant to fly," I said.

"I'm human," she reminded me.

"I'm not sure if *I'm* meant to fly."

"*Everyone's* meant to fly."

I closed my eyes and concentrated harder. I even tried flapping my arms. I just felt dumb.

"You can do it," Caydia said. "Lift off, be light."

I tried to meditate by slowing my breathing until I felt as light as a feather. Nothing changed. After, I imagined the ground was gone. A moment later, Caydia took me by the hands and whispered, "Open your eyes." I opened my eyes and she let go. We were floating over the ground. I grabbed onto her hand for an extra moment. She held my hand until I was comfortable.

"I got you," she said with a smile.

"How am I doing this?" I asked.

"You tell me," she said, as she joyfully pushed me up into the sky. I flipped and spun then flew back over to her once I regained stability. I felt like I was like playing underwater. We flew over the woodlands.

"Having fun?" she asked.

"This is incredible," I said. "It's unlike anything I've ever done before."

"You're really good at this," she told me.

"I want to go higher."

I zoomed up and kept my eyes on the stars.

"Stay with me," Caydia yelled from below.

She chased me. She twirled and soared around me when she caught up. We could barely see the ground from the altitude we were at. Caydia floated on her back and shut her eyes. I saw the stars on the other side of the sky. They looked so close. Nearly tangible. I thrusted up like a rocket and flew towards them faster and faster.

"Wait, don't go that high," Caydia warned.

The light around me grew brighter and brighter. My body temperature was increasing. I closed my eyes and continued until, all went quiet. When I opened my eyes, I was mesmerized by the vibrant glare of the sun shining over the planet. The sight was breathtaking. I broke the planet's atmosphere and could still breathe. I was floating in another universe, viewing a different solar system. There was no sound. The sun was nearly blinding. I was watching the sunrise from space. The neighboring planets appeared to be so close. I could see their surfaces. On one planet, I saw advanced civilizations along with layers of cities and lights. From far below, I could see Caydia mouth the words, "I can't go up that high."

I flew away from Galaxius and zoomed in the direction of the futuristic looking planet. An individual wearing a helmet, jacket, and jetpack soared alongside me. *Battle Ranger* was written on his sleeve. He looked to be patrolling the sector. I was flying right beside him.

He halted me the moment he noticed me. He seemed amazed by the sight of me. "You're flying," he came to his senses and said, "in a restricted area." There was a microphone built into his helmet. "This is a no-fly zone. Change your course, or you will be shot down," he said.

He pointed a large laser cannon at me. I didn't want to agitate him but didn't want to leave. I was still sightseeing and taking everything in.

I pouted and flew back to Galaxius. I put my legs forward, and dropped back into its atmosphere. I fell towards the ground and stopped when I reached Caydia's level.

Once we met up again, the two of us dropped down together. We descended back down slowly. I gently floated from side to side like a leaf.

We returned to the garden terrace built above our bedrooms. We made it back just as the sun began to rise and shine over the Observatory. There were two staircases. One that led you to my bedroom and one that led you to Caydia's. I hovered down the stairs that led to my room and saw Atrixia lying in a bed. She was asleep. I landed on the bed beside her, shut my eyes, and went to sleep. I'll remember this as a dream when I awake.

CHAPTER 20

11:10

I awoke later that morning under the rays of a bright sun. Light was peeking through the window. I felt good. Atrixia was still asleep. I quietly slipped out of the bed and grabbed a random cloak. After, I walked out of the bedroom. There was a red glass brick window that shone into Caydias room. Its curtains were open. I threw on the red cloak she gave me and snuck past it. Caydia was sitting up in her bed. She didn't notice me. I headed down the stairs and snuck out the front door. Fresh grass had grown around the building overnight. The muddy landscape had turned into grassy terrain that went on as far as the eye could see. I ran off into the woods with no destination. I was just trying to get lost. The morning was as calm as any other in Ossynthore. The sun was out, birds were chirping. Still, something about today felt different. It was time to prepare. Once I was sure I was completely alone, I fired up my powers. I snapped my fingers and accidentally set fire to a tree. I freaked out and a handful of water streamed from my hand. I threw the water at the tree and a massive tidal wave flew out of my hand and washed out the flames. I quickly spun my wrists around each other. When a red flare formed in my left hand and blue flare formed in my right, I flew from the floor and smashed the energy into the ground. A hot purple starburst sprung up. The feeling was exhilarating. I felt alive. I wanted to practice creating things on command, so I concentrated harder and imagined a gold necklace. I focused until a small black box appeared in my hand.

I opened the box and thought, *Atrixia is going to love this one*. I pocketed the box and carried on. I walked with my hands in my pockets down a dirt path. I held my head low while I thought about everything. After some time, I began to wonder about Atrixia. I started to miss her. 'Why don't we have cell phones here?' I asked myself. I was about to fly back to the Observatory when I heard crumbling dirt. I didn't think much of it until I realized they were footsteps. I looked around, ready to take on whatever came at me.

"Oh, good morning," I heard from behind.

I turned around and saw Caydia smiling at me under her hood.

"Where' you off to?" she asked.

"Nowhere special," I told her. "I'm just takin' a walk."

She sat down on the edge of a small hill and patted the grass, welcoming me to sit down beside her. I sat down next to her and asked, "What's up?"

"I have a surprise for you."

I got excited the moment she said that. Knowing her, I couldn't imagine what it was.

I closed my eyes and held out my hand. "Surprise me," I said.

She placed something cold and circular in the palm of my hand. I opened my eyes and saw a bronze pocket watch.

"What's this for?"

"That watch you hold in your hand is indeed special. Its hands can tell you the current time in any place. They can point out the date of any event, even if the event has yet to happen. It's how I was able to tell today was your birthday."

"Today's my birthday?" I asked. "I mean it's incredible," I told her, referring to the watch.

I could tell that it was handcrafted. "Why would you want *me* to have *this*?"

She smiled and shook her head silently. She didn't have an answer.

I looked back down at the watch. The time was 11:10 am and the large hand was about to change.

"Make a wish," I said to her.

I had to think fast. *I wish for this year to contribute to an even brighter future.* I looked up at the clouds feeling a bit doubtful then looked at Caydia and smiled. I hugged her from the side and thanked her.

We walked back to the Observatory. We could have flown but we wanted to take our time. Atrixia was standing in the front doorway. She randomly seemed to be in a great mood. The sun shone over her. She looked so bright. Her eyes and her smile just welcomed the day. Her face was the perfect start to my morning. She met me on the stone steps and kissed me on the cheek. She was so happy to see me. She was so delighted, she didn't even care to ask where Caydia and I went last night or this morning. Atrixia stepped onto the ground and felt the grass under her heels. She waved a flat hand over the grass then trees and flowers began to emerge.

After, a whole forest, full of twists and turns, stood around us.

"The world is balanced once again," Atrixia said. She looked at me and added, "for some reason, it's been balanced ever since you arrived."

"I received your notice," Atrixia told Caydia, "as did many other foresters when you made your firecall. When should we be expecting them to arrive?"

"I'm not sure," Caydia said.

Caydia stepped inside the Observatory and clapped her hands twice. All the dust and cobwebs cleared away instantaneously.

"We have some minor preparation to do," she said.

The three of us spent the morning tidying up the place. Later that day, Atrixia stepped outside to grab some fresh air. A short man passed by. I stood in the front doorway and noticed him talking with Atrixia.

He was wearing all green and resembled a leprechaun. I wasn't sure what he wanted but Atrixia called me over to their conversation.

"He has something to share with me," Atrixia said. "It's about you. It's something you don't know about yourself."

"Only catch is you can't know what it is," the man said to me.

"And if I tell him?" Atrixia asked.

"You'll both forget," the man assured.

"It could be the place of something I lost or the day I die," I told Atrixia. "I think you should hear what he has to say."

"What if I whisper it to him?" Atrixia asked the man.

"It will still be wiped from both your minds."

"Fine, then just tell *me* and I'll keep it to myself," Atrixia said.

When she finally agreed, he leaned in close and whispered into her ear. Instantly, Atrixia started to cry. She grabbed on to me and held me. She buried her face in my chest and sobbed. The man adjusted his hat, nodded at me, then continued his way. I looked at the man with confusion as I held her. I watched him disappear into the green.

"What did he tell you?" I asked, once he was gone.

She shook her head no like she didn't want to tell me.

"It's okay," I told her. I rubbed her back. "I *wish* you could tell me," I said.

She looked up, held back her tears, and said, "It was your name."

A part of me felt weird when she said that. I totally forgot about my name. Another part of me felt bad for her. She could never say my name and I know she wanted to.

I tried to remember it. I kissed her head and she stopped crying. Once she did, I backed away from her. I wanted to lay down. I felt weird about being here again. I headed up the bedroom tower. Caydia's bedroom was scarlet. Inside, I could see her books neatly shelved and her cloaks hung up. On the opposite side of the hall was the heliotrope room I slept in last night. There, I found my belongings, as well as Atrixia's. I noticed the display case encasing my soul gem had been moved from the jewelry tower to my bedroom.

I unfastened the chain around my neck and locked the stone away. The end of the display case's key was shaped like a heart with a star engraved into it. I hid the key in a drawer under my clothing. I looked over at the four-post king size bed I slept on last night. Its covers were a royal purple. I jumped on the bed and rolled over on my back.

Shortly after, I fell asleep and found myself floating in that dark empty world. Except this time, I didn't jolt. I knew where I was. This wasn't my first time here. Still though, I was completely lost. I looked around the infinite ongoing void. I appeared here right after I fell asleep when I got home from school. I can remember how dizzy I was when I woke up. There wasn't a thing in sight. I was suspended in mid-air, floating above the abysmal darkness. I looked down on my sneakers. They were visible. I was wearing the clothes I fell asleep in. All except for my necklace. I recall locking it away. Nobody was around. At least so I thought until I was hit with a cold gust of wind from behind. I turned around and I was face to face with the phantom. It appeared out of nowhere. I floated under its towering stature.

It looked down over me through its hood. I couldn't tell if this was a dream or not. "It's time I return to my world, to the exact moment I left, that is," I said. Its red eyes grew brighter and brighter within its hood. The phantom reached out a bony hand and clenched its fingers in front of my chest. Right where my necklace would be hanging if I hadn't taken it off. I looked deep into its eyes as a deep roar gradually grew louder and louder from within its hood.

Suddenly, I awoke from the dream, terrified. I sat up. The stars were out. I slept the entire day.

The deep roar I heard was continuing outside my window.

I rubbed my eye. After, I looked over at the display case and made sure my necklace was right where I left it. I looked over and saw that an entire outfit had been laid out on a red leather chair for me. It consisted of a pair of black jeans, a tight black V-neck t-shirt, and my midnightblue cloak. I found a washroom and quickly bathed. I felt fresh after. I threw the clothes on and walked over to the locked case. I unlocked it, lifted its glass top, and pulled out the necklace. I lifted its long silver chain and the heavy stone flashed slowly. Once I placed the stone around my neck, its light remained on.

"Where's Atrixia?" I asked myself. I stepped out of my bedroom and called for both Atrixia and Caydia. Caydia didn't seem to be in her room. I knocked on her door and didn't receive an answer. Instead of heading downstairs, I chose to head upstairs. I've yet to see what was making the loud rumbling. I ascended to the garden terrace. The moment I stepped out onto the patio, I had to have been looking over a million people. Hordes of creatures, knights, witches, wizards, warlocks, ghouls, goblins, dryads, fairies, and pixies, anything and everything, had all gathered in the woods around the observatory. They all cheered once they saw my necklace. It was lit up and shining purple.

"You slept well?" Atrixia asked.

"I slept all day."

"You sure did," she said. "Enjoy yourself now."

I looked around the large crowd. I didn't recognize anyone but most appeared to be around my age. They were clearly drinking, this was a party. I held my arm out to escort Atrixia down the stairs the way I like. She held onto my arm and, with pleasure, she descended the stairs with me. We walked through the large crowd. I heard a caw and saw a dark bird circling above.

"Ignore it," Atrixia told me, "it's only a crow."

I made sure my gem was still tucked under my cloak. Concealing it allowed me to keep a low profile. Atrixia and I found Caydia. She was wearing a red dress with a black bodice. A red hooded shawl was worn around her shoulders. She was drinking her favorite wine, 'Angel Kiss', while making new friends and talking to old ones. When I looked back at Atrixia, she was reconnecting with people from her forest. I walked over to Caydia and looked into her bluishsilver eyes. She looked gorgeous tonight. I noticed that her hair was no longer gray, but black.

Her natural color. She passed me her wine and I took a sip.

"You know," I told her, "when we met in the woods and you mentioned a gathering, I thought you meant a meeting or a rally."

"Yeah, what's your point?"

"This is a party," I told her.

I passed her back the bottle and she took a sip.

"Having fun?" she asked.

"I'm having a blast," I said, honestly.

"What have you and Atrixia been up to?"

"Just hanging around."

Right then, a giant spider dropped down behind me. I turned around, jumped back, and screamed. Everyone looked at me oddly. It was the spider I saw from the terrace earlier. "It's okay," I heard Caydia say, "that's my boy, Baz."

"Ya boy Baz is a giant fucking spider," I said.

"I know, I know, everyone sees a giant spider and freaks out," Baz said. "It's never 'Hey, good morning mister spider,' or 'Hey, I see that ass.'"

My eyes widened as the spider turned around to show us all his dorsal side. "But don't worry," Baz said, "Ima keep 'them mosquitoes away from y'all. C'mon baby," he said to an attractive girl accompanying him. The girl gave me a nasty look then the two walked off. The spider shook his abdomen as he did so. Caydia looked at me and shook her head. She passed me back the bottle. I took a sip and began to feel light headed. I felt like I was levitating. The purple light under my shirt began to go out. I looked down at my hands and they were fading away. The backs of my fingers were translucent. I could see through them. I stuffed my hands in my pockets before anyone could see and broke away from the crowd.

"Next sip's mine," I told Caydia.

She smiled at me. "I'll hold it for you," she promised.

I found a shed, sat down beside it, and leaned back. I pulled out one of my hands and felt so relieved when I saw that it had reappeared entirely.

The phantom's doing this. They're doing anything to prevent me from using my power. If my soul disappears, my power goes with it. If they can't take my power, they can surely prevent me from using it. My power is probably the only reason I'm still alive. I don't know why this world is coming to an end but I think the knight has something to do with it. I'm sure the phantom plays a role in it as well. I don't think we met by coincidence. Now, I have secrets I can't share. Atrixia knows some of the things I'm capable of but not everything. That girl hates superpowers. She has no idea I can wish for anything I want. I laid my hood over my head, wrapped my arms around my knees, and put my head down. A group of young girls walked past.

They were amused by how paranoid I was. They probably thought I was some fool who got too drunk. I just hid in the shadows. Eventually, Atrixia found me.

"Hey," I heard her say to me. She was happy to see me. She pulled me away from the party. Everyone was looking at me. People were stopping to stare. A few women smiled at me. I looked down and realized my necklace had been showing this whole time. It's a color they're not familiar with. I concealed it and continued through the crowd. Atrixia and I climbed to the top of a hill and only then were we finally alone.

She handed me a silver ring and said, "Happy birthday."

"Thank you," I said.

"I checked on you while you were asleep and that ring appeared beside you, right before my eyes. You must've been wearing it when you transferred to this universe. Do you recall it?"

I studied it for a moment and tried to. The memory flashed as soon as I placed it on my pinky and rolled its spinner. It was my sister's. The first time I saw it I tried it on, liked it, and she let me keep it. She had plenty.

"Thank you," I said.

She pulled out a flower that was holding back her hair. After, her gorgeous blonde hair fell behind her back. She shook it out. I pulled a small part of her hair forward and let it hang over her shoulder. She was perfect. She opened my cloak and revealed my soul gem. Its light reflected off her green eyes. She laid her arms around my shoulders and looked at me. 'Was she waiting for me to kiss her?' I wondered. There was no one around. I looked at her for a moment.

Her eyes were warming.

"They're all rooting for you," she said.

"Why?"

"They're all counting on you," she told me.

"They're counting on you as well. You're a part of the team too," I reminded her. I wanted her to feel credit too. I made it this far because of her and Caydia.

"They don't know about me or Caydia. They don't even know who you are yet. You've been concealing your power and you've yet to introduce yourself. Your power is what they're putting their faith in. Somehow, your power is what's reversing all the darkness in this world. When the curse was placed upon it, it was set so that no one's power could reverse it. The caster didn't account for yours because they didn't know of its existence. Now that they do, it's probably why they're after you. They either want you dead, or your power, or both."

"I feel like this battle's not even mine," I said frustratedly. "I was dragged into it."

"I'm not surprised you feel that way. You didn't ask for any of this."

"And you? Do you have faith in me?" She leaned in and kissed me. Suddenly, green storm clouds gathered in the sky.

"DAMON RAYMOND, COME FORTH!" I heard someone yell in a loud crashing voice. I heard a loud siren go off inside of my head the moment I heard the name. The storm clouds cleared over the observatory and the face of a god-sized demon appeared in the stars. Its eyes looked over the massive crowd. The demon had just spoken to the entire realm.

He said one name and one name only. My name. I turned my head and saw the massive eye of the monstrous being peering into the woods. Ever make awkward eye contact?

Atrixia didn't know what to do. "It's him," was all she said.

"Who is *that*?" I asked.

"The one behind the gloom. The one who's been arranging all the fires. You're the only reason he hasn't destroyed the entire world yet. You're the one thing preventing him from doing so. Or at least that stone is," she said, referring to my soul gem, "He's been waiting to tear this planet apart. He could with ease. He wishes to salvage your stone and all the unknown power that comes with it. He wants it for himself."

I took hold of my stone and thought, *It's mine*.

"There's a reason he wants your power. Whatever that reason is, find it, and put an end to all this."

"Me?"

"You clearly must be some form of threat to him."

"I'm not a threat."

"He just rose from the dark world to make a call to the entire realm. He said one name: D."

I looked at the double-horned demon currently gazing down over the entire crowd. He was looking for me. When I looked back over at Atrixia, she was gone.

CHAPTER 21

THREE RED HOODS

I descended the hill and walked out of the woods. I took off my cloak once I locked eyes with the monster. My soul gem lit up. I looked at everyone else. Their faces and bodies were frozen. They were under a spell. They couldn't see me. They were all looking up with shocked facial expressions. I was walking through a sea of mannequins.

It was creepy. The demon's fiery eyes rained down on me. I flew from the ground and ascended into the sky. Finally, the demon and I were face to face. He had both Atrixia and Caydia trapped in a bubble. Their bubbles were floating in the air. He knew about our trio. He's been watching us.

"What do you want with these people?" I asked.

"I want nothing from these people," the demon said in his dark voice.

"Word is you wanna take over their world and start anew."

"I've already taken over their world and soon I'll have you. He reached down to grab me.

I flew back and fired up my hands.

"It's okay," Caydia silently mouthed to me.

I switched off the flares. "Forgive me, I don't believe we've met," I said to the demon with a kind smile. "On top of that, I don't see why you'd wanna tear this world apart. I'd be delighted to give you a tour of the place. I'm seeing it for the first time myself.

"I'm quite familiar with this world," said the demon.

"Then why would you ever wanna destroy it?"

"The planet will be destroyed but it won't be fully obliterated. A new kingdom shall be built from its remains."

"Kingdom?" I questioned back. It was the first time I heard the word in this place. It made me wanna yack.

"My fighters will have you and I will be the holder of your power before you can even discover its true meaning. I'll have your soul stripped from your body before the end of the month. Time is ticking. You have nowhere to hide and your friends can't keep you safe. Leave your friends and family out of this. It's best you don't drag them into this."

"I can't remember my friends and family."

"This is between you and me," he said, looking around the frozen world. "It's just you in this world. You're alone."

"JUST STOP!" I yelled at him.

He grinned at me. He had flames in his smile.

"Be at the Cloud Palace the night of October 31st," he said before disappearing like a giant hologram. Atrixia and Caydia descended slowly. Their bubbles popped the moment they touched the ground. I hovered to the ground and the world was in motion again. The night sky returned to normal. No one around had any idea what happened or who I was. I ran inside the observatory. I wanted to lock my stone away in the glass case. I no longer wanted it, while at the same time, I was too afraid to take it off and risk having it get stolen. I climbed up to my room and sat down on the windowsill. The party went on outside my window. Everyone looked so happy. They were oblivious. I wished them all a safe world and a happy life. Atrixia and Caydia walked in and I stood up from the windowsill.

"You're not scared, are you?" Caydia asked me.

"Never," I said.

"Good, because that guy was a joke." She laughed. "Everyone down there is prepared."

Atrixia looked at Caydia in disbelief; she didn't take the demon as anything to underestimate.

"Why do you think all those people showed up here tonight?" Caydia asked Atrixia.

"It's an assembly, not a party." Caydia turned to me and said, "He's hiding. That was a hologram."

I looked back out the window, my mind elsewhere. After a few minutes, I said, "I need to get some air." I climbed to the top of the tower and walked out on the terrace. I unveiled my necklace and overlooked the entire crowd. I was up too high for them to see my face but they could see the light shining off my necklace. After a moment, I kissed two fingers and held up a rock symbol. Everyone looked at me, returned the gesture, and cheered.

Bless y'all, I thought.

I turned around and popped back into my room. I tossed my midnight-blue cloak and changed into my fiery red one. After, I headed back down the tower stairs. I reached the bottom and noticed the secret side door Caydia used last night. The door was on the other side of the glass sphere. I walked across the floor of the sphere quickly. I looked up at the sky as I did. I stopped before the door, raised my cherry-red hood, and snuck out. I kindly moved through the crowd. No one knew who I was. Just the way I like it. Eventually, I reached the woods and found a trail to get lost on.

I lowered my hood as soon as I was alone. From there, I disappeared into the night. I didn't think anyone was gonna miss me. I didn't wanna go too far from Atrixia and Caydia. I was just trying to take a walk and get away from everything for a moment.

I walked with my hands in my pockets, wanting nothing more than to look at the stars.

The night was peaceful. I saw three lights on the trail up ahead. I continued walking until I reached them. I came to three jack-o-lanterns stacked on top of one another. The bottom one, the largest, resembled me. It had large angry eyes and a menacing smile. A silver necklace holding a purple stone was placed around it. The middle pumpkin, the medium sized one, resembled Atrixia. Its eyes were kinder but its smile was nothing to trust. There were leaves around the crown of its head and its eyes locked directly on me. The top one, the smallest, reassembled Caydia. A hood was laid over its stem. Its facial expression was confident. I knew it was her. They depicted us as evil. Jack-o-lanterns are used to ward off evil spirits.

The demon was watching us, I thought.

I smashed them with my foot, turned around, and headed back. When I got back to the Observatory, Atrixia and Caydia were still awake and looking for me. I was happy to see them again. As much as I aimed to be alone, there were times I didn't like the feeling of it.

"Where have you been?" Atrixia asked. "I've been searching everywhere for you."

"I went for a short walk. I didn't go far."

"Nice cloak," Caydia said. "Where'd you get it?" she asked sarcastically. "This isn't yours, is it?"

"No," she laughed. "It's the one I gave you. It's yours to keep."

"Thank you," I said. I looked at the crystal ball ring she gave me. I personally liked to wear the crystal ball ring she gave me backwards, you know, with the ball facing me when I looked at the inside of my hand. I closed my hand around it and held it.

Caydia was still wearing her shawl and Atrixia was wearing the red hoodie I gave her.

She and Caydia pulled up a chair and sat down. I did the same but sat backwards on my chair.

After I raised my hood, we were three red hoods putting our minds together.

"Soo…" I said, "A knight, a flamedame, a barbarian, and now to top it all off, a demon."

I kept the phantom to myself. That was personal.

"Are you guys still with me?" I asked.

"Of course," Caydia said fearlessly.

"Always," Atrixia said to me.

"Well they're gonna be coming for us," I said, holding onto my soul gem. I let go of it and hid it under my cloak.

"What now?" I asked.

Caydia didn't seem to know, nor did Atrixia. I didn't know either. I started to feel worried. I looked around at the other people. Then, I stood up on a table.

I yelled out "Hey!" to the crowd and no one looked up. I flew up from the table and ascended into the sky. I flew higher and higher until I reached space then released a massive purple starburst that everyone below could see. It was the first time they were ever introduced to my power. When I returned to the planet, I had everyone's full attention. My hood was concealing my face. They've yet to discover who I am. I looked at everyone unsure of what to say as they all looked back at me. I looked at Caydia. "It's okay," she mouthed to me.

"I'm not gonna say a lot because I'm not much of a talker," I said to the million people below. I felt the speech would be easier to make with a bullhorn and one appeared in my hand. "What I will say is, that demon intends to kill me and take over your planet before the end of the month." I looked at each of their faces. I still saw so much hope, love, and courage in all their eyes. They seemed to be proud of their home.

"If you were to be granted three wishes the moment you came across a genie, what would you wish for?" I asked them. "Would you wish for something everlasting? Would you make a wish for someone else? Or maybe even put one towards a brighter future? Not just a future that's brighter for you, but for everyone else as well. That demon is gonna come and it's our job to be ready for him. And I know we will be."

I kissed two fingers and again, I held up a rock and roll sign. Others returned my gesture one by one, until everyone was holding their pointer and pinky to the stars. Some howled up at the moon. Many cheered. They all looked ready for whatever was to come. I called Atrixia and Caydia and headed inside the observatory.

CHAPTER 22
HOW TO BUILD A BROOM

I awoke the next morning alone in my room. Atrixia wasn't lying beside me. I walked out of my bedroom and Caydia walked out of her room at the same time.

"You know where Trixi is?" I asked.

"Haven't seen her."

Caydia and I walked down the stairs together. Atrixia wasn't in the glass dome or in the other towers. Caydia and I called out her name.

"Where could she be?" I asked.

We walked outside to see Atrixia headed into the woods.

"What's she up to?" I asked Caydia.

"I'm not sure."

We followed her. "Trix?" I asked once we nearly caught up. She turned around and presented an old open book. *How to Build a Broom* was written at the top of the left page.

"I have a favor," she said.

"Yes?" I replied.

"It's a special favor."

"You're generous and don't ask for anything. What's the favor?"

"I need a tree branch, some straw, and a secure place to craft something."

"A broom? Is that what you intend to make?" Caydia laughed.

"What's wrong with that?"

"Nothing," Caydia said. "It's just been generations since someone traveled by broom. A bit outdated. Usually when one needs to travel quickly they just snap their fingers and zap to their destination instantaneously."

"Well, I wish to fly," Atrixia said. "If you can't help, it's fine. I don't need you to assist me."

"Let me help you so this doesn't end with you getting hurt," Caydia insisted.

"You don't have to worry about me getting hurt."

"A tree branch and some hay, that's all you need?" Caydia confirmed.

"And some twine," Atrixia added.

Atrixia walked further into the woods for a branch, leaving me alone with Caydia. Caydia and I shared a look before I hurried after Atrixia. Caydia chuckled and walked off alone.

"Hey," I said once I caught up with Atrixia. I looked at her and smiled. Her face took my breath away every time. I tried to hide it.

"Care to help me find a broomstick?"

"Why do you wish to fly?"

"Why did you feel the need to pierce the atmosphere?"

"Wuh?" I played dumb.

"You wanted to challenge your limits and go beyond them. Maybe even realize you don't have any."

I couldn't argue. I just looked back at her not knowing what to say. I reached out my hand for the book and she passed it to me. I studied each page.

"By the looks of this book, I can guess the broom you intend to make isn't meant for cleaning up messes."

"Who said it was?" she asked.

She selected a sturdy dead tree branch from the ground. She rubbed her hand down it. After, its bark was smooth and no longer rough. It returned to a healthy color. The branch was alive again.

"There's much to do," she said.

She turned around and returned to Caydia. Caydia was on her way back to us.

"I couldn't find any string but I was able to gather some wild hay," Caydia said.

"Thank you. This is perfect," Atrixia said. "Do you know anything about activating a witch's broom?"

"No," Caydia said. She snapped her fingers and reappeared next to

Atrixia to demonstrate her ability to teleport. "I never needed one. Like I said, they're outdated."

Atrixia read the next line in the book; suddenly, the tree branch flew into Atrixia's hand without her looking.

"When did you learn to do *that*?" Caydia asked.

"Just now," Atrixia said.

I looked at them like this was wild. Atrixia took the hay. Then with the tree branch in one hand and the hay in the other, she connected the two using vines. The vines grew across the entire length of the broom, wrapped around the hay, and sprouted green leaves, lastly forming a broom.

"Incredible," I said.

"It's still not done," Atrixia said.

"How do you make it fly?" I asked.

"Some wiggitty-waz," Caydia said.

"What?" I asked.

"A little skippity bop wit' a bop," Atrixia said to me with a smile.

"What are you talking about?" I asked.

"The book says that the broom needs to be awakened by a force," Atrixia said.

"A force?" Caydia asked. "What kind of force?"

"I don't know. That's all it says." She looked at the book again. "A force. A force of what?"

"Maybe you need a witch to activate it," Caydia suggested.

"You wanna give it a shot?" Atrixia asked.

"Why not?"

Caydia tried all sorts of methods to get the broom to hover on its own. Wind, levitation, even telekinesis. She was afraid of accidentally setting fire to the broom if she tried anything else.

"You try," Caydia said to me.

I took hold of the broom. I tried starpower, levitation, I even dropped it on the ground and did the genie gesture where I fold one arm over the other and bow my chin. It was out of humor.

I wasn't surprised when nothing happened. *I wish the broom would fly,* I thought to myself.

Nothing happened.

Atrixia got frustrated and picked up the broom.

"Relax," I told her. "It's okay."

"No. I found this book upstairs in the witch's house. I went over the book's rules and we gathered the broom's materials. Now the broom is assembled and the book says the broom needs to be awakened by a force."

Out of frustration, she threw the broom on the ground and turned away. After she turned around, the broom never touched the ground. Instead, the broom remained floating in the air.

Caydia and I didn't say anything at first. The vines on the broom began to light up yellow.

"Uh Trix," I said over to her excitedly.

Atrixia turned around and her eyes lit up. The broom needed to be awakened by a force of nature. She tossed the book to Caydia and Caydia read on. Caydia searched through the table of contents.

"Preparation, activation, and User settings," she said, and flipped to the settings page.

"Navigation, Stability, Jet stream color," she read aloud.

Atrixia hopped on the broom and took off instantly.

"Wait!" Caydia shouted.

Caydia and I took off after her. Atrixia was flying fast and high. Caydia and I flew from the ground and caught up with her. Atrixia was smiling.

"Stabilize," Caydia commanded the broom.

After, the broom flew straight and steady. The book was still in Caydia's hands. Caydia laid on her back and continued to fly at the same pace as Atrixia. Caydia read each setting to her. Caydia said the word "link," aloud. After, she gave Atrixia a shove. Atrixia did a full roll and didn't fall off the broom. Her body was linked to it.

"You're attached to your broom now," Caydia informed Atrixia, "you can never fall off it while flying."

Atrixia flew upward and did two full loops. I was amazed.

"Pick a color," Caydia said.

"Pink," Atrixia said.

Nextly, the broom started leaving a pink stream of light.

"You want to add a seat and some handlebars? Caydia asked.

Atrixia cringed her nose and shook her head no.

"Navigation," Caydia read. "Is there any place you want to set as your current home?"

"The observatory," Atrixia said. She looked at me. I looked at her and smiled. She smiled back at me warmly. She swung around a red maple tree. When she came back around, her clothes were different. She was wearing a long clear cloak with red leaves sewn into it. Maple leaves fluttered endlessly off her coat tail and flew into the wind. Atrixia's hood was made of translucent fibers, almost like a bridal cape. I could see the side of her face through it. She was wearing a dress made of orange and yellow leaves under her cloak. Her dress was short and tight.

She looked gorgeous.

She flew back to me. "You want a ride?" she asked me. I flew above her broom and landed right behind her. She stretched her arms out over the broom and I held onto her from behind. She rolled the broom like a stunt pilot.

"What else does that book say?" Atrixia asked Caydia.

"There's a way to make it indestructible, if you wish."

"I wi-"

Right at that moment, we were hit with a fireball from below. Quietly, the tip of the broom began to dip and the wind on our faces picked up. We were crashing. We were high in the sky and we began to dive downwards.

"Pull up!" I yelled.

Even though Atrixia was trying all she could, we continued to fall. She pulled up on the broom and we began to spiral out of control. We were about to smack into the trees. At the last second, I grabbed Atrixia and flew off the broom. The broom got lost somewhere in the woods.

"Are you okay?" I asked Atrixia.

"I'm fine, the broom should be fine too. But how are you?" she asked.

I held onto her in midair and looked down. "I feel like I'm on top of the world," I told her.

I felt adrenaline, and I could tell she felt the same. I smiled at her and we both laughed. After a moment, I looked down and got serious. Someone just fired at us. We descended with caution. "Stay close," I said once we reached the ground. I felt like this place wasn't safe for her.

After all, someone did just try to shoot us down. We could hear distant explosions.

"I think we crashed into a warzone," Atrixia said.

"We almost did," I reminded her.

Caydia caught up to us and dropped down. "We can't stay here," she said once she touched down.

"We need to find the broom first," Atrixia said.

The ground beneath us began to rumble and shake. The sound of charging horses was moving closer. We heard battle cries and horns blowing. I raised the hood of my blue cloak and the three of us moved closer in the direction of the sound. Outside the woods was a flat grassy field where multiple warriors, wizards, warlocks, and knights were battling ghastly skeletons. The wizards cast spells at dark forces, banishing them back to wherever they came. The knights fought with shields and swords. Some even had sorcerer staffs. Archers fired arrows from afar.

One army was dark and shadow streaked, mainly composed of skeletons and evil spirits.

The army on the other side wore blue and silver armor. They were an assembly of humans.

Strong, courageous humans.

"What are they fighting over?" I asked.

"Good and evil," Caydia said, "it's a never ending battle."

A knight in blue armor wore the emblem of a dragonfly on their chest. They stood over all the other men and women, commanding them, giving them their every order. After the silver army acted, the blue knight began aiding the wounded soldiers. I thought I was hidden when I managed to get spotted by the blue knight. The blue knight looked up at me and seemed to recognize my face. The knight wore a helmet so I couldn't see *theirs*. Still, its body froze the moment they noticed me. The blue knight took out a horn, lifted its visor, and blew a victorious sound. The humans fought off the evil spirits until they heard the sound and all the dark forces stopped fighting and retreated. The silver knights began to cheer and celebrate around the blue knight as one giant rally. I backed away. The blue knight has yet to take their eyes off me. They knew who I was.

"Found the broom," Atrixia said. She raised her hand and the broom flew to it. "Let's go," she told us.

We weren't staying much longer but first, I held out my hand for Atrixia to pass me the broom. She handed it to me and I scanned any damage to the broom. I turned to Caydia and said,

I wish to make this broom indestructible.

The broom momentarily lit up purple. After, it looked good as new and nothing could even scuff it.

"Wow, that was easy," Caydia said.

I figured it was just a minor safety precaution for Atrixia. It couldn't hurt.

Atrixia snatched the broom from me and studied it closely. "Did you just wish for that to happen?" She asked me. She looked shocked.

"Uhh-" I dragged on until I looked up and saw the black knight standing silent, still, and atop a rock before an army. It was the first time I saw the black knight in the daylight. The black knight was frozen in position and appeared to be looking at something behind me. I turned around and saw the dragonfly Knight.

"That boy is property of Zorcus," the black knight said to the dragonfly knight. "I'm ordered to obtain him."

It was the first time I heard him speak. The black knight drew its sword.

"Whoever you are, you've never been more wrong in your entire life," the dragonfly knight replied. The dragonfly knight drew her sword and an ambush broke out.

The black knight's soldiers charged with rage. They showed no hesitation. The blue knight stood tall, strong, and confidently, when their men came pouring out through the trees by the dozens. They all ran with their weapons raised to the sky.

Swords sliced through the air. Axes slashed and hammers smashed. I kept Atrixia and Caydia close. I didn't want them to get hurt. I didn't know what to do. I looked at the blue knight.

I didn't want to see anyone killed. The ones that were getting killed were already dead.

The dark side was no match for the blue knight's army. They fought with honor and loyalty for the dragonfly knight. The shaded thick woods allowed for Atrixia, Caydia, and I to disappear quicker than steam. After a few moments of us running through shrubs, trees, and spider webs, an arrow landed in the ground right before us. We backed away and regained our breath. The end of the arrow began to release yellow smoke. We were breathing heavily. The fume made the three of us fall asleep instantaneously. When I awoke, I was alone on a grassy field. Atrixia and Caydia were nowhere in sight. Before me stood a purple skinned muscular man. He wore enchanted armor. He looked at me with two irises filled with blue and red lightning. The sky was the same as his eyes. "I'm here to help. My name is Rubrix."

CHAPTER 23

I FOUND MAGIC

"**W**hat is this place?" I asked him.

"My place," he told me. "There's someone who wishes to speak with you."

"Let their wish be granted," I said. I rolled my eyes. I didn't want to be in this place much longer.

"Not yet. There's much preparation that needs to be done before the two of you meet."

The sky cleared and multiple warriors appeared around me. They were all participating in training sessions. The sun was out. I was being held in some form of mind trance.

"What do I need preparation for?" I asked.

"Not preparation for you, preparation for her."

"Her?"

"This is where you'll be staying for the next few hours."

I looked over and saw Caydia practicing with other wizards. She was demonstrating her skill at defense and strategy. Atrixia was sitting by a huddle of girls. I walked over to her. The other girls appeared to be teasing her. Atrixia reached for me and smiled the moment I approached. I took her by the hand. She looked so happy to see me. The top of her hair was a gorgeous maple red. The hair below was blonde. I was noticing it now for the first time. I was happy to see her. She gave me the same smile from the night we first met.

"Come with me. There's something I wish to tell you," I told her.

"Okay," she said. I helped her up and she followed me behind a tree. I was nervous.

193

"What is it?" she asked.

"Not here," I said.

"Where then?"

"I know where," I said. I whispered in her ear the exact place I wanted to go and she smiled. She looked at me and I felt a connection between us.

"Stand back," she said.

After, she waved her hand in an upward motion and a large tree spun out of the ground.

The tree had a wooden door, which she opened for me. The inside of the tree was glowing purple and she told me the door was safe to walk through. I stepped through and entered a whole new world. I took her by the hand and pulled her into a hickory colored wood forest. Its trees were green. Up above, yellow glowing vines dangled from the tree branches. The sky was in a nighttime state and the stars were out. It was the perfect place. Atrixia closed the door and the tree disappeared. She walked over to me, took me in her arms and said, "So, what did you wanna tell me?"

I felt a bump in my chest. I didn't know how she was gonna take it. This was the first time I was sharing a secret I've yet to tell anyone before.

"Soo…" I mumbled, "I have…"

"Yes?"

I looked away not knowing what to say.

"You don't wanna talk about it?" she asked.

I stepped away, looked down at the ground, and shook my head. I didn't know how to talk today. She stepped over to me and held me in her arms again. This time she didn't let me walk away.

I reached behind my back and a flower appeared in my hand. I kept the flower behind my back and closed my eyes for a moment.

I held out a heliotrope rose and opened my eyes. Typically, I'm not a fan of roses but this rose was different. Its pedals changed from blue, to purple, and back to blue, with specks of silver sprinkled over them. The flower was unlike any other.

"Where did that just come from?" she asked.

I handed her the flower, then gently placed my hand on her face. I kissed *her* for the first time. The kiss was long and meaningful. Her eyes widened and the next moment, the deck of a mega yacht appeared behind her. She was lying on her back with me in her arms. She wore designer clothing. Her high tops were worth more than my entire wardrobe. We were deep out in the ocean. It appeared to be the first time Atrixia had seen an ocean. "What just happened?" she asked. "Where are we?"

"Paradise," I told her.

I kissed her on the neck a single time and a string of pearls appeared around it. I looked down at her. Her eyes were purple. She appeared to be very exhilarated. She was trying to control her breathing. I told her to relax and control her thoughts. I just unintentionally inserted my power into her.

"Just breathe, don't think of anything truly desirable right away. Just hold that power in your heart. Don't keep it inside for long either. Just find a nice time to release it and don't tell a soul about your wish."

She closed her eyes and tried to concentrate. After, we just kissed and kissed. I told her to imagine something special. She imagined a place and we appeared there before I could even kiss her again. Turns out when I kiss someone, they gain the power to wish for anything they want a single time. The wishes rack up with each kiss. Atrixia would have plenty at this point. We were standing in a meadow underneath a breathtaking sunset the next moment. There was a garden nearby.

"What is this place?" I asked.

"Paradise," she told me, "as long as you're with me."

Her clothing had changed. She was no longer wearing the clothes I wished. She was now wearing a dress made of purple leaves. She seemed more comfortable.

"This garden is where I was born," she told me.

"It's gorgeous," I told her.

"I'll eventually have to return there," she said.

We stayed for a moment. I loved it. Eventually, I took her by the hands, closed my eyes, and kissed her. I imagined we were back in the enchanted hickory forest. After I kissed her, we were there before I opened my eyes. I was familiar with the forest. There, I felt secure. I found comfort there. There, I had privacy. We continued to kiss, and as we did, I realized something. Something strong. Something powerful. I wasn't sure of it at first. It was right here, right now at this moment. I found *magic*. I looked at her and felt so happy to be with her. I looked around at the vast forest. *What a world*, I thought. Before we left, I kissed her one last time.

She accepted me. I thought my power was going to be a deal breaker with a girl like her.

CHAPTER 24

I'M THE LUCKY ONE

We met up with Rubrix. Everyone else was still at the training camp. Atrixia sat down on the grass.

"Ah, you're back just in time," Rubrix said to me.

"Back in time for what?" I asked.

Rubrix banged his staff and we all transported to a circular field surrounded by pink trees.

The trees shed pink pedals. Daylight shone over the field.

"Why is she competing?" one of the girls asked, referring to Atrixia. Atrixia was sitting on the grass.

"What's your power?" another girl asked her.

Atrixia smiled, folded her hands over her knee, and said, "Baby, I'm the lucky one." She looked blissful. She's been in a good mood since we got back. Rubrix banged his staff again and multiple weapons appeared on the ground. Each one sparkled on the grass. I didn't like where this was going.

"Select a weapon," Rubrix yelled to everyone.

I looked at Atrixia and Caydia. These were deadly weapons. It'd be a shame for even a drop of blood to be shed in this place. Caydia pulled a spell book from her book bag. Atrixia looked around at the swords, axes, and hammers. She noticed a bow and picked it up.

"What were Thatcher and Deliah's steps again?" Atrixia asked.

I lifted a staff with a heavy glass orb at the top. The orb lit up a bright purple and I dropped the staff. They all looked at me.

"All ready?" Rubrix yelled out.

"All in!" everyone yelled back.

Everyone began to charge and dash. I quickly picked up the staff unsure what to do with it. I tilted it and defended myself with it.

"What now?" Atrixia asked.

"Let's just run around and make it look like we're participating," Caydia suggested.

I loved her idea. The fighters attempted to hurt each other. They swung and hurled their weapons at one other. It was an ugly sight.

"Stop," I screamed out.

I waved the staff at the warriors, forgetting it was a sorcerer's staff. Multiple starbursts were released from the sphere. A girl ran into one and it changed her into a swan. Another transformed a warrior into a genie. His legs disappeared, replaced with a long smoke tail. The ones who noticed turned and looked at me oddly. They figured it was the power of the staff that transformed the individuals into other beings, not me. Those who didn't notice continued to fight. Caydia threw green electrical sparks at those who tried her. It was wicked. Atrixia was standing still. Rubrix urged Atrixia to involve herself.

"It's not real," he assured her. She pulled an arrow from a quiver and drew it back with her bow. She raised it, not even knowing who to aim for.

"No," I screamed out.

I instinctively waved my hand and the motion changed her hunting bow to a bow made of rose-gold. The bow shimmered with yellow light. The tips of the arrows in the quiver were shaped like hearts. It didn't know what the weapon could do after.

I banged the staff and commanded all to freeze. I banged the staff a second time then all the weapons vanished, disarming the warriors and warlocks. I brought the girl who turned into a swan back to her human form, then lastly, changed the genie back to a warrior.

"Aw, I kinda liked being a genie," the warrior said.

Atrixia healed the wounded with a restoration spell.

"Damon," the instructor yelled out mid-drill. "Are you crazy?" He banged his staff on the ground twice and beamed us all back to the camp. The sun was setting. Rubrix looked at me with red and blue lightning in his eyes. After, the world around us disappeared and it was just him and I on a grassy field under a lightning filled sky. I felt like I was trapped inside a plasma ball. Using the power of our minds, he was able to pull me, and only me, to the side. Seemed like a useful quality for a coach to possess. He was frustrated. He looked at me like he wanted to kick me in the chest and put me on my back but he didn't out of respect.

"You seem like you were mommied, babied, sheltered, spoiled, overweight, overprivileged. You lacked discipline. I see the fire you're fighting with, but you're not using it. On the other hand, your power is unchanneled and you must learn to control it."

I didn't question him. In fact, I was amazed by how he read all that. The lighting in his eyes cleared. His eyes were naturally dark blue. We returned to the training camp. I looked around at everyone else and wanted to find Atrixia and Caydia.

"Wash up," Rubrix said.

I was confused. I looked around for a bathhouse. There wasn't one in sight. Instead, they had me shower alone under a waterfall. Night had fallen. The moon was my only light source. I brushed my teeth then found some clothes that had been laid out for me. I wore a red thermal with a pair of black jeans. They weren't mine but they had all been fitted for me. I grabbed a red pom-pom hat from my bag and met back with Rubrix.

"Who wishes to meet with me?" I asked.

"Come, it's time," he told me.

He brought me to a grand palace. The light in every window was royal purple. He led me to a garden outside the palace.

"Wait here," he said.

"For whom?" I asked.

I looked around the garden. I stood on a cross-path between four topiary squares. Rubrix had already vanished by the time I looked back and when I did I couldn't believe who I saw. In red lipstick and a white fur coat, stood my mom. She wore lime-colored eye shadow around her green eyes. Her hair was brunette in this universe, not blonde. She carried the pendant of a dragonfly on her chain. The dragonfly encased a sapphire. The sapphire was her power gem.

"You look nice," I told her.

"Why, thank you," she said back.

"Your shoes are nice."

"Thanks, Lovey. When I die, don't bury me in shoes. They're uncomfortable."

"Okay?" I said questionably. I had too many questions on my mind to ask what she even meant by that. I hugged her. "I wanna talk," I said.

"Let's talk."

She led me through a courtyard filled with flower planters. My mom told me how she's been watching me since my walk home from school. She saw me get flushed down the well and wasn't worried. She knew I'd turn out okay. I pricked my finger on a thorn and no blood came out. Nothing could hurt me here. She kept an eye on me every minute up until this moment. She apologized for having to leave so suddenly without notice. We walked into a green jungle. This is where I liked to talk.

"I love you," I told her once we were away from everything. "I missed you," I said. "I came home and the house was empty."

That's usually how I liked it but, still, something was strange when I left. I looked over at the high-standing palace. There was a massive party going on inside. Men were inside cyphing. The smoke coming from the house smelt funky. I chose to continue further into the jungle. My mom was okay with it. She chose to stay with me.

"I've made friends," I told her. Friends was an understatement.

"I see," she said.

"I've also made enemies."

"Don't worry about them," she said. She removed her fur coat and hung it on a tree. She was wearing a long dark blue dress. Green and black glitter was speckled at the bottom. I noticed it when her dress spun in the moonlight.

"Welcome home," she told me while I interacted with the luminescent plants.

I had a connection with this place.

"The rest of your family's inside," my mom told me.

I paused for a moment. "Let's head in."

"Let's do it," my mom said.

She grabbed her coat and we entered the palace. The first person I wanted to see was Atrixia. I couldn't remember my family but I knew I didn't wanna be alone with them. I walked with my mother down a long hallway. In the room to my left, I noticed someone I saw on the battlefield earlier. He had long brown hair and a long brown beard. His cape was crimson red.

Many people were gathered around him.

"His name's Ruarkson. He lives by the water," my mom informed me. "He's your brother. He'll leave in the morning. You should spend time with him while you're here."

I thought about it. A child wearing a small pink hood ran past me. I recognized her cloak.

She was the girl who disappeared into the giant jack-o-lantern when we were looking for Jaxin's house. She was also the one who created the tall flower forest, the rainbow, and the sky coins. I've yet to meet her. I saw another man that looked like Ruarkson except he was leaner and his hair was blonde. His outfit was made from vines and leaves. There appeared to be conflict between him and another individual on the other side of the room, wearing a black tactical suit equipped with advanced technological gadgets. He looked like he was from the future or an alien planet. He wore a dark helmet with a glass visor.

"You're brothers with the two of them as well," my mom said, "the one in the helmet is your oldest brother."

I watched him vanish out a nearby window. The blonde one turned away and walked into another room. Everyone else was dressed in formal clothes. I was wearing my black and white sneakers. My black jeans had tears in them. I kneeled to tie my shoelace and noticed that the white floor was made of marble. When I looked up, I saw Trixi and Caydia. I stood and kissed them both on the hand. That's how the other men greeted women here. I snapped my fingers when I saw that both Atrixia's and Caydia's hands were empty and a drink appeared in each of them.

"My family's here," I told Atrixia nervously.

"I know. I've met most of them already," she said. "I think they're lovely."

"I'm happy you're here," I said to both. We walked outside to the pavilion. My mom later walked out holding a glass bottle. It was a beer from home. It was for me. My mom walked over, handed me the beer, and looked at us.

She looked at Atrixia for a moment. "You're gorgeous."

She looked at Caydia and said, "You're beautiful too." I could tell she really liked Atrixia though. It was the first time they've met.

"Thank you," I said as my mom passed me the bottle. "Love you," I told her.

"I love you too."

I slipped away from Atrixia and Caydia for a moment so I could have a chat with my mom.

"Mom?"

"Yes my dear."

"Why was I kept from this place?"

Memories and recollections of my family began to return from a time when I was seven. They weren't memories of earth, they were memories of Ossynthore. I remember wearing the emblem of the sun on my chest.

"Arrangements were made to protect you."

I took a sip of my beer. We all walked inside and entered a tavern-like room. There, we found men drinking from chalices. One sat sipping from a small barrel rested on his shoulder. He appeared to be very happy and very drunk. I blew a small kiss in the air as I passed him and wished him the best of luck. Shortly after, I found Ruark. He was talking with a few of his fellow shipmates. He noticed me as I approached him.

"I'm Raurkson Henry," he said.

We're brothers who saw each other the other day except that was back on earth, before I crossed over to this world. My memory was still blurry. He invited me to smoke. I thanked him and told him maybe later. Turns out, Ruark is a sailor, a pirate, and a pioneer. He's found ancient treasures in the past and battled the most brutal monsters of the sea. (So he claims.)

"You must come aboard my ship sometime," he told me. He gave me a head nod and said, "I *wish* to catch up with you as we sail the seas. I'll show you every cavern, island, and reef. This planet is much larger than Earth. Its waters are wider and much deeper."

I thanked him for the invitation and stepped back into the hallway. My other brothers were nowhere to be found.

"Be careful while you're here," my mom told me. She came in from out of nowhere.

"Why?"

"There are evils in this world. Darknesses you don't even know about. Evils that can consume the very best of us."

Right then, a gorgeous woman who looked to be about ten years older than myself entered the room. She looked like she just woke up. Her face resembled mine. The only difference was her brown hair. I knew she was my sister. She looked at me. This was her first time seeing me in this world. She looked at mom and asked, "when did he get here?" She sounded annoyed.

"After a phantom threw me down a well," I answered. "Question. What if that never happened?" I asked my mom.

"All find their way here eventually," she told me.

"I'm really happy to see you here," my sister finally admitted. "You probably can't remember, but we saw each other the other day. Seeing you *here* is like seeing you for the first time."

I complimented her dress and found Atrixia and Caydia again. I don't know why but I felt distant from my family. I love them but I didn't wanna stick around much longer. I wanted to go back to the observatory but I didn't show it. I stuck around and had a few more beers.

"Rubrix said he wants you back on the training field tomorrow morning," Caydia told me. "Who's the girl you were talking to a moment ago?" she asked.

"That would be my sister," I told her.

"Your sister?"

"My sister," I confirmed.

"Keep an eye on her," Atrixia advised.

I watched my sister leave the room. It got late and we decided that it was time to go. My mom offered us rooms and insisted we stayed. I told her we were going back to the Observatory and she asked about it.

"The large blue one made of glass?"

"Yes. It's not far from here is it?"

"It's your father's. There's a door that connects to it. You're the only one here who can access it. Not even I can. You don't have to worry about any of your other siblings breaking in. Trust me, your father did all he could to prevent that from happening."

My father passed away when I was young. I remember him. I didn't think now was the proper time to ask about him while everyone else was around. Still, something was off. The door to the jewelry tower was also made so that it could only be opened by me. I didn't know why it was left open, and I wished to. My mom brought the three of us down a hall and led us to an old grandfather clock. Its hands and weights were made of gold. She moved the hands to 11:11 and the front of the clock opened like a door. The weights raised and yellow light shone through. Atrixia and Caydia stood back in wonder. The door led to the glass orb that served as the observatory's center.

"I love you," my mother told me.

"I love you too," I said.

We stepped through and entered a small hall. On the other side of the bright hall was another clock. The two large clocks stood back to back. We walked through the second clock and entered our home. I was the last to walk out and I closed the door behind us. Its weights dropped down and rattled. Atrixia, Caydia, and I walked up to our bedrooms. I lay in bed with my arms around Atrixia. She was warm. I could tell she was tired. She rested her head on my chest. She wasn't afraid of me.

CHAPTER 25

RED'S DEFINITELY YOUR COLOR

I woke up and Atrixia was gone. I sat up, walked out of my room, and knocked on Caydia's door. She wasn't in her bedroom either. I walked downstairs and called out to the bottom floor. I didn't receive a response so I walked outside. The day was clear. I still couldn't find either of them, but I heard laughing from the woods. I took a few steps into the wick and found them. Atrixia was growing flawless blue flowers the same color as Caydia's eyes. She was placing them very carefully in Caydia's hair, which was styled differently. Her bangs were gone and her hair was curled and parted. Her face was unveiled. You could see her eyes clear as day. She was wearing a sundress and a flowery anklet above her barefoot. Atrixia placed one final flower. "And done."

I was shocked by how different she looked. I tried to hide my expression but I couldn't keep from smiling. She looked gorgeous. Caydia created a circular swarm of silver light that reflected her face. She investigated it like a mirror. Once she was done glancing at her new look, the illusive mirror dissipated and disappeared. After, she turned to Atrixia, with a small black book on her lap. The book's cover was blank. Caydia held the book and thought it was an appropriate time to give it away. She crossed her leg over the other, pulled the book from each end, and the book duplicated an additional copy. After, she was holding a book in each of her hands. They were identical to each other.

"I wanted to give this to you at my cave," Caydia told Atrixia. "Please take this book. Whatever you write in it, will appear in mine."

Caydia passed one to Atrixia and hugged her. Atrixia thanked her and walked away. Atrixia looked over each blank page with delight. Once Atrixia was gone, Caydia passed me the other book and smiled. Her teeth were pretty and white.

"This one would be for you," she told me.

I took the book and looked down at its hard cover. After, I hugged Caydia tightly. I was so grateful for it.

"Thank you so much," I said.

"Don't mention it," she said sincerely.

"No, you're really special, and you deserve something just as special. I don't know how I could ever repay you."

She looked down and thought for a moment. "Save my world," she finally said, tears forming.

That cut me deep. She walked back to the observatory with Atrixia. I remained outside and thought about what Caydia said. I opened the book and felt the pages with my fingertips. There's something I love about blank pages. Without even thinking, I wished for a red pen. I was amazed, shocked, and a little scared when one appeared in my right hand. The first thing I drew was a heart. After, I wanted to change the color of the pen's ink to purple so I could draw a star within the heart. When nothing changed, I wondered why.

Everyone met on the training field later that morning. Everyone looked prepared, except me. I looked like I just rolled out of bed. I was wearing a long loose black hoodie and worn out black jeans. I'm sure my hair was a mess as well. I never have a clue what's about to happen here. I looked around and saw weights and weapons. Rubrix came up to me. He was wearing his chest plate. He called for everyone's attention. The others approached, one by one.

"Hope you slept well," Rubrix told me. He was excited. An obstacle course had been prepared.

"I hope everyone stretched," Rubrix said to the pack.

Like Rubrix, they were all wearing armor.

"Everyone pair up," Rubix said. I looked around for a partner. Everyone had a buddy.

Atrixia paired with Caydia.

"I'll be your partner," Rubrix told me. He seemed to be the most fitting.

"The course is simple," he said. "You've all done it before. D, are you ready?"

By the time he asked, I had already broken away from the crowd. I snuck into the woods and I just kept walking until my head was clear. I walked and walked. It was all I wanted to do. I checked behind me and made sure no one was following me. I placed my hands in my pockets and kept going. I passed two chairs on a rocky ocean shore. I walked a little further and noticed a nice house close by. I hoped I wasn't trespassing on private property. I noticed a guy ahead. He was tossing weights across a grassy field. He wore a white compression shirt. He had short blonde hair and large shoulders. He appeared to be my age and looked to be throwing weights for distance. Clearly, he was a man of strength. I didn't want to intrusively interrupt him. He dropped the weight, walked over to a pull up bar, and began to do pull ups.

"What's going on man?" I asked in the middle of his set. He didn't mind. He looked at my clothes and laughed. He hopped back down, took out two water bottles, and passed one to me. I thanked him. He wore one of the finest rope chains I had ever seen. It was one of the very few gold things that I've ever liked in my life. I liked him.

"My name's Damon. Are you a warrior?"

"No I'm not," he said. "I'm an athlete. My name's Bolt," he told me with a smile.

I showed him how to dap hands and after, he told me about the sports he played and the competitions he's been in. He had a nice work ethic and kind attitude. We were complete opposites but we got along well. After a while, I looked at the pocket watch Caydia gave me and thought it was a good time to head back. Before I left he said, "You know, if you ever wanted to train," taking a sip, "feel free to come by."

When I got back to the training camp. Everyone was looking for me. Atrixia, Caydia, and Ruark were grateful when I returned. My mom was wearing all her armor, except her helmet. Her hair was down. My blonde leaf-wearing brother, whose name I've yet to learn, was standing there and appeared to be furious.

My sister appeared on the training field out of thin air. "What'd I miss?" she asked.

"Where have you been?" my mom asked me.

"I went for a walk. What's the deal?"

"You can't run off like that," she told me.

"I came back."

"Back is where you need to go," my mom said.

"Back to where?" I asked.

"Back to Earth. Back to the other world. You were never meant to come here. I'll arrange for you to be sent back. I'll have you beamed back to earth first thing tomorrow morning. You'll see us all there tomorrow and you'll have no remembrance of this place whatsoever."

"I'm not leaving."

"Your power will be extracted before you leave as well."

"Won't I die if you extract my power? Is it not attached to my soul?"

"You'll be fine. You won't feel a thing," she assured.

"'You won't feel a thing,' that's something a mom says. Will my power be destroyed?"

"It won't be destroyed, it just won't be yours anymore."

"It never was," my blonde brother added. It was the first time I heard him speak and my immediate response was to give him an evil eye.

"Come," my mom said to me. She placed her arm around me and tried to take me back to the house.

"No," I shouted. I pushed her gauntlet off me. She moved in closer and tried to calm me.

"Back up," I yelled. Everyone entered a defensive position. I took off into the sky.

Caydia flew after me and Atrixia followed on her broom.

"Wait!" my mom yelled. "Don't go that way!"

I didn't know *where* I was flying to, I just flew until I felt comfortable again. As time went on, the trees beneath us started to look gray, not green. Atrixia flew beside me. Caydia sat backwards on Atrixia's broom and played with the colorful stream of sparks that were released from its straws.

"What does that feel like?" I asked Caydia.

"It's tingly," she told me.

Suddenly, the sparks stopped flowing and the broom began to rock. "Something's wrong," Atrixia said.

The tip of the broom dipped down. Then *all of us* began to fall.

Something was preventing us from using our powers here. None of us could fly and I was unable to imagine something that'd break our fall. We fell through the trees. The branches broke our fall. We landed on the ground and tumbled in the leaves. The fall was rough but we survived. The trees were gray and their leaves were black. We could hear sorrowful, ghastly moans all around. I began to feel lightheaded. I was unable to stand up. There was a toxin in the air. It wasn't safe to breathe in. I looked up and saw terrifyingly large spider webs. I covered my ears and tried to block out the sound of the moans but the moans and cries only grew louder. There was nobody around except for the three of us. I started to feel dizzy. I realized now that this place was noxious and haunted. I feared for Atrixia and Caydia. This was my fault. I rolled over and faced the girls. I saw Caydia lying on the ground beside me with her eyes closed. She was still.

"No," I moaned as the dead leaves blew past her scarlet red cloak. "Get up," I whispered to her. My eyes began to feel heavy.

"Baby!" I yelled out, hoping Atrixia was around. I didn't receive an answer.

"Thank you," I whispered to both and shut my eyes.

Suddenly, I was swept off the ground by something that had swooshed by with a jolt. The broomstick flew under me, picked me up, and scooped up Caydia. I didn't know what was happening. The broomstick began to carry the two of us away as Atrixia ran after the broom like a bus she was late for. She possessed a natural immunity to the poison. She hopped on top of me and tried to steer.

Caydia had her back on the end of the broom. Her arms and legs dangled. She had yet to wake up, but I was. Atrixia rested her head on my shoulder and asked if I was okay. I still felt dizzy. Thankfully, Atrixia was immune to the poison. We flew upward until we were well clear of the woods. I looked down and cringed my nose at the sight of multiple giant spiders crawling over the treetops. They were long and thin with black and yellow legs. They weren't furry like Baz.

"Where are we going?" Caydia asked from the back.

She had finally woken up. I was so happy when I heard her voice. I couldn't get the image of her laying on the ground out of my head.

"I'm not sure," Atrixia said. "I'm not controlling the broom. We're being transported to an unknown location."

"Should we be worried?" I asked.

"Not sure," Atrixia said.

After a short time, the broom began to circle over a fairy land that appeared out of nowhere. From above, the land was like the eye of a hurricane. The area was hidden deep in the middle of the poisonous woods. The broom descended into the vibrant yellow glow of the small village below. The trees here were full of green leaves. There were little homes with windows and doorways built into the trunks of each tree. They housed fairies and pixies. I peeked inside one and found a fairy lounging. I looked inside another and saw two pixies slow dancing in their living room. They were hovering over the floor.

"They seem to be living peacefully. Perhaps we shouldn't disturb them," Caydia said.

"I didn't land here," Atrixia said. "For some reason, the broom was compelled to land here."

The fairies began to open doors and fly from their homes. They glowed and each one of them possessed a different color. They looked like Christmas lights and flew around slowly.

They seemed to be happy we were here. They arranged themselves to form a light pattern. The light sequence lured us in a specific direction and guided us. We walked deeper into the forest. We followed their pattern and I felt deja vu. I remembered the fireflies when I was down by the water with my boys. The fairies guided us to a tree with a large wooden door built into it. Grassy steps lead up to the door.

"I love these," I said, once I saw the tree's door.

Bioluminescent butterflies had been encased in glass jars and placed on the ground to light the walkway to the door. Atrixia began releasing the butterflies from their jars, one by one, as we approached the tree. After, the three of us stood side by side at the bottom of the doorsteps.

"Maybe we should go back to the observatory," Atrixia suggested. "Something about this place just seems, witchy."

I knocked on the door. Whoever wanted our attention was receiving it now. A girl answered the door.

"My name's Amanda. You can call me Mandy," the girl in the doorway said. She had long dark hair and brown eyes and wore a bright red shirt with long loose sleeves. Her pants were black and tight. She wore black leather boots with tall heels.

"Do enter. My master's expecting you," Mandy said to the three of us.

I nodded at Atrixia. She still had doubts so I took her by the hand. I felt like she was nervous. The ceiling was too high to see once we entered the enchanted tree. Mandy reminded us that our sizes hadn't changed. The tree is under a spell so its interior was much larger than its exterior. Like the map room in Jaxin's study, the inner walls of the hollow tree were lined with bookshelves. Each shelf was crammed with books. Mandy informed us that it was her job to keep them in order. I rubbed my thumb over Atrixia's hand and let go of it. I caught up with Mandy and walked beside her. Mandy's high-heeled boots tapped against the floor. Her sleeves swayed. She intrigued me.

"Vocasta," Mandy said suddenly. I looked forward and saw a tall elegant looking woman standing in the hallway. It was unexpected. Her hair was straight and black like her dress. Her dress was tight and her smile was welcoming. She was older than I was, perhaps mid-thirties. "Are you the one who saved us?" I asked. I was grateful.

"You're safe here. I protect these woods. I do hope you find comfort and sanctuary while you're here. Follow me," Vocasta said. We passed books about witchcraft and potions. Atrixia found them disturbing so she looked down at the floor as we walked. I walked beside her as we all followed Vocasta down the stairs into a large pit. I looked down over the railing and saw a lab. We reached the base of the pit and the first thing I noticed in her lab was a black cat once it popped its head out of a jack-o-lantern. The cat's pupils disappeared and its eyes were all white.

The cat leaped out of the pumpkin, walked across the countertop, and sat. The cat looked at Vocasta with its white eyes and when it did, its eyes turned bright green and their pupils returned. The cat looked at Caydia with its green eyes and their color changed from green to red. The red shifted to yellow once the cat looked at Atrixia. Vocasta turned her back and finally the cat looked at me. The yellow in its eyes changed to a bright purple while Vocasta wasn't looking.

A fish appeared in front of the cat and they began to nibble at it.

"I've seen this cat before," I said.

Although I couldn't remember where, I could recall seeing its eyes. I looked around the lab some more.

"Her name's Sage," Vocasta said.

I watched bottles bubble as Vocasta explained to the girls how Sage could adopt anyone's power. "Even yours," Vocasta told me, thinking I wasn't paying attention. She thought I was uninterested in what she was saying. On the contrary, I found her very intriguing. I looked closely at each bottle as they boiled. Vocasta kept a live black widow in a sealed jar. I stepped away from it. I read the labels on the other jars. 'Newt eyes' 'Spider legs' 'Cat whiskers' 'Bat blood.' The list went on. I see why Atrixia finds these things disturbing. Vocasta was different but I found her fascinating. Caydia looked at a few of the books Vocasta kept in her lab. One of the books was red and had a ruby built into its spine. The jewel reacted and lit up when Caydia walked past it. 'Dyeheart' was written on the book's spine. She looked at the lettering on the side of the book and recognized it. She ripped the book off the wall and it opened on its own. 'Dyeheart,' is a last name she stopped going by years ago, she said. It made her sad. The book looked very fancy, almost as if it came from a royal library. The outer layer of the pages were coated in gold paint. The inside of the book was complex. There were locks preventing one from turning the first page. The book possessed a small chamber with a bronze cover in the center of its texts. The cover could only be lifted by Caydia or someone from the same bloodline. It was stated in the print. Caydia twisted off the cover with ease. After, the locks fell off and hit the floor. The chamber held a ruby soul gem. The gem was large and shaped like a heart. Words were written in a circle around its chamber. I was unable to decipher them.

"That book was dropped off at my tree, along with many other books, years ago," Vocasta said. "Unlike the other donated books it came with, it was stated that the book's true owner will come to claim it one day. I tried for years to pry it open and I could never even crack the book. It's always been sealed. I figured it was some old spell book. I guess *you* found it, or better yet, *that book found you.*"

"What?" Caydia asked. She was very confused.

"Most find their books, but that book, that book found you," Vocasta told her.

"That was easy," Caydia said.

Caydia lifted the gem and looked back at the book. She flipped through some of the pages. She stopped on one that held a picture of a girl wearing the same exact necklace. The girl in the book looked nearly identical to Caydia. They each had the same dark hair and the same light eyes. The resemblance was clear; yet, she still wondered if her and the girl in the book were related. The ruby looked the same exact way as it did then, brand new.

"Those things never age," Vocasta said, referring to the ruby.

The name on the book was slightly different from how Caydia remembered it.

"This can't be mine," she said, "My last name is spelled Dyart and it's pronounced Dy-art, not Dyeheart."

"It's Dyeheart," Vocasta assured her.

"My last name's Braxton," Atrixia said. It was random but she was happy to say it.

I walked over to Caydia and said, "I believe irrefutable was the word you used when I wasn't sure if my gem was mine or not."

She eyed me, swapped her previous necklace with the ruby heart, and asked how it looked.

"Like you were born to wear it," I assured her.

She took my word for it. She placed her original necklace inside the book then looked at her great great grandmother's photo one last time. The girl in the photo had a black cloak and straight black bangs. Caydia shut the book, snapped her fingers, and changed into a black cloak. Her hair was no longer curled. It was straight. Her bangs hung above her eyes. Her necklace shone brightly. It was nearly blinding. I smiled. The girl looked like a star after. She found a mirror in Vocastas lab and looked at herself. The mirror was lit by candles. On the table in front of the mirror sat a skull with bat wings and a music box.

"Red's definitely your color," I said.

She looked at me with pale blue eyes and smiled. Atrixia stood with the tip of her broomstick on the floor. She was leaning on her broom with her arms wrapped around its stick. She admired Caydias new look. Vocasta seemed to be a bit intrigued by it as well.

"Come children," Vocasta said.

"Children?" Atrixia questioned.

Vocasta walked over to a clear glass bowl filled with a clear boiling solution. Vocasta pricked her finger with a pin and released a drop of red blood into the bowl. The liquid had an immediate reaction. It turned green and released a cloud that formed into the shape of a spider.

Vocasta looked up from the solid green liquid and read its cloud. "Evil, bewitchment, darkness." She walked away from the bowl and said, "I'm a bitch. I mean witch." She rolled her eyes and smiled. "You try," she said to Caydia.

Caydia looked at her and smiled back.

"Blood spells?" Atrixia asked. She thought it was demonic.

"It's not a blood spell," Vocasta said. "It's a test to display what type of power your blood holds. Green is a more wicked color. It usually pertains to alchemy and witchcraft. The solution usually turns black when one practices dark arts. That kind of activity will rip the life out of you if you're not careful. The form of power is addictive. Necromancers may use it from time to time. Red shows when one is destructive and disastrous. You'll see it from many sorcerers. And you," Vocasta said to me. "I don't know what you are."

Caydia walked over to the bowl, passed her family's book to Atrixia, and pricked her finger with the tip of a small blade. The liquid solution changed from green to a rosy red with just a drop. Fiery red flames arose from the bowl and a puff of pink smoke shaped like a heart emerged from them.

"Sorcery, alteration, and of course, heart," Vocasta read.

"Wow. Just like your ancestor, according to this book," Atrixia said. Both Atrixia and I looked at each other. We were both unsure about going. Vocasta called Atrixia to do it next.

"This is dark," Atrixia said.

"Oh c'mon," Caydia said, "it doesn't hurt." Atrixia remained by my side.

"Why not give it a shot?" Vocasta asked Atrixia.

"It's not our thing," I told Vocasta. "What else can you show us?"

Each root of the tree Vocasta lived in was hollowed out like a tunnel. The place was a labyrinth. One hall held an alchemy unit with a cauldron the size of my house.

Another hall was a never-ending closet of enchanted robes, dresses, and cloaks. One root held an indoor garden. I noticed one of Vocasta's bedrooms in another root. Her room was behind a wood door with a green stain glass window on each side. I looked behind me and saw Atrixia holding her finger over the glass bowl. A drop of green blood fell from Atrixia's finger and the substance turned yellow. Vocasta looked impressed by Atrixia's color as well when a cloud of yellow smoke appeared and multiple smokey butterflies flew away.

"Your blood type is complex," Vocasta said, "it's always difficult to read. Dryad, biomancer, asexual, you're in the early years of your third century-"

"Stop!" Atrixia screamed out. All was quiet for a moment.

"You descended from a tree?" Caydia asked.

"You're two hundred years old?" I asked.

"I came from… a tree of dreams," Atrixia whispered. None of us knew what she meant.

Atrixia turned to me. "And I told you, I'm about your age, in tree years. We went over this."

"And how long ago were you born?" I asked.

"A little over two hundred years ago. That's early twenties for me. I know others over a thousand years old," she told us.

I was a little freaked out but I didn't see Atrixia any differently. If anything, I was *even more* fascinated by her. I kissed the top of her head and held her.

"I think it's your turn," Vocasta said to me.

"Sorry, but I ain't tryna turn your little blood bath black." I laughed when no one knew what I meant.

"What do you mean?" Vocasta asked.

If my soul was vanishing, or if the phantom planted something dark in me that prevented me from using my power, this was when everyone was going to find out. I approached the bowl, pricked my finger with Caydia's dagger, and no blood came out. Vocasta didn't let me walk away so easily. She grabbed her bottle of bat blood from the shelf. That alone was enough to make Atrixia nervous. Vocasta poured a small amount of blood into a beaker. Atrixia covered her eyes and turned away as she did so. Vocasta approached me with the beaker in one hand and a long cotton swab in the other. She rubbed the swab around the inside of my mouth then stirred the blood with it. She dumped out all the blood in the beaker, not just a drop, and the substance in the bowl began to glow purple. Purple smoke oozed from the bowl. It was enchanting. Nextly, a small star appeared above the bowl. The star grew bigger and brighter until Vocasta felt the need to contain it. She placed a force field around the star right before it exploded so her lab wasn't destroyed. No one said anything for a moment. Vocasta's lab wasn't damaged, but she still looked angry.

"The blood you possess is of something immortal," she said to me with suspicion. It was a surprise to me, too.

"I desire to know why your blood is purple and you should know I was never fond of liars," she said thoroughly. She tapped her nails on the table.

"My blood is red, the same color as yours," I said.

"Why haven't I seen your power shade before? You're him!" Vocasta finally shouted. She was in shock. "The world is counting on you, what are you going to do?"

I backed away from the question and looked at Caydia. "This is crazy," I told Vocasta.

I flew from the ground and laid my hood over my head without even having to touch it. I looked down and held out two purple solar flares. When a curse was placed on this planet, it wasn't to prevent my power from reversing it. The gloom began clearing when I arrived. Darkness doesn't react well around stars. No one knew about my power before.

"I can do whatever I want here. *Anyone* can be whoever they want to be. I'll do whatever I can to make sure that'll always be the case."

"The attack on the realm is planned to be on Halloween," Vocasta said.

"Halloween?" I asked.

"It's a universal day. An evening where the dead return to the physical world," Vocasta told me, "Zorcus sent three fighters after you. He plans to unleash darkness all over the planet. There will be little time to escape or prepare for it."

"Zorcus and I have met," I laughed. "I'm well aware of his plans."
"Zorcus expects you to be at the cloud palace the night of October 31st."

"What's the cloud palace?" I asked.

"It's a castle in the sky," Caydia informed me.

"It's located in the Towny," Vocasta said.

"The Towny?" I asked.

"The Towny! It's the most enticing place on this planet," Caydia said. She seemed excited.

"Do you know how to control your power?" Atrixia asked me.

"Of course," I said.

"Really, you learned how to control *all* your powers?"

I looked at her and she took my lack of response as a no.

"In a few weeks, this world is going to fall apart. Its woods will burn to ashes and its skies will turn black," Vocasta said.

I looked down at the floor and said, "It's *me* they're gonna be coming after."

"What's that supposed to mean?" Atrixia asked.

I walked over to her and handed her the small black box I wished for in the woods the morning of my birthday.

"What's this?" she asked.

She opened its lid, covered her mouth, and gasped. The box contained a rose gold heart attached to a chain. She lifted the chain and I took it from her. I gently laid the chain around her neck and fastened it. "Something that I wanted you to have," I said.

She grabbed the pendant, walked over to Vocasta's mirror, and looked in it. She pulled her hand away, looked at the heart, and saw the word 'Faith' engraved in script. She held it and wept.

"I didn't want you to have something that just makes you smile. That's too simple. I wanted you to have something greater. Something that contributes to your charm. That way, no matter what, it'll always be a part of you. I feel like this heart symbolizes your core. Keep it for me. Hold it close when I'm not around. You're one of the few left I trust to hold my heart. Keep it dearly. Not just for now, but forever and always." The heart also possessed a small chamber capable of sealing a tiny object. Using my own star power, I was able to break a small shard off the front of my soul gem. After, my gem was round-cut. It was no longer pointy and I liked it even more. I took the small shard and encased it in the heart's chamber. "This will protect you," I promised. I kissed her and the gold heart lit up purple. Caydia and Vocasta were shocked. Atrixia pulled away. "From what?"

"Bad energy," I simply said.

I looked Atrixia in the eyes. She had my power under control more than I did. I loved her. I knew what I had to do now. I wanted to be with her even if she would outlive me. If I wanted to spend the rest of my life with her, I had to keep her safe. If you're in danger, you don't get to decide that.

"Go to the Observatory," I said to her and Caydia. "You'll be safe there."

I took both Atrixia's hands and kissed them. "Look after each other," I begged.

"What's happening right now?" Atrixia asked. "Where are you going?"

"I wish to see you again," I told Atrixia. I flew to the exit and stepped out into the world. I raised my hood with my hands just as it started to rain. I flew into the cloudy atmosphere and couldn't see a thing up there. It was a little difficult but I eventually flew back to my mother's palace. I touched the ground and received word from Rubrix that my mother had gone missing. "One moment she was here. The next moment, she was gone," Rubrix told me. "Some say she went searching for you."

I rushed to the castle in a flash. "Mom!" I called through the halls. There was no answer.

I searched through the whole house. I checked every floor and found no one. No one was home. *Everyone* was gone. I started to freak out. I began to breathe heavily. I climbed to the highest room in the main tower. The room was circular and made of cinder blocks. There was no one. As a matter of fact, there was nothing in it. There was no furniture. What I did find was a blue spell book on the floor in the middle of the room. I browsed it as I walked outside.

I didn't wanna stay at the palace so I ran into the woodlands. It was the only place I felt safe. The crystal ball on my finger began to shine, which meant Caydia was trying to contact me. I ignored the call. I flipped through the blue book and tried to decipher its texts. Its wording was written in another language. A language I couldn't comprehend. The book held symbols I didn't recognize. It contained charts and tables I couldn't read. I stored the book in my bag for now. I snapped my fingers and changed into a pair of light blue jeans and a red flannel. I watched Caydia do it enough until I got the hang of it. I needed to get my powers under control. I pushed up each of my sleeves then tried to create a starburst with my hands. I spun my wrists around each other and accidentally banged my hands into one another in doing so. The failure resulted in a massive explosion that blew up in my face. It was a good thing I moved to a secure environment before I did it. I tried something different. This time, I tried creating a gumball machine. It was random, but I felt like it was a safe thing to wish for.

I tried to test my power again and a portal appeared. *Strange*, I thought. The portal wasn't my creation. I waited for a moment. I was expecting something evil to step out. *Maybe I'll get some practice*, I thought.

Nothing came out of the portal. Whatever was on the other side was waiting for *me*. I stepped into the forest burned down by the flamedame. The observatory wasn't far. Suddenly, the flamedame appeared out of thin air. There wasn't a need to engage in battle. She seemed like she just wanted to talk. She spun around and looked at me.

"Why do you come?" she asked me.

"I didn't invite myself. I was brought here."

"You have no business here. Why care for a world you were kept from? Rule with us. Be on our side. I'm sure Zorcus would have a nice place for you."

"You think that's what I care about? A seat at the king's table? Let's pretend that *was* true. Who would ever wish to rule a dark world?"

"A dark world? A new world," she corrected me. She took hold of my hand that wore the crystal ball and replenished the woodlands. Using my ring, she reconstructed the trees using some form of time reversal spell. The ring was more powerful than I thought. It didn't just show one their fate, it also allowed one to reverse it.

"How did you do that?" I asked.

"You wouldn't even know the full potential of your powers. Makes more sense for you to just hand them over. You'll be sent home without a scratch. Leave your power in our hands and leave this world behind. You won't even remember it. Or die for it, your choice."

Nothing was said for a moment.

"Hand it over," she said, referring to my soul gem. "Other nations and realms have already begun preparing for battle. You can prevent all of this by a simple exchange. It's been said that if anyone enters the cloud palace with you, the entire world will be destroyed instantaneously. There's nowhere for you to run and there's no place for you to hide. The woodlands won't guard you. Your friends aren't safe even if you leave them out of this. Hand over the gem. After that, you'll have your mother, your friends, your freedom, whatever you wish." She blew a kiss at me.

I launched two star bolts at her. She dodged them both. After, I flung my arms out and unleashed a massive tidal wave to wipe her out. She vanished before the water could reach her. The next moment, I was back in the previous woodlands. When I got back, the first thing I saw was a gumball machine. I looked over my shoulder and saw my mom's castle.

This is my home, I thought to myself, *this is* my *home*. It was time to hit the books and study hard.

CHAPTER 26

THIS IS MY WORLD

I got lost. Days went by. Sage came to keep me company from time to time. I bathed in a nearby river and changed my clothes with a snap. It was warm out so I changed into a pair of dark blue jeans and a gray tank top. I also threw a sleeveless back hoodie over me. My hair dried in a frizzy way. My hair had grown past my eyes. I had eaten the last of my apples and I was hungry. I've yet to understand a single word in the blue spell book. I've also read books on sorcery, illusion, conjuration, restoration, and even destruction while I was here. None of those lessons compared to the ones in the mysterious blue book. I flipped through its pages and came to an image of a star. I looked up at the sky. The stars weren't out yet. I looked back down at the book, turned the page, and the next image struck me. It was the symbol of a heart.

I shut my eyes and Atrixia was the first one to come to mind. Second, was Caydia, and the third was my niece Gara. The fourth thing I thought of was this planet, my girl's home. I hadn't seen Atrixia since the day I left. I missed the sound of her voice. Even in a crowded room, I could tell when she was talking. I opened the black book that Atrixia and I had received from Caydia. I peeked at the red heart I drew. I saw that Atrixia had drawn a violet star in the center of the heart.

I figured the farther I was from her and Caydia, the safer they were. I thought if I returned to the Observatory or flew back to my mother's palace, I'd go back to nothing. Halloween is tomorrow. I needed to get my act together and make it to the Cloud palace by then.

How? I wondered. I've yet to find out what the cloud palace even is or where to find it. I'm sure Vocasta can point me in its direction. She seemed to be familiar with it. I placed my hands in my pockets and felt something small. I pulled it out and held the penny I found on the street the day before I came to this world. I took out the blue book and glanced at it again. I tried to sound out each word. I realized this book had been coded for my power. My power has yet to exist before me. This book is the first and probably the only of its kind. I looked up to the sky. "Help me," I said desperately.

I watched something silver fall from the sky and walked in its direction. The glistening silver object landed in front of a tree. I saw the silver object shimmering back at me as I approached it. I wondered what it could be. I reached down and picked up the glass magnifier and its holder. Immediately after, the blue book flew from my hand and floated in the air. On the cover of the book was a heart and within that heart was the symbol of a star. A saying had been circularly printed around the heart in a language that I couldn't read. I looked at the book through the magnifier to have a larger view of the lettering and the wording appeared in English. 'It's written in the stars,' the book's cover stated. Suddenly, the clouds above disappeared entirely. I looked back at the book and read on.

The pages listed rules and instructions. The first rule read: *True wishes are made from the heart.*

Rule number two: *Love is compelling and doesn't always arrive on time, making it off limits to wish for.*

Rule three: *Bringing anyone back from the dead is considered necromancy and falls under the category of dark spells. FORBIDDEN,* the book clearly stated.

Rule four: *If you're the type to wish for unlimited fortune and power, know that there isn't enough to satisfy you and there never will be.*

Rule five: *Wish for anything, not everything.*

At the end I found a note. *Damon,* the note read, *I wrote these rules for you the moment I found out you were going to be born. Follow them. Nothing is more important than health. Your health was the most important thing to me. You are very smart. - Dad.*

The pages were covered with an invisible coating that protected them from power and prevented them from being destroyed by any acid or dirt. A tear fell onto them and slid down.

The book contained a small pocket within its spine and in it was a wearable magnifier holder. Almost, like a pair of glasses with only one lens. I inserted the magnifier and tried it on. I wore the magnifier like a monocle and the spell book hovered over my palm. I read the pages as each one flipped past my eye. The book and I had a connection. I was able to macro-process it. I could instantly read it, repeatedly. I read until night came. By then, I was speaking the book's language. I was making shooting stars appear above. I looked up and saw a sky full of brightly colored meteor shards. Each was composed of calcium. I made a wish on every one of 'em. One for each person I loved here and on earth. I closed my eyes and wished for four cups of semisweet chocolate chips. They appeared in a long red bag. I chewed on a few. It was the first thing I had eaten all day. Once I had enough, I made the bag disappear. I felt cool after I closed my eyes again and imagined my favorite hand-held video game console and was playing it the next moment. I looked both ways.

I tossed the console to the side and it disappeared in a puff of purple smoke. I closed my eyes and imagined myself with a nicer hairstyle. One appeared and when I opened my eyes, I was holding a mirror and wearing a new pair of sunglasses. I looked at myself in the mirror and could see my eyes glowing purple behind my glasses. I felt scared when I lowered my shades and saw each of my eyes shining a bright starry violet. Once I felt my hair was on point, both the mirror and sunglasses vanished. I bowed my chin a single time and changed the color of my jeans from blue to black. I snapped my fingers and I was wearing a black collared shirt with a red vest. I conjured a brand new pair of pearl white high top sneakers. I created a dark blue cloak with actual stars sewn into its fibers. The color of the stars changed with whatever power I used, whether it was blue, red, or purple. I placed my thumbs through its thumbholes.

I flew into the skies and wrote Atrixia's name in cursive using starlight. I was about to fly away when I heard the most beautiful voice below. I landed and covered my soul gem. I walked in the direction of the girl's voice. Judging by the salty scent in the air, I could tell I was near the ocean. I came across a girl with long beautiful orange hair. She was alone in a warm steamy hot spring. She stopped singing and said, "You there," once she noticed me. I approached her. I wanted to be kind. Her eyes were blue and friendly. She seemed nice.

"What are you doing all the way out here?" she asked.

"I was just wandering around and wanted to make sure everything was okay. You haven't seen anything strange or eerie going on, have you?"

"I'm not sure. I haven't been here long. I'm not from here. Where are you from?"

"I'm from another world."

"I come from another world as well, though I wish to travel around this one someday. Do you own a vessel?" she asked.

"What?" I laughed.

"Do you possess a ship?"

"I don't, but you do."

She didn't know what I meant. I told her to turn around. She looked behind her and saw the most glorious ship floating in the harbor. The ship's sails were the color of the night sky. Its multiple stories had fancy glass purple windows. The ship's interior lights were amber. A blank banner hung across its back. The banner was reserved for the name of the ship.

"It's yours," I told her. "Sail wherever you wish. Name the ship whatever you want. Write 'Just married,' on the back of it. I don't care. Run free." I blew her a kiss.

"I wish I could run," she laughed. "You're sweet but I don't need a ship to travel the ocean." She raised a shimmery orange mermaid tail out of the water.

I kneeled and took her by the hand. "Close your eyes," I told her.

She closed her eyes, peeked, and asked, "What are you gonna do?" She had no idea what was going to happen.

"Close your eyes, take a deep breath, and think of what you want."

She closed her eyes, submerged herself under the surface, and took a deep breath. She held onto me tightly. I shut my eyes and bowed my head. The next moment, she came to the surface and looked at me in shock. She looked over her back and lifted a single leg out of the water. She curled her foot and bent her leg towards me. Her smile was warm. She caught a glance of my purple gem and looked at its color with fascination.

"You're him," she said.

I swished my hand around and made my bag appear out of thin air. I reached into it, pulled out an unused cloak, and passed it to her. She covered herself, stood up, and climbed out of the pool. I helped her out of the water. Her toenails were painted orange. She had trouble standing at first. I held her in my arms until she got the hang of it. I let go of her and she stumbled a bit so I held her hand the way Caydia held mine until I learned to levitate. She learned to walk on her own surprisingly quickly.

She looked down at her legs and said, "You really can have *anything* you want here."

"You can just jump back into the water whenever you wish to be a mermaid again."

She stepped back into the water, regained her tail, and swam over to me.

I backed away and started to walk off.

"Wherever you are, wherever you go, if you ever need another wish, just look up at the stars," I whispered.

"Wait," she yelled. "You just helped a mermaid, don't you know what happens now?"

I nodded my head no. She took out a pink conch shell and placed it on the ground. She smiled and called me back over to her.

I kneeled in front of the shell. "What's this for?" I asked.

"This is your chance to wish for the impossible. Sadly, your wish can't interfere with the power of another," the mermaid said.

How does one think of the unthinkable? Are there questions we don't know to ask? Wishes we don't even know to make? I believed I already could wish for anything. I never considered wishing for the impossible.

I got one. I was on the fence about it but I picked up the pink conch shell and brought it close to my lips. My heart was racing. "I wish to be forever young," I whispered. "Are you sure?" she asked. "Forever is - you know, forever."

"Forever or never," I said, with an old song in mind.

She smiled and clapped her hands together. A bright orange light shone throughout the woods. I felt no different after.

"Enjoy your life," she said. "It's going to be a long one."

"I will. What's your name?" I asked her.

"Melody," she said.

"I love your voice," I said.

She laughed and smiled back at me. I motioned over to the ship floating in the distance.

"If you're going to climb aboard that ship, you might wanna hire a captain, a crew, a cabin boy," I told her.

"There are plenty around here but you should take that ship," she urged.

I liked the thought of it. What I'd do to just sail away. I liked this girl. She was like a combination of Atrixia and Caydia. I began to miss them.

"I have to go," I said sadly. "Perhaps our roads will cross again someday."

"I wish," she said.

I blew her a kiss, put my hands in my jeans pockets, and carried on. I felt something small and round in my pocket. I pulled it out and found the penny I picked up on Earth the day I came here. I kissed it and threw it down on the ground. A wishing well appeared. I hopped up onto the rim of the well, crouched, and looked down into it. Instead of darkness, there was a bright purple light at the bottom. I dropped down into the well and popped out of another well that emerged close to the observatory. After I climbed out, the well shrunk down and transformed back into the penny. The penny sat in the grass. I picked it up and placed it back in my pocket.

The sky was getting light. Day was approaching. I ran inside the observatory and met with Caydia. She was the only one I could find. She was sitting in the central dome with the lights off.

"Have you seen Trixie?" I asked.

"No, she told me she was going home. I wasn't sure what she meant. She seemed upset the last time we spoke. I tried to contact your ring after she left."

I had a feeling I knew where Atrixia was. I didn't know how to get there but I knew she was safe. I sat down in front of Caydia and presented a red velvet cupcake. Its icing was vanilla and its rainbow sprinkles lit up.

The significant part about this cupcake was its candle. It shall truly grant its user anything they desire. Its flame served as the only light in the Observatory.

"What's this for?" Caydia asked.

"Happy birthday," I told her.

Most send money when they don't know what to buy someone. 'Well here's a cupcake that will grant you anything you wish for,' I figured.

She seemed so overjoyed that I remembered.

"-and happy Halloween!!" I added.

"I don't know what to wish for," she said.

"Ask your heart what it wants," I whispered.

After a moment, she smiled, shut her eyes, and blew out the candle with certainty. Nothing changed physically and she didn't tell me what she wished for either. She knew how it works.

"Thank you, Damon," she said with a long side-hug.

I stepped away. "I need to find Atrixia. I don't know where to start. I doubt she'll forgive me for running off again."

"If she's a girl, you would know what to do and you wouldn't be talking to me right now. Grant her pearls and diamonds. Except she's not just some girl, she's your girl. You don't know what to do." She laughed and found it amusing. "It's okay," she reminded me. "Give her your love. I know you're filled with it. Don't lie. I know that girl of yours is out there waiting for you. *You* that is. Not your power, not your gifts, but you. That's what she wants."

She unboxed the wand I found in the witch's house. I thought it had been left there. Caydia saw it as a cool souvenir and decided to keep it.

"Go get your girl," she said.

"I don't think she'll like us playing with this while she's away."

"A love spell shouldn't hurt."

"I read that love spells can be dangerous."

"Then be sure to get some distance first."

"That's not what I meant."

I walked deep into the woods. Once I was away from Caydia and the Observatory, I took the wand out of its box. I wasn't even sure what to do with it. I only walked into the woods because I felt silly attempting this in front of Caydia.

I was never taught how to use a wand. I made sure the end of the wand was pointed away from my face. I waved the wand and the tip lit up. I didn't know of any love spells. I just needed one that would bring Atrixia back to me.

"I love you?" I asked the wand.

"I love you too," I heard from behind.

I turned around, saw Atrixia, and hid the wand behind my back.

"Did that work? Wow, that was fast."

"Did what work? You're talking to a stick."

"I'm sorry," I said. I looked into her eyes. Her hair was entirely red now.

"You told me you would never leave. I don't know how many times you've broken that promise since you made it."

I had nothing to say. She was right. I was just doing my best to protect her. I wouldn't be able to live with myself if anything happened to her.

"Tell me, what exactly do you do during the time you're away?" she asked.

"Atrixia, I've kept things from you. And yes, I even broke the promise I made, but everything I've done was to protect you and the future of your world. *Our* world. I don't wanna leave it." I walked over and held her. "I don't wanna leave you." I closed my eyes and rested my head on her shoulder.

"I forgive you," she whispered.

She walked over to a plant and grew a large pink flower. Her red hair turned blonde and a pink dress formed around her the instant the flower blossomed. Her orange eyes turned green.

She twirled around and sprinkled some glowing pollen on all the greenery.

After, multiple brightly colored orbs grew out of the bushes. The orbs lit up one by one. Each rang a soft bell. Together they formed a melody and she began to dance to it. Flowers bloomed around her. The flowers continued to grow on and on. The grass beneath her feet grew taller. She took a step towards me, spun around again, then passed the dance over to me. I snapped my right fingers, snapped my left fingers, then smacked the top of my left fist. I rubbed my palms together, spun around, and smacked the top of my right fist behind my back as I did so. I smacked my hands together again upfront and snapped both my right and left fingers. Lastly, I smacked the top of my left hand, rubbed my palms together, then spun my wrists around each other. Once I built up enough energy between my hands, I threw the starlight into the ground with my left hand. Purple smoke appeared and miniature stars formed around us. The smoke cleared and I saw Atrixia's gorgeous face. I spun her to my right then spun her to my left. We took each other's hands and held our palms against each other's. We kissed and an enchanted forest had formed around us.

CHAPTER 27

A WORLD OF HARMONY

I held her in my arms. "I loved your necklace," she said. "I never got to tell you that."

There's so much I never got to tell her. She saved my life. "You're welcome," was all that came out at first. "I'll stand by you," I promised. "I'm gonna be alive for a while."

"What do you mean?" she asked.

"I told a mermaid's conch shell that I wanted to be young forever."

"When was this?"

"You asked what I do when I run off."

She looked at me with surprise. "I'll have to go to sleep for the winter soon," she said sadly.

"I'll wait for you. I'll be there when you wake up."

She looked at me and smiled. We kissed. Afterward, Atrixia and I hurried back to the Observatory. She ran in while I waited outside. I looked up at the sky. Atrixia walked to the front and stood in the doorway.

"Caydia's gone," she told me.

"Gone?"

"She's not inside."

I got nervous when I called out Caydia's name and received no response.

"Where could she have gone?" I asked Atrixia.

I looked over and saw that Atrixia was no longer standing in the spot I saw her last.

"Atrixia!" I yelled out. I began to panic.

"I'm right here," Atrixia said.

She was standing right by my side. I looked her in the eyes as storm clouds gathered in the sky. I didn't know what to do. Suddenly, darkness began to spread over the land. I looked over to where Atrixia was standing last. She had vanished as well.

"No," I yelled.

I knew what was happening. Everyone was vanishing. It was only a matter of time until the same happened to me. The Observatory vanished as though it never existed. Suddenly, darkness began to sweep over the land. I was about to fly away when the clouds disappeared and the sky turned black. The darkness had surrounded me. There was nowhere to go. All light had been obliterated and everything went dark. I couldn't see anything.

I heard ghostly sounds from deep in the dark. I made a miniature star appear for light and saw the striped tail of a hideous creature soar past me. I stepped back. I looked to my left and a pair of vicious bloody teeth snapped at me. I leaned back like a boxer, shut off the light, and figured it was best to remain hidden.

I took too long. I was too late, I told myself.

The light in my soul gem began to die out and I started to disappear. I looked at the back of my hands as my fingers started to vanish. I backed into a tree. It wasn't very heroic but I sat down on the ground against the tree and wrapped my arms around my knees. The woods around me started to disappear. I closed my eyes and rested my head on my arms. I imagined the night I met Atrixia. The night I unfolded the burlap and laid it over the wobbly log. I wished I was next to her. We never stopped believing. I'll probably never get another chance to see her. She wore so many dresses and I only got to spin her in one. I imagined us dancing, and heard a shimmer close by. I thought I was hallucinating when fairy dust flew and formed the shapes of our bodies dancing over the water of a nearby pond. My figure spun her. We held each other as the dust disappeared. I put my head down and waited to disappear. When I opened my eyes a moment later, I was still sitting on the ground, except my soul gem was missing.

The phantom, I figured. What would a soulless figure possibly do with a soul gem? In the distance, I saw a jar light up blue. The jar held a fairy. Another jar lit up and then another. The leaves on the trees began to light up yellow. Vocasta's tree appeared ahead. I was so confused but now wasn't the time to ask questions. Like Atrixia, I set each fairy free as I approached the front door. The light inside the door window switched on. Vocasta was home. I reached the grassy steps and Vocasta opened the door before I could even knock.

"How does your place still exist after the darkness wiped everything away?" I asked.

"I told you, I have the fairy woods protected."

"Why keep the fairies in jars?"

"Only the mean ones," she laughed. "The fire starters, the hair pullers." She took me down to her lab.

"Has the entire world fallen apart?" I asked.

"Only the parts around you. You're safe here, and your friends are safe as well. The entire planet has been teleported to the Towny, the city where you'll find the Cloud Palace. Everyone's there to witness you and the black knight face off."

I looked down at the ground. "I could use a drink," I told Vocasta. I laughed at first until I said, "I might die tonight."

She could tell I was scared and fear wasn't an emotion she expected. I looked around her lab and remembered the last time I was here. I walked over to a bookshelf holding various potions and elixirs. I wondered if Caydia left any of her 'Angel Kiss' behind. I saw a steel black bottle and picked it up. 'Hatred' its label read.

"Why keep a bottle of hatred?" I asked. "Why not a bottle of love? A bottle of happiness?"

"Love and happiness can't be kept in a bottle. It's our hatred and sadness we keep bottled up."

I looked at her questionably and put the bottle down.

"Where'd you say Atrixia and Caydia were again? Caydia went to the cloud place. She's probably there looking for you as we speak."

"And Atrixia went with her?"

"I can't make any guarantee on Atrixia's location. She mentioned something about going home before the darkness reigns over the entire planet. She didn't specify where she meant by home, but she said returning there would increase her chances of survival."

"She just left without saying goodbye?" I asked.

Vocasta smiled at me.

"There's someone here you should meet," she said.

She led me down one of her hallways. On the way, she explained how some alternate universes work a lot differently compared to ours. Her lecture was advanced and complex. I didn't understand a word she was saying to me. She spoke of a dimension where time flowed backwards.

"Tomorrow he'll be a day younger and you'll be a day older, but today, the *two* of you are the same age," she said.

"Who'll be a day younger? Who are you talking about?"

"Go. He's waiting."

I walked over to a wide window. The window was impenetrable. It allowed one to view another dimension. I couldn't pass through but I could see through it. I saw the mountain range of another planet. The rocks were pink. The sky was starry. In the distance, I saw someone wandering. He appeared to be lost. He was wearing white futuristic clothing. It was nearly skin tight like it was designed for one to fly fast. His hair was blonde. He appeared to be neat, clean, and bright in appearance. He turned and looked at me and the two of us froze. That was when I realized who I was looking at. He was looking right back at me. The wanderer was *me*. I was looking at another dimension. The other me approached the window. Finally, I was standing face to face with myself. In his eyes, he looked like he had already lived an eternal lifetime of adventure. He placed his hand against the invisible barrier and I placed my hand over his. He looked at me and smiled. Suddenly, I felt confident, like I had the brightest future ahead of me. It was the most hopeful look I've ever received and it was given to me by my future self. His body began to glow. His light diffused through the barrier and into my hand. He was no longer standing there. His energy flowed through me. I turned to Vocasta feeling more alive than ever.

"It's time for me to go," I told Vocasta.

I went to grab my bag. Right then, an old book labeled *Spirits of Darkness* fell out of my bag. It opened on a particular page when it hit the floor. I picked it up and studied the page. On it, I found a ghastly image of a documented ghost.

Name: (No name)

Origin: Unknown.
'Absence of sound when present.'
'Sudden drops in temperature when present.'
'Lack of form'
'EAP: Run.'

I dropped the book and wanted to kick it away from me.

"You okay?" Vocasta asked. She sounded sorry for me.

"You lose your body, you're left with your soul. You lose your soul, what are you left with?" I asked.

"Your spirit."

"Your spirit?"

"Your soul is linked to your body and your spirit is linked to your soul. We don't have much time. This might be confusing right now, but some can detach their soul from their body." Vocasta picked up the book. "Is he a friend of yours?" I closed my eyes and shook my head no. "It says here, he traded his soul, but before he sold and traded his soul, he managed to detach his spirit from it."

"That sounds too complex. Even here, how is that possible?" I asked.

"Cheaters find ways. He owed his soul and when it was time to pay up he submitted an empty, blank one. Clever."

I pulled out the penny, threw it on the ground, and the well appeared. I thanked Vocasta for pulling me out of the darkness. She wished me good luck and I hopped down the well. Instead of arriving at the cloud palace, I emerged in the meadow Atrixia brought me to. I had a feeling she would be here. I remembered this place. After I entered the nearby garden, I felt like I was walking in a dream. I crossed multiple isles of hedges. Each one was centered with a different tree. I passed each one, wondering which one was Atrixia's. I called out her name. No one was around. Eventually, I came to an isle with a short wide oak tree. There was a red hoodie hanging from one of its branches. My hoodie, the hoodie I gave her. There were flowers all around. Here, it felt like springtime. Mums of red and yellow were arranged around the base of Atrixia's tree for the fall. That's when it hit me. This is where she was born.

"'D'," I heard a voice say. I looked behind me and saw Atrixia. Her hair was entirely red again. Her eyes were orange. Even though she looked a lot different from the first time we met, I still thought she was the most gorgeous girl ever.

"I'm so happy to see you again," I told her. The necklace I gave her still hung around her neck. She held its heart in her hand and looked up at me.

"I wasn't leaving for good," she said. "I was only visiting this place in case it gets destroyed tonight. I wanted to see it one last time. These lands are blessed. There's enchantments in the soil that should withstand the darkness."

I told her not to worry. We kissed and her necklace lit up. We made love. So much love. We each learned to control the power.

"I lost my soul gem," I said. "Somewhere in the darkness. I'm pretty sure the phantom snatched it from me."

"Who?" she asked.

"Never mind. My gem just vanished from my neck in the pitch blackness. There's no saying what happened to it or where it even is."

"We must move fast. Your gem can be anywhere."

"Why would someone else steal my gem? What could they do with it? It's not like whoever took it can access my power through it."

"Whoever took it might not be able to access your power, but they can certainly hide it from you to prevent you from using it."

"We need to find Caydia," I said.

"She'll be waiting for us at the cloud palace. Everywhere else is obscured."

I pulled the penny out of my pocket again.

"What's that?" Atrixia asked.

"This penny can take us anywhere we want to go." I threw the penny on the grass and the well sprung up.

"Just jump," I told her, "it's fun."

The two of us hopped down the well. She went first. The two of us arrived at a highly populated town, referred to as the Towny by its residents and visitors. All were celebrating and partying. I didn't know why. No one knew who I was. Other girls were eyeing me as if they liked me. Atrixia pulled me closer and stared at them until they looked away.

"Why are they drinking and laughing?" I asked. I was so confused.

"What would you expect people to be doing together if their world was coming to an end?" Atrixia asked me.

I looked around and saw shops and stands. I noticed a familiar color shimmering inside one of the shops.

"Hold on," I told Atrixia. I wanted to get a closer look at whatever was shining inside the gift shop. Its violet light was blinking back at me. I got close enough to see that it was a purple glowing rock. I was close enough for the soul gem to react to me. It wouldn't be hard to prove it was mine. The shop was run by a young graceful looking girl. She looked at her customers with kind eyes and greeted each one with a warm smile.

"My name's Harmony," she said as I approached the counter.

"It's a pleasure," I said.

I had to find a way to obtain the gem without indicating it belonged to me. I asked if she accepted sky coins and she didn't know what I was talking about.

"I couldn't help but see that stone. I think that necklace would make the perfect gift for my girl. I'd love to buy it from you."

"I'm sorry, but that stone isn't for sale. That stone is a lost item we displayed on the shelf with hopes that it would be reunited with its owner."

"Well how will you be able to tell if whoever comes to claim it is telling the truth or not?" I asked.

"You're right. There's no certainty who the gem belongs to. Anyone within fifty feet of that stone can be the one causing it to react."

Smart girl, I thought.

"It's a soul gem. Only the stone's true holder can wield its power," she added.

"Its power," I repeated back. I looked at her. She was oblivious of the stone's capabilities and I could tell. "What if I didn't have any money to offer, but I could provide you with *anything* you desired?"

"You can't bribe me and you can't bargain for it," she said.

"I know one thing you would want in exchange for that rock, a world that didn't end tonight. Let me have it and I promise you, tomorrow morning you'll wake up in a world of harmony, Harmony."

She looked at me wide-eyed and handed me the soul gem without question. I looked at the stone and placed it around my neck. "I kid you not, when God made you, he was sure to make your eyes and your teeth together at the same time. I think the person you are on this planet couldn't ever possibly fit anymore to the name that you carry. I wish you a splendiferous life."

"And I wish you the best of luck, Starheart."

Starheart. It was the first time I ever heard it. I liked it.

The phantom never took the gem for itself. The phantom never even hid it. They just used it to lure me here. I found Atrixia and ran my fingers through her bright red hair.

"Where are we supposed to find Caydia?" I asked. There had to be a million people drinking in the center of the town. On a hilltop, not far outside the city, I noticed a blinking purple light. Someone was signaling us from a shadowy woodland.

"There," I pointed out. Atrixia and I moved through the crowd. Each time a person took a sip from their bottle, a color would appear in the sky above. Atrixia explained to me that the skies were reflecting the emotions of those drinking beneath it. Almost like a mood ring. I looked up and saw ten thousand different colors colliding. Atrixia and I headed up a small hill and entered shadowy woods where the trees had no leaves.

"Cayde?" I called out. I didn't see her anywhere.

"Over here," I heard Caydia say.

She walked out wearing a new red cloak. Her hood was raised and her necklace was charged. She was wearing a black dress with purple stockings. Her boots were tall and black. She looked like a sorcerer. I was relieved once we finally found her.

"We need to stay together and out of sight," I said.

The cloud palace could be seen in the distance built on a cliff edge. The night was black. The cliff and cloud palace appeared as one. The palace had so many floors, I couldn't see the top story. The building was built into the clouds, hence its name.

I wanted to face off with the knight now. I was ready for them. I raised my hood and we blended in with the crowd perfectly. We walked through the witchy town. I made sure both girls stayed by me. We were by the ocean. I could smell it in the air.

We walked past an empty dark church. We heard a loud bell ring in threes from above the church. Inside, I could see the flame dame sitting on a throne made of flames in the front of the chapel. I told the girls to wait outside just as a raven flew overhead.

"If you don't know what you're doing, I'm coming in," Caydia said.

"I wish for the two of you to stay together. Protect each other. Do you understand?"

They both nodded their heads at me. I walked through the door and passed a top hat on my way in. I picked it up, put it on, and looked around. *It's showtime*, I thought.

The room was filled with lit candles. I bowed my head and approached the altar.

The flamedame sat up in her chair. I melted each candle down to a puddle. I didn't just blow them out. I passed each row of pews until I reached the front. I looked at the flamedame and smiled. I took off my hat and reached into it. A purple light shone from within the hat and I pulled out a rabbit. The white rabbit hopped away. I placed the hat back on my head and the flamedame and I were face to face. She was intimidated. The rabbit was cuddly. It was the fact that I mastered my power that frightened her.

"I see you found your soul gem," she said.

"How'd you know it went missing?" I asked.

She remained silent.

"Speak less than you know, huh?"

She smiled.

"Well then." I threw both a red and blue starbolt at the flamedame and a great purple starburst blew her out of her throne. She fired flames out of her hands from the air. I dove and ducked behind a church pue. I looked up and imagined torrential downpour. A violent storm appeared above and rain came crashing down. The flamedame wasn't washed away by the rain, but her flames were useless. I tossed my hat and the white rabbit hid inside it. The rain felt good on my face while the flamedame was burned by the water. I could hear the loud sizzle of each drop landing on her. Caydia came in through a side door and unleashed a massive tidal wave that wiped out the flamedame. I blew away the storm and multiple black chunks of cooled lava fell from the air and compiled on the floor.

For a moment, the rocks remained on the ground. Soon after, the rocks reassembled into the flamedame's form. I thought Caydia had just beat her. The rocks ignited and fire spat out everywhere. The monster was back to life and more enraged than before.

"Stay back," I told Caydia. "I thought I told you to stay with Atrixia, where is she?"

Atrixia was flying around on a broom above our heads.

I grasped onto the flamedame's arm and flew through the ceiling. I ascended into the sky. The oxygen got thinner and thinner the higher we went. We entered space. There, the flamedame had no oxygen to burn off. She quickly crumbled into a thousand pieces. I blew on her remains and the rocks dispersed in their own directions like shooting stars. "That's one down," I said, once we regrouped.

We passed a saloon. Live music could be heard playing inside. Inside was filled with knights and warriors, gathered for a rally. I only stopped because I heard my brother's name being said inside. "Ruarkson… Ruarkson…" I peeked inside a window and saw him sitting at a table with multiple men standing around him. They were studying a map.

We headed through the doors and a man pushed us out.

"What's the problem?" I asked.

"Are you old enough?" he asked.

"I'm two hundred," Atrixia said.

"I'm twenty and Ruarkson's brother," I said. "Just a quick word with him is all I need."

"You two are good," he said to Atrixia and I. "But you," he said to Caydia, "you're outta here."

"I turned nineteen today," she said. She rolled her eyes and crossed her arms.

"Fine," the man said to us. "Get in quickly."

I rushed in.

"This isn't the place to just barge into," Atrixia said, "You're brother's clearly attending other matters. He doesn't seem like the type of person one just approaches."

"I'm his only younger brother," I said strongly. I stood dead center in the bar and shouted,

"I'm looking for Ruarkson!"

The whole place fell silent. People stepped back and a path to the table was formed. I heard music play. My brothers sat in the back of the saloon. Ruark had a tear in his eye. The man standing beside him was tall and thin, wearing a long dark coat. The tall thin man turned and looked at me with anger. He had his bony hands placed flat on the table. Between them was a knife pinned into the map. The map displayed invasion lines on sacred kingdoms and lands that have been taken over by enemy armies. Figurine armies were arranged across the map. I regretted barging in here. The door man took hold of my arm and asked my brother if my presence was allowable. My brother nodded his head yes and told the man to unhand me.

"Come forward," Ruarkson said. I approached his table. The crowd stared at me in silence.

"No need to introduce yourself," Ruarkson said. "They all know who you are."

"You have to tell your army to stand down," I urged, "The fight needs to remain between the knight and I. If not, they'll destroy the whole planet."

<h1 style="text-align:center">CHAPTER 28</h1>

<h1 style="text-align:center">THE PALACE</h1>

We arrived at the cloud palace. I lowered my hood and showed my stone. That drew everyone's attention. They stood back and cleared a path to the front door. I said not a word. I was scared, but I refused to show it. The entire realm was gathered around, ready to engage if we faced danger.

"It's time to finish this," I said to Atrixia and Caydia when we finally reached the front doors, locked until I stood before them. Soldiers operating the ram were so confused. "Wait," Caydia said, before I stepped through. "What happens when this is over?"

"I guess this is our last night together, whether I win or lose," I said.

Caydia's eyes filled with tears. Atrixia looked at me like she already missed me.

"I'll return," I said. "And when I do, it'll be to a world we can call our own. A bright one that belongs to all of us." I looked at Atrixia and said, "Don't worry. I'll be there."

I took her by the hands and looked into her orange eyes. They were nearly brown. I whispered, "Nobody compares to you. I can't wait to see you again." I smiled.

"You won't remember me once you're back on Earth. There's no certainty you'll even retain your powers. You'll age," she said. "Just don't ever say goodbye forever."

I kissed her and her charm necklace lit up.

"Remember to kiss me one last time before you go," she said. " I'll save every wish until you return."

The doors opened on their own and everyone backed away frightfully like I was being welcomed in by two ghosts. Everyone was watching me now. I entered and with no prelude a battle broke out outside. Phantoms and ghostly spirits came flying out of the palace. They attacked the massive army assembled outside. Witches drank from their bottles as they flew down on their broomsticks. Explosions went off and sparks rained down. From a distance, it would have looked like a firework show. Skeletons wearing helmets charged with swords. The warriors and knights clashed. The phantoms flew around, sabotaging the opposing army.

"Go!" I heard Caydia yell out from behind.

I hurried and the doors slammed shut behind me. The palace was empty. I walked along the black and white checkerboard flooring. I thought I entered alone until I heard others walking behind me. I turned around and saw Atrixia and Caydia. Neither of them could let me walk in alone. It turned out the flamedame was bluffing about the world ending if I brought allies with me. There's no way Zorcus would risk my power being destroyed with the rest of the world. We passed statues of knights, marble sculptures of angels, and walked along the finest carpets. Caydia told me the Cloud Palace was used for blessings and worship. I bet the Knight is going to be waiting for me on the top floor. I heard a loud rumble above and the floor shook. The barbarian was nearby. I looked at the girls.

"This is between me and them. Like I said, stay together and have each other's backs while I'm gone. Please," I said desperately. I rushed ahead without them. I kicked off the floor and began to fly. I ascended the stairs. The girls remained on the bottom floor. I flew fast. I passed multiple floors and finally stopped on one when I heard a loud roar from behind a set of double doors. The tower was built into a mountain. I opened the doors and stepped onto a mountain top. I was high in the clouds. The snow fell and the wind blew. I walked through the snow.

I heard a loud thump from behind. I turned around and there stood the massive monstrous barbarian holding a battle ax. He and his ax grew to the size of a house right before my eyes. I raised my hood and levitated off the ground. He rested the ax on his shoulder and began to walk towards me. I looked him in the eye. He leaped high in the air and I flew to the side. He slammed his ax down into the ground and missed me. From the air, I imagined a large concrete weight. One appeared and landed on his head just as I'd hoped. His skull was made of some strong bone marrow. Still, he was hurt. He held his head and slammed his ax into the side of the mountain. Rocks rained down from above and I had to fly out of the way. I swooped down and punched the giant in the chest. He fell and landed on his back. I punched him in the face while he was down. He grabbed me and threw me off with ease. I threw a hot starburst at him before he could even get up. The impact resulted in a large explosion. When I thought I had won, the being began to twitch and move again. He slowly rose to his feet and released a loud roar the entire realm could hear. He picked up his ax and when he did, its rod was flimsy like a noodle, as though it were to be made of rubber. He growled and tossed the ax. He jumped over to me and tried to pound me into the ground with his fists. I had to evade every one of his smashes. I flew quickly, put my feet together, and kicked him in the face. He stumbled back, and when he tried to come at me again, I wished for a sheet of ice, and moved out of the way. A crystal blanket of ice spread across the ground and the monster lost balance. I landed on the snow and watched him slide right past me. He skidded into the rocks. I flew as fast as I could and he still managed to catch me by my cape. He tried to crush me. I looked at him when we both realized he couldn't. He was angry. I could tell he wanted this world. I'm strong, but so was he. The crystal ball on my ring flashed twice. Caydia was trying to contact me. The brute threw me to the ground and stomped on my chest. It knocked the wind out of me. He went to stomp on my head and I flew away before I could even catch my breath. He grabbed my cloak again and threw me down onto the ice. My necklace began to die out. I rolled over on my stomach and tried to get up and the beast began pounding his fists into my back. I flipped over, laid on my back, and looked up at him. I charged a violet star bolt in my chest. The giant went to punch me. At that moment, a flash appeared before both of us. I looked around and I was back on the first floor of the palace. Caydia was there. She had her shiny red hood up.

"Where's Atrixia?" I asked. Atrixia was nowhere in sight. I didn't hear any clatter or commotion outside. The world I was in seemed to consist only of Caydia and I.

"Where are we?" I asked. "what just happened?"

"I rewound the time back five minutes," Caydia said.

"I didn't have to be pulled out of that fight."

The clatter and commotion of people battling outside resumed. We heard the same thump from above that we heard five minutes ago. The thumping of the giant.

"Now's not the time," Caydia said, "now's the time to act fast. You have a crystal ball on your finger, maybe you should use it."

I raced over to the stairs and flew up the stairwell. I reached the doors and stepped out onto the mountain top. The barbarian dropped down, and again, he and his ax grew to the size of a house. When he did, I charged at him faster than ever. I flew fast. I aimed straight for his horns.

Once I was close enough, I put my feet forward, grabbed onto his horns tightly, and had enough strength to flip the monster over and smash him down on his hideous face.

"Do I look like I'm being pulled out of this fight by a girl this time?" I asked. I was angry about it.

The beast looked up and roared. It didn't speak my language. I felt no fear. I flew by him as he stood up and spat. I fired a hot solar flare in his face, blinding his only eye. He held his face with one hand and tried to grab me with his other. He managed to get hold of my cloak, except this time a star fire burned through my cloak fibers. The monster released me and held his hand in pain. I was doing damage but not enough.

I remembered Caydia telling me about soul trapping. I read about how risky it could be and how I could possibly lose my soul in the process. I dropped to the ground and pulled out the dagger Caydia gave to me. Its blade was only five inches long. The dagger wasn't long enough to kill the beast. Even if I were to penetrate the beast's skin, I wouldn't be able to cut deep enough to reach its heart. Plus, I didn't want to kill him. I didn't feel the need to do so.

I looked into my crystal ball and checked my greatest chances of striking him. His ribs would be my easiest route but not close enough to do the trick. Striking the being over its heart was my cleanest way of accomplishing the objective. The monster went to strike me. The moment he changed his body position, I flew like a shooting star. I shut my eyes, and with enough luck, I somehow managed to strike the being directly in its chest. Only thing was, I felt the strike more than he did. I screamed like it was my heart that got struck with the dagger.

Caydia forgot to mention that part. Now, the battle was between whoever had the stronger soul. We both fell to the ground. I held onto the dagger with one hand and looked at the world around me. This might be the last time I ever saw it. I watched the snow fall. I turned and looked the monster in the face. "Where's my girlfriend?" I asked. Not that he would know. "She's got a face a lot prettier than yours," I shouted.

He snapped his sharp crooked teeth at me. I weakened him. The soul gem in the dagger was growing brighter with purple as the light in my necklace began to die out. If you have a light in you, don't lose it. If not, you're wrong: find it.

"Get up!" I heard Atrixia yell from above. She was circling around on her broom. I looked to her and mouthed the words, "I'm happy you got to know me."

She looked at me sternly. Her face was the last thing I saw before I shut my eyes and all went dark. When I opened my eyes, I was in a different place, and everyone was gone. My clothes were different. I was dressed in all white. I was in a forest where the flowers were pink, green, and white. The trees shed pink petals. The tiny pink petals blew in the air and felt icy cold on my face. I heard Atrixia cry, "Damon! Damon!"

I woke up and was laying in the snow. The cold flower petals I was feeling were snowflakes falling on my face. I looked over at the dagger and saw its gem flashing with gray light that wasn't mine. It was the light of the barbarian's soul.

"I love you," was the next thing I heard. I looked to my side and saw Atrixia sitting beside me. I pulled out the dagger and stood up. I extracted the gem and studied it. I lowered the gem, and kissed Atrixia long and softly. "We aren't finished yet," I said. "There's still one more to go."

The black raven flew over our heads.

"Find safety," I told Atrixia.

Atrixia hopped on her broomstick and said, "I'm not leaving you."

"We need to go after that raven."

She flew me to the top floor. We reached a flat circular pad used as a port for airships. I hopped off the broom and floated down. The raven swooped by and flew out of sight. The black knight appeared from nowhere.

"Get out of here!" I told Atrixia. "Now!" She blew me a kiss and flew away.

"Whatever your name is, this ends tonight," said the Knight.

"Damon," I said. The knight looked at me and didn't say a word. "My name is Damon," I repeated. I hovered off the ground and charged a purple starbolt in each of my hands. "Here I am," I said.

The color of the stars sewn into my cloak changed to the color of the dark violet starlight I had activated. The knight backed away, frightened. I not only possessed the ability to control the energy and heat of a star, I was able to make anything appear by simply wishing for it. I launched the bolts and blew the knight off the ground. I reached into my pocket and pulled out the gem with the barbarian's soul. "Your fighters," I said as I launched the gem into outer space, "are gone. This world will never be yours. Soon this will all be over and done with."

The knight drew a long black sword with an edge sharpened just for me.

"What do you receive out of this? That's my only question," I asked the knight.

The knight flipped into the air and sent his sword straight down over me. I froze the knight and tossed him to the side.

"Try again," I told him. "I just wanna know, why are you so mean?" I asked.

The knight rose and leaped towards me again, the rage evident. The knight punched me in the face with its heavy gauntlet. The punch didn't leave a mark, but it hurt. I flew off the ground and punched the knight in the center of their chest plate. There was a big purple explosion. It blew the knight back, but only a few feet. The knight sliced me in the arm. I looked at my wound and saw yellow shining from it. We were both surprised. I was off-guard and the knight drove its sword straight through my core. I fell to the ground.

"You were never killed on Earth. You were simply summoned here, brought here to die.

You're to be slain by my hand. This is where your final chapter ends," said the knight.

"This is where you're wrong. Things don't have to be this way. There isn't a reason for it to end like this."

"I'm not one to reason with. I'm not one who negotiates. I get what I want and what I want is your power and you lying still in cold blood. Dead."

I recognized his voice this time; it was dark and whispery. The knight picked me up by my neck, looked me in the eye, and choked me. I grabbed onto its gauntlet tightly. I broke free from its clasp just enough to ask the knight one question. "Who are you?"

The knight dropped me on the ground and I was too weakened to get back up. Both the phantom and the raven arrive, and I was surrounded. I had to get up now. The knight let me take my time. Somehow, I managed to. The four of us were at a standoff. I didn't know who to target first. The phantom's cloak flew away with the wind as though it were to be empty. The raven vanished into a puff of feathers. The knight unfastened its helmet and removed it.

I was speechless when I saw nothing where its head should be. There was no face. The headless knight stood over me. I watched the gray clouds drift past his shoulder guards. There was no head to block my view of them. I was freaked out. The knight pulled an empty vial off its belt. The vial was no ordinary vial. Its glass was thick and its shell made of steel, used to trap one's power. I've seen an image in one of Caydia's books. The knight intended to seal my power in it. All he had to do was point the bottle at me and remove its cap. My power would no longer be mine.

"You?" I questioned. Although the knight lacked a face, I recognized him the instant I saw he possessed no physical form.

"How long have you been after me?" I asked.

"Getting close to you was easy. I was always near," the knight said in his whispery voice.

I was shocked. I had nothing to say. He transformed into the raven and held the bottle in its foot.

"I followed you home from school. I stood in your room and watched you sleep. I entered your dreams. I stood in the doorway as you left your house, but you didn't see me. You forgot to close the front door. I was at the shore before you arrived. Your friends couldn't see me. They think you're crazy. They forgot about you."

I blasted him away. They transformed back into the knight and stormed me in an instant. I was knocked off the building. I free fell for a few moments while my head pounded. I came to my senses and began to fly. The knight flew in and grabbed me by the neck. He began to fly towards the ground. I tried to punch him in the face on the way down. It took awhile but we finally reached the ground and when we did, he drove me into the dirt. While I was down, he asked me if I was scared.

I recovered slowly and backed away.

"No," I said. I was so confused by the question. "Why would I be scared of…? You're literally nothing," I laughed. I reached out for his hand. "Can you help me, help you?"

He turned away and drew his sword. When he did, I pulled his power from him.

On the way down, I snatched the bottle from him. It was only after I took the bottle that I began to laugh. I didn't feel safe until I had it. He tried to bottle my power: I now held his. He had no power to even store within a gem. He turned around and faced me. I heard the wind whistle and blow through his hollow armor. He now had nothing. Only the knight's empty energetic form remained. A few years ago, my science teacher explained that energy couldn't be created or destroyed. I couldn't obliterate the knight entirely. I didn't have to. I already beat him. Plus, there was nothing left for me to destroy. All that mattered was that he could no longer use his powers against others. We ended on that. Whoever he was, whatever he was, I watched him walk away. He still had his sword in hand. I was expecting him to come at me again. Instead, the sword fell to the ground. The knight detached their cape and let it fly away. His entire armor set came apart piece by piece. He had no body. No form whatsoever. He still made noise when he climbed atop his black horse's back. The boot holsters rattled and the horse rode off into the night. The battle had ended. My mom was aiding the wounded. When I met back with Atrixia, I held her. I loved her. I felt her red hair. I was so happy and overjoyed to see her again.

"I love you," I told her. I looked deep into her burgundy colored eyes and meant what I said.

"I love you too," she said back.

I was thrilled. The sun shone brightly the next morning. The entire realm was gathered around the cloud palace. The chancellor of Ossynthore wished to meet with me. He was standing high up on a platform above the entire crowd. I approached him with both Atrixia and Caydia. I made it clear that Atrixia and Caydia were the ones to thank the moment we met. He knew of them as well. He was an older, shorter man with short curly white hair. Once he was faced with both Atrixia and Caydia, he gave them each a flower crown made of gold vines and leaves. He handed me a golden cloak the color of the sun. I put it on the instant I received it. He smiled and told me he remembered me from when I was younger. "Sunboy," he called me.

I stood between Atrixia and Caydia. Both girls wore flower crowns. I took both their hands and raised them high over my head for the world to see. They cheered. They lived in harmony. This planet's people were free. They didn't seem to have a problem in the world. There was no one in danger. There was a surplus of food. The lost spirits found their way. Now was the time to go. It hurt but I knew it. I said goodbye to my family as Starheart one last time. They all told me I'd see them again in a few minutes. I said goodbye to Caydia. I held out the crystal ball ring she gave me.

"I'm bringing this with me," I said, "you saved my life." I kissed the side of her head. "Thank you so much."

I hugged both girls and said, "I wish I could take the both of you back with me."

I walked over to Caydia, held my palms against hers, and said, "You're one of my best friends. I'm gonna miss you so much."

She could feel my energy. She always could. Tears began to fall from her sky blue eyes. I felt so bad. I unfastened my chain and handed Caydia my soul gem. "I know you'll protect this," I said.

"Don't ever let the light die out," she said.

"You're the girl from the graveyard? The one with the pointy hat and the jack-o-lantern?" I knew it once she said that. She started to laugh. She hugged me.

"Thanks for getting me out of that cave," she whispered. She wiped the tears from her face.

"I wish I could have found you sooner," I told her.

"I'll always be watching you. I'll be hoping you don't fall and when you do, I'm gonna be there in a heartbeat. I don't care if we're worlds away. A part of me is always gonna be missing you until you return." She gave me a final hug that lasted a long moment. I kissed her cheek while she was in my arms. "Watch over the Observatory," I told her lastly.

I let her go and walked over to Atrixia. I met her behind a tree. We teleported to her meadow. There, we kissed and kissed. It was all I wanted to do.

"I love you," I said. "I love your world."

"Our world," she corrected me.

I looked at my pocket watch. The time was 11:11.

"I referred to you as my girlfriend last night," I said.

"Why'd you do that?" she asked.

"Are you not at this point?"

"You never asked me."

"Do you wish to be?"

She laid her arms around me, kissed me, and said, "If you wish."

"Thank you so much for everything. You saved me. Thanks for that."

She smiled at me with the same warm smile she gave me the night we first met. That night we met on the log seemed so long ago. Her lips were perfectly shaped. I couldn't resist the urge to kiss them. Her rose gold heart lit up like a star.

"I know distance is only space, but you don't think it's gonna be awkward having a girlfriend in a dimension you don't remember?" she asked.

"I may forget you. I may even forget your face a few times at first. But the one thing I could never forget is the feeling I get from you. It's a feeling I don't get from any other person. I'll remember you by that. I'll know you by the feeling. Every time."

"Even when you're back on earth, I'll still be the only one you love?"

"No matter where I am, you'll still be the only one I love," I assured her to her surprise. "No power compares to our love. It's worth more than anything I could ever wish for. I'll see you when I look at a flower. I'll see you when a leaf blows past. A part of me will remember you when I'm lying in bed alone. You'll always be kept in my heart, Atrixia."

When I said that, I remembered the black book Caydia gave to each of us. If I remembered correctly, whatever I wrote in my book would appear in Atrixia's. I pulled out mine and Atrixia pulled out hers. She read as I wrote in pen: *Regardless of how far we traveled, no matter what we faced along the way, you, you made it a journey and it wouldn't have been a journey without you. I wouldn't have made it this far if I didn't have you by my side.*

Underneath I wrote, *P. S. I'll never forget the color of your first dress. Things like that happen once in a minute, twice in a moment, but never in a thousand years. Sure things were up and down, off and.. What I'm trying to say is, don't forget about me. - D*

I gave her one final long lasting kiss.

"I can't wait to see you again," I whispered, with her in my arms.

"We'll see each other soon," she promised.

She stepped away and I took her by the hand before she parted.

"I wish you didn't have to go," I said sadly.

"We both have to go. You have a life to return to and I must go to sleep soon. We won't be apart forever."

I kissed her one last time and let go. She walked over to her tree and hung the red hoodie on a branch. She turned to me and said, "I love you."

"I love you too." I smiled and hid my sadness.

The trunk of her tree split open. She looked at me with her maple red eyes one last time, then stepped into her tree. The bark closed behind her and I was alone. Once she was gone, I walked over to the red hoodie and ran my fingers down it. I left it hanging on the branch. I walked over to the tree's trunk and placed my hand on the tree's bark. I closed my eyes, rested my head against the tree, and tried not to weep.

"I'll see you in the morning, baby," I whispered.

"You okay?" I heard someone ask from behind.

I turned around and saw Caydia.

"That's it," I said.

"What do you mean?" she asked.

I shook my head. "I don't wanna be here anymore."

"Before Atrixia left, she told me to keep an eye on you. You know?

Keep you busy. I'll see you around."

I hugged her and tried hard to remember this moment and the feeling of holding Caydia in my arms. 'She's real. She's right here,' I told myself.

I looked into her blue eyes and let go. I left without saying a further word. I threw the penny on the grass and my well appeared. I hopped down the well and the next moment, I found myself laying on the grass of a random person's lawn.

I looked around a familiar looking suburban town.

'What is this?' I asked myself when I looked down at a flashing glass ball I was wearing on my finger. In my other hand was a red book. *Stories of Ossynthore*, its cover read.